BRITTLE MIDNIGHT

BOOK TWO
OF
CITY OF MAGIC

Cover by Yocla Designs

Prologue

The punch, when it came, broke his nose. Monroe heard the sickening crack almost before he felt the flash of pain. The onlookers didn't bother to mask their shocked gasps. Whatever. They could think what they wanted. He ignored the spray of blood that splattered onto the ground in front of him and turned to face the young werewolf once again.

For all his swagger and bravado, Nero suddenly looked rather nonplussed. From the expression on his face, the last thing he'd expected was to land such a blow. Monroe bared his teeth. The boy's alpha should be doing more to teach him to guard against displaying his emotions too obviously. But then again, Julian had always been something of a soft touch.

Monroe shook his head slightly, his dark-red curls damp with sweat. He could see with the easy clarity of experience that Nero's left side was vulnerable. Not only did the kid hold himself stiffly, favouring that side as if bothered by an old injury, but he also had his fists lowered. A simple jab to his kidneys and he'd be floored. Then it would all be over.

Monroe let the kid hit him again, a teeth-knocking blow to the side of his head which was followed up by a sharp kick to his ribs. That was better. Nero was pressing his advantage. It was about time. As Monroe spun from the force of the first hit, more blood from his wounds arced out, spraying at least three of the watching crowd. One of them, an older-looking vampire, appeared delighted and used the tip of his finger to smear Monroe's blood onto his tongue. He smacked his lips, ignoring the glares from the werewolves next to him.

Monroe ignored the lot of them. He wasn't there for them. He pivoted onto his toes, exposing his right flank just enough for Nero to notice. The shock and dismay that the younger werewolf had displayed at managing to beat the older maestro was being replaced by the heady combination of bloodlust and power. This time he was going to go in for kill. Monroe was going to let him.

'Enough.'

There was a collective groan from the crowd. Julian's eyes narrowed, his bristling anger forcing them all to slink away into the shadows from where they'd come. Monroe's glare matched Julian's, spark for furious spark.

'What did you do that for?' Nero burst out, barely able to contain himself. 'I had him! I was beating him! It was a fair fight and I was better! You—'

'Don't be a fucking idiot,' Julian growled.

The censure in his alpha's voice finally made Nero drop his shoulders in submission. 'I didn't start it.'

'I don't care.' Julian's eyes hardened. 'Get out of here.'

At first Nero remained, a flicker of tell-tale indecision rippling through him. Then, with a final huff, he did as he was told and bent down to pick up his jacket before following the others out of the room.

Once the kid was out of earshot, Monroe spoke. He still had enough decorum – just – that he wouldn't get into an argument with another alpha while there was an audience. 'You should not have interfered. This has nothing to do with you.'

Julian folded his arms in irritation. 'It has everything to do with me. That boy is in my pack. He's my charge and he's my responsibility.'

Monroe spat out blood. 'There's not a single mark or bruise on him.'

'That's not what I'm talking about and you know it. I have enough problems with his ego as it is. Now he's going to think he's stronger than you, that he's more powerful than Monroe himself. I don't need that kind of angst in my life. And Nero certainly doesn't need that kind of belief. He'll go around picking fights with everyone and he'll end up getting himself killed.'

'I'm not responsible for the actions of others,' Monroe said. 'Not any more. And if your pup is picking fights then he doesn't belong here.'

Julian looked at him without speaking for several seconds. There was a time when there hadn't been a single soul on this planet who would have dared to eyeball Monroe in such a fashion. Truth be told even now Julian, as alpha of the Yorkshire werewolves, was probably the only person who would dare. Still, it was a mark of how times had changed.

When Julian did speak, his voice was low and without emotion. 'You are throwing your toys out of the pram.'

Genuine anger lit Monroe's face. 'You dare to equate the loss of my entire pack to having a tantrum?'

Julian's expression didn't alter. 'I'm not talking about your pack. What happened to them was a tragedy. I'm talking about *you*. You told us to settle here, away from the others. You promised safety and a new society.'

'No one's died,' Monroe snapped. 'Not recently anyway. And we have a society.'

'Such as it is.'

'Not everything is on my shoulders.'

Julian raised his hands, palms facing outwards. 'Exactly. You're hurt. I get that. You think everything that brought us here is your fault. Whether that's true or not isn't for me to say. But you have a responsibility to pull yourself together. We came here because of you, Monroe. We need *you*.'

'You came here because the magic in the atmosphere suits our kind. I had nothing to do with it.'

'Now you're being facetious. We came to Manchester for the magic. We settled here in the north because you persuaded us to. You promised lots and you've delivered very little. Not in the last few weeks, anyway. If you want to cry at night that is up to you, but you cannot pull others into your grief. This won't wash.'

'This is *my* city,' Monroe said. 'This is *my* community.'

'Start acting like it is, then.'

Monroe stared him down. 'What exactly,' he asked icily, 'are you saying?'

'Sort yourself out,' the other werewolf replied. 'Or there's no place for you here.' And with that, he turned on his heel and walked out.

***

An hour later, Monroe was on his fourth whisky. It was perhaps indicative of the British that, even with the aftermath of a three-month-old apocalypse to deal with and a lack of normalised infrastructure, several bars and clubs had already opened up in this part of Manchester. Whether there were any in the southern part of the city, Monroe couldn't say for sure. He was fairly certain that there would be, though, even if they weren't frequented by the werewolves and vampires that hung around this one.

'Hello darling,' drawled a familiar voice.

Monroe didn't bother turning round. 'What do you want?'

'G and T, of course. I'd give my right fang if it included ice and a slice. Unfortunately,' Julie said with a light laugh, 'I fear those days are gone.'

'There's still a single exit point out of the city,' Monroe grunted. 'You are more than welcome to depart that way whenever you choose. Leave, and you'll be able to get all the ice and lemon that your heart desires.'

'Except then I wouldn't be able to get back into Manchester, would I? Although I'm sure that would delight you.'

'You can do whatever you want. I don't care.'

She hissed through her teeth. 'Except you should care, darling. A couple of months ago you'd have happily chopped off my head.'

'You'd have deserved it.'

Julie shrugged, although there was a darkness to her expression. 'I'm not denying that.'

He swung his head towards her and gave her a long, measured look. 'So you're finally owning up to your part in all this? In the magical collapse of an entire city?'

Julie looked away. 'I always did,' she answered softly. 'And I am trying to make amends.'

'Then do so away from here.'

Her mouth curved into a sad smile. 'Except that here appears to be where I am most needed.'

'I don't need you.'

'No,' she said mildly, 'but you do need something. Or rather someone.' She paused. 'Charley has been struggling lately.'

'What Charlotte does is nothing to do with me.' Monroe took another sip of his drink, rolling the heavy glass in his hands. 'Is she alright?' His voice remained casual but his body was unnaturally still as he waited for the answer.

—

'She's taken a lot on her shoulders,' Julie said. 'And there's a lot of pressure on her to keep her new little community going.'

'Then perhaps you should be there helping her.'

'Perhaps,' Julie retorted, 'it's not me who she needs.'

Monroe inhaled deeply, holding the breath in his lungs for several seconds before exhaling. 'You seem to have lots of opinions about what other people need.'

'I'm smarter than I look.'

He snorted. 'I doubt that.'

Julie reached behind her, taking a tall glass from another punter and admonishing him with a stern wag of her finger before he could complain. Then she tossed the contents in Monroe's face.

He sprang to his feet, knocking over his bar stool as he spun round to face her with his fists clenched. 'I wouldn't normally hit a woman,' he snarled, 'but you're a vampire. That makes you fair game.'

'Stop with the hissy fit,' she dismissed. 'I had to do something to get your attention. You're falling apart at the seams, Monroe. You were fine and coping when you had something to focus on. Now your little community is finding its feet, you're adrift. You're letting your grief get the better of you. You're heading for collapse and, sooner or later, so will Charley. I understand why you've set up separate enclaves but the pair of you need to stop avoiding each other if this new Manchester is going to survive. The north needs you and the south needs her. If you're not going to sort yourself out for the people who are here, then sort yourself out for her before she burns out. You don't need more on your conscience than you already have.'

Monroe took a napkin from the counter and wiped the worst of the liquid from his face. 'What Charlotte does is not my business.'

'Keep telling yourself that,' Julie murmured, 'and you'll soon be an even better liar than I am.'

The door to the pub jangled and two new customers walked in, their eyes landing almost instantly on Julie. Their unnatural pallor and close-mouthed expressions marked them immediately as vampires. Both of them had a vaguely dangerous air, although the taller vamp's Metallica T-shirt somewhat dampened down the threat of his companion, whose scarred face told of promised threats and perilous risk.

Julie's face paled slightly but she shook out her hair defiantly and sniffed. 'I have to go. There are several people in here who are about to bounce up and ask me for my autograph and frankly, darling, I can't be arsed with that.' She gave Monroe a meaningful look. 'Be a good little werewolf and go and see Charley, even if it's for her sake rather than your own.' She whirled out, giving the other vampires as wide a berth as possible.

Monroe glowered into his empty glass. By all accounts, Charlotte was doing perfectly well without him. And sooner or later, the north would do perfectly well without him too. Setting up here and taking charge had seemed like an excellent idea a few months ago; now he simply couldn't be arsed. It was time everyone took responsibility for themselves instead of looking to others to sort out their problems.

He pushed away the glass and walked to the door, flinging it open with more force than he'd intended. It crashed against its frame but he ignored it and stepped outside. Dawn was already here and the first few rays of winter sunshine were hitting the quiet street. He pursed his lips and strode over to the nearest sunbeam, raising his head slightly and sniffing. He stayed there for a moment, letting the weak warmth wash over him.

Maybe the vampire actress had a point. It wouldn't hurt to make sure Charlotte was alright. Besides, no matter what else was going on with life, sunshine always smelled good.

Chapter One

'The taps are spouting blood again, Charley.' There was a glint of delight in Cath's eyes as she declared this unwholesome little titbit. 'Very skeevy.'

I sighed and pushed back my hair. 'I thought that was all sorted by now.'

'Guess not.' She grinned at me. 'At least Julie will be happy.'

I grimaced. I had a sudden vision of the soap actress cum vampire with her head tilted over a sink and her mouth wide open as she gulped down sticky red ooze. It wasn't a particularly pleasant image, although I supposed that at least it would stop her temporarily from skipping over to the northern side of the city every couple of nights to feed her hunger pangs. Every time she went, I couldn't stop myself worrying about what she was up to – or who she might be hurting. She treated the northern community like some sort of blood bank. I should have been pleased that she wasn't bloodying up my doorstep but unfortunately my imagination conjured all sorts of unpleasant scenarios about what she was up to when I couldn't see her.

The front door banged open and Albert, an older gentleman who had taken up residence a couple of streets away, came in. He whacked his cane against the walls as he stomped towards us. The kilt he insisted on wearing, despite his lack of Scottish ancestry, was swinging from side to side. 'Blood,' he snapped. 'Taps.' He glared at me. 'Fix it.'

I gestured at Cath. 'I only just found out about it.

I'll try and sort it as soon as I can.'

Albert waggled his bushy eyebrows at me, conveying that I had better get a move on and solve the problem immediately, then he huffed and stormed out again, nearly colliding with Jodie who was on her way in. I sent myself a brief, happy thought of the pre-magical apocalypse days when people didn't barge into my house without so much as knocking first and raised a hand to her in greeting.

'Red shit is coming out of the taps again,' she said without preamble.

'Yeah,' I said, 'I've heard.' It wasn't the worst thing that had happened in the three months since the British government had built their walls and closed off the wild magic of Manchester from the rest of the world – but it was bloody irritating. Especially given the trouble we'd gone to in order to maintain running water in the first place. The last thing we needed was overflowing sewage and outbreaks of cholera on top of everything else. And it was nice to be able to get clean, even if hot water was nothing more than a dim memory.

Jodie crossed her arms and stared at me as if it were all my fault. 'I wanted to wash my hair. Anna was going to do the laundry.'

Lizzy appeared from behind Jodie. Her normally blonde locks were dripping with bright red ooze. 'The taps…'

'Yeah, I got it,' I said drily. 'I'm about to head over to the reservoir.'

'I'll come with you.'

I shook my head. The blood clinging to her skin and hair would only attract predators. Her company would be more hassle than it was worth. 'You get yourself cleaned up,' I said, not unkindly. 'I'll deal with it.'

Lizzy looked relieved more than anything else. I didn't blame her; last time it took several hours of muttering nonsensical incantations and waving my hands around before I fixed the problem. Even then I couldn't say what I did to clear up the water, so goodness only knew what it would take this time.

I still didn't have a proper handle on the magical powers that had been bestowed on me after I'd spent the night curled up with the little sphere that a crazy faery had planted on me – and which had almost caused the destruction of the entire world. You've heard of a learning curve? Well, as far as magic was concerned, this was a learning cliff face and I didn't possess so much as a single rope.

I grabbed my handy backpack, which these days always sat by the front door ready for the emergencies that seemed to occur on an hourly basis, and scooted past the small assembly. I took care not to brush past Lizzy on my way out and end up plastered in the same gunk that she was.

Jodie called out after me, 'If you could make the water drinkable this time, that'd be fab.'

Unlikely. I'd try my best though – and everyone loves a trier. Or so I liked to pretend. I gritted my teeth, steeled myself against the growing lump of cold lead that seemed to be constantly expanding in my belly, and closed the door behind me.

***

I took a bike. There were still plenty of cars lying around with usable petrol in their engines but these days it was usually faster and more convenient to cycle. Teams of people had been clearing the roads of abandoned cars for weeks and, for the most part, they'd done a grand job. It was getting to the point where the stationary vehicles were looking less like forlorn reminders of all that we'd lost and more like relics from a bygone age. All the same, I couldn't stop myself feeling a twinge when I passed the odd car with a tree sprouting through its roof. Every month Mother Nature had a growth spurt and the trees and bushes stretched upwards and outwards by another few feet. Winter might have been almost upon us but no one had told the trees.

Thankfully my journey was uneventful. I caught sight of the odd passing shadow, indicating that I was being watched by a few of the magical creatures that had appeared from nowhere to inhabit this new world. Shadow beasts, hell hounds, giant rats, mammoth pink elephants, swampy canal monsters. There was no end to the nasties that lived in Manchester these days. Right now we were working on a live-and-let-live theory: if they left us alone, we would do the same. It worked most of the time. I pretended not to notice anything out of the ordinary and pedalled slightly faster. Every day I wasn't chomped on by a monster was a good day.

When I finally arrived at my destination, I propped the bike against a wall by the main waterworks building next to the old reservoir and craned my neck upwards. I couldn't see anything malevolent or dangerous. In fact, I couldn't see much at all.

'What's the betting,' I muttered to myself, 'that whatever magical beastie is causing all this crap is hiding somewhere and laughing at me?' I wrinkled my nose. 'Three to one. Easy.'

'You know that talking to yourself is the first sign of madness,' drawled a familiar Scottish brogue.

I half-jumped out of my skin and spun in Monroe's direction. I'd barely seen him for weeks. We'd met up a few times initially, and he'd given me some basic fighting lessons as he'd promised, but they were a distant memory. We'd both become too busy doing other things. The fact that he'd decided to show up here could only mean that his half of the city was also affected by the water problems – and that for once he actually gave a shit.

I wanted to be able to say that he was looking good, but there were heavy dark shadows under his eyes and faint bruises across his jawline. Given what I'd learned about the fast recovery time of werewolves, he must have taken a hell of a beating in the last few days to still be showing the effects. Worry flickered through my belly, although I knew he wouldn't thank me for the sentiment.

'Been in a fight?' I asked, trying to sound casual.

Monroe ignored my question and walked over, stopping a few centimetres before our bodies touched. 'How have you been, Charlotte?' He tilted his head towards mine and inhaled. 'You smell good.'

Gah. Even though he looked like he'd spent the last three days in a ditch, he possessed the skill to make my heart skip a beat. Those eyes were too damned blue for their own good. 'I'm fine.'

He didn't remove his searing gaze from my face. 'You shouldn't be here on your own.'

'I'm the enchantress of Manchester South,' I said. 'I can look after myself.' That came out far snottier than I'd intended and I winced. 'Sorry.'

'Don't apologise. You are indeed the enchantress.' He smiled at me. 'I'm not suggesting that you can't look after yourself, just that this water thing could be a big problem and it would be handy to have some back-up.'

I made a show of looking over Monroe's shoulder for his own seemingly invisible back-up. He nodded ruefully and acknowledged my point.

'This is the third time we've had an issue with the water,' I said. 'I managed perfectly well on my own on the first two occasions.'

Monroe suddenly looked uncomfortable. 'It's my turn to apologise. I would have helped you out both those times but I was rather … busy. By the time I was free, you'd already solved the problem.'

'So why come now?' I asked softly. 'Why not send someone else in your place?'

He offered me a lazy shrug, although the light in his eyes intensified. 'I wanted to see you.'

Feeling oddly embarrassed, I shifted under the weight of his gaze. 'I might have delegated sorting out the water problems to someone else.'

Monroe snorted. 'As if. Delegation isn't your thing.'

'Apparently it's not yours either.'

He watched me for a moment. 'Maybe we're more alike than either of us realise.'

I doubted that very much. Bonds had been forged between us in the first days of the magical apocalypse that had struck Manchester back in September, but there were fundamental differences in how we saw our future in this brand-new world. I was focused on building a community where everyone was welcome; Monroe's intention was to create a safe haven for those whom he deemed worthy – and who would toe his line and follow his rules. Not that the bruises on his face suggested anything remotely safe about his northern quarter.

In any case, our differences were the reason he had set up in the opposite end of the city to me. Most of the 'normals' clung to my side, while most of the magical beings stuck with Monroe. Birds of a feather flocked together, I suppose. There were a few outliers who'd elected to avoid both communities. And, of course, there was the Travotel run by Timmons, the sole faery left in this world. The hotel acted as a neutral ground between our two areas. It was the Switzerland of Manchester – but with fewer cuckoo clocks, less chocolate and more mini-soaps. Somehow Timmons had an endless supply of mini-soaps.

I wasn't in the mood for a session of home truths with Monroe. That way just led to angst and, from his bruises and the heavy shadows under his eyes, Monroe needed more light-hearted fun than soul-searching commentary. To that end, I lifted my chin and offered him a small grin. 'Well,' I said, 'my hair matches your eyes if nothing else.' I fluffed up my blue locks and fluttered my eyelashes.

Monroe snorted but I was certain I detected a faint loosening around his shoulders. I'd take what I could get. 'Come on,' I said. 'This isn't my first bloodied-water experience. I'll lead the way.'

He swept a bow, indicating his acquiescence as I turned and headed for the narrow metal staircase that led to the top of the small reservoir. I could feel Monroe's eyes on my back as I climbed. I suspected he was looking at my arse rather than my spinal column but I could live with that. Part of me hoped that was the case.

Although I held a remarkable amount of information and number of facts in my head, all of which I'd garnered in my career as a semi-professional gambler, until recently water hadn't been one of those things that I knew much about. I hadn't needed to; I turned on the tap and water poured out. I'd taken it for granted completely. More fool me.

Neither did we have any plumbers in our community who understood anything about the pedestrian magic of running water. There were therapists and yoga teachers, electricians and professional dog walkers, but there wasn't a single plumber. It had taken considerable research in the Manchester library, as well as considerable work, to even begin to understand the mysteries of large-scale plumbing and water mains. I was proud of myself for that.

When the city had run at capacity, water was pumped in via a massive reservoir more than a hundred miles away. It was quite a feat of engineering, which I'd have admired if it weren't so damned out of reach. Thanks to the cordon the British army had set up around the city, technically we couldn't get out of Manchester. There was one exit point that we still controlled from the inside but if you left that way you couldn't get back in. You'd probably also be thrown into quarantine until the government decided you weren't a magical risk to the rest of the country. No, a reservoir up in the hills wasn't any good to us whatsoever.

Fortunately, before the population of Manchester boomed in pre-Victorian times, there was another far smaller reservoir here on the outskirts and it remained accessible to those of us within the city boundaries. Until very recently, this little reservoir had been almost unnecessary. It didn't hold enough water for a normal city and it was more a point of historical curiosity than anything useful. Not so now. With considerable patience and a lot of work, we'd got it up and running again so that we could turn on a tap and at least get a trickle of something in return for our trouble. The water wasn't very clean, as we didn't have the expertise or the equipment to treat it, and it ran at temperatures between 'fuck it's freezing' and 'my lips are turning blue' – but it was better than nothing. Apart from when it turned to blood, of course.

I clumped up the rickety stairs until I reached the

walkway that led across the front of the reservoir. Even without the small sea of red rippling in the light winter breeze, the blood would have been unmistakable. The smell was certainly … tangy. From behind me, Monroe let out a small growl.

'This is exactly like the other two times,' I told him. 'I have no idea what's causing it and I don't really know how to stop it. I try lots of different things and sooner or later the blood just dissipates.' I waved a hand. 'It's probably the magic in the air that's affecting the water.'

'No.' There was a tautness across Monroe's jawline. 'If that were the case, it would happen more often. Or it wouldn't be fixable. The fact that you've managed to clear it up twice before suggests that this isn't an environmental problem.' He grimaced and ran a hand through his hair. 'If I'd realised that earlier, I'd have done something about it. I've been … distracted.'

Distracted by what exactly? I glanced at him. Certainly grief was the root cause. There was no question that Monroe was still suffering terribly as a result of the loss of his werewolf pack, who'd all been killed by some crazy faeries when Manchester was first plunged into magical hell. But Monroe blamed himself and deep-seated grief, especially when you felt responsible for the deaths in question, could cause a myriad of other problems. I bit my lip and wondered what in hell was really going on with him. Not to mention if there was anything I could do that could help.

'Well,' I said briskly, 'you're here now. If you have any ideas, other than me waving my arms around for a few hours, they'd be very welcome.'

Monroe frowned and cast his eyes across the surface of the water. His gaze eventually settled on a small patch towards the far left. 'There,' he said.

'Something is there.'

I squinted. I couldn't see a thing.

'See?' he said.

'Uh…'

'The ripples on the surface don't match the direction of the wind.' There was a note of self-satisfaction in his voice, enhanced no doubt by the fact that I still couldn't see what he meant. Clearly his eyesight was far better than mine. I had no reason not to trust his judgment, however.

I nodded decisively and swivelled round to walk to the end of the gangway. Monroe grabbed my elbow to hold me back. 'What are you doing?'

'Investigating. Solving.' I flicked him a look. 'That is why we're here, after all.'

'It could be dangerous.'

I laughed briefly. Everything about this new Manchester was dangerous; that was what made it such dubious fun. 'Then,' I said, 'you stay back here where it's safe and I'll check it out.' I yanked back my arm.

'That's not what I meant, Charlotte, and you know it. Have you forgotten what happened with the Canal Monster?'

I could hardly forget. It had grabbed hold of me out by Old Trafford and I'd come close to drowning and being eaten at the same time. We all avoided that area now if we could help it, but there continued to be reports of its presence lurking up and down the old ship canal. Fortunately no one had died in its saliva-laden jaws. Alas, I suspected that was probably only a matter of time.

'I remember,' I told him. 'But I escaped unscathed. I'm sure this will be exactly the same.' I flashed him a brilliant smile and took off once more.

Monroe huffed under his breath. Then he followed.

———

It wasn't easy getting close. Although the steel walkway allowed us access to the top of the reservoir, it didn't stretch all the way round the sides so we were forced to slip, slide and squelch across a narrow section of mossy mud. Even Monroe wasn't as sure-footed as normal. At one point his foot gave away and he crashed into me, his arms going round my waist as he tried to steady himself. I dug in my heels to avoid us both tipping into the reservoir of dark blood – but it was a close thing.

'Thanks,' he muttered.

'Any time you need rescuing, I'm right here,' I chirped.

I thought he was going to snipe something sarcastic at me but instead his head dipped down to my ear. 'I appreciate that, sunshine,' he murmured. His arms tightened fractionally around my waist before he let go.

I coughed and kept my face resolutely turned forward so he couldn't see the sudden stain of embarrassment on my cheeks. Except I wasn't sure it was embarrassment; it might have been pure lust. Either way, it certainly appeared that the masculine arrogance that Monroe had displayed the first time we met had vanished for good. That warmed me no end.

'All the same,' he continued, 'you should let me take things from here. You've tried twice and failed. I'll deal with this problem once and for all. Sometimes it takes an alpha werewolf to save the world.'

Oh for goodness' sake. I rolled my eyes but, rather than argue, I gestured at the blood. 'Go on then, maestro,' I said. 'Have at it.'

Monroe smiled, ignoring my sarcasm, and cast around the ground before reaching for a long branch that was snaking its way across the verge behind us. He gave it a tug but it resolutely refused to budge.

'Want some help there, genius?' I enquired.

He grunted and yanked harder on the branch but it stayed rooted to the ground. 'Go ahead.' He spoke as if he were merely giving me something to do so that I didn't feel entirely useless. All the same, when he straightened up and glanced at me, there was a glint of self-mockery in his eyes.

I grinned at him. I didn't understand much about my newly fledged magical capabilities but retrieving stubborn objects was something I'd become an expert at in recent weeks. It simply took the right amount of force – not too much so that the object in question went flying out of reach but enough to release it from whatever was holding it in place. 'Watch and learn,' I declared before flicking my wrist.

The branch snapped free and, with unerring speed and force, almost whacked into Monroe. He only just pulled back in time. A fraction of a second later there was a fat plop as it landed in the blood lake, splattering both of us with fine red droplets. Oops.

'Nice going,' Monroe murmured.

Hmm. Maybe both of us needed an exercise in humility. 'Sorry.' I grimaced. That was what I got for showing off.

I lifted my head. There was another branch a few metres away. Second time lucky, I decided. Not that I believed in luck. I raised my hands once more and prepared to concentrate harder this time around.

Just then, there was a ripple in the blood behind us and the original branch flew out again, landing with a wet thump between Monroe and me.

We exchanged looks and slowly turned to look at the reservoir. More undulations disrupted the surface of the blood. Keeping his eyes trained on the patch where the ripples were the strongest, Monroe crouched down, took hold of the branch and threw it back in.

This time the heavy, blood-soaked branch flew out of the water far faster – and with far more force. I squeaked and leapt to the side to avoid being smacked in the shin. Monroe didn't move a muscle; he simply folded his arms and glared at the rippling lake of blood.

I followed his gaze and spotted a dark shadow moving underneath the surface. My stomach tightened but, before I could say anything, a strange humming sound reached my ears. It was an annoying, grating buzz and it set my teeth on edge. I grimaced and glanced at Monroe. He'd dropped his arms to his sides and was suddenly slack-jawed. I blinked. There was a dreamy expression on his face. Well, that was new.

'Uh, Monroe?'

He ignored me and stepped towards the reservoir's edge. With the sudden certainty that he was about to throw himself in, I lunged forward and yanked him back. 'What the hell are you doing?' I hissed.

He shook me off as if I were nothing more than an irritating fly, and started forward once more. I cursed under my breath and reached for him again. This time I didn't bother trying to grab him; I just elbowed him sharply in the ribs. Fury spasmed across his body and he snarled, fur sprouting out across his jawline.

The humming stopped abruptly and the surface of the reservoir broke to reveal the head of an extraordinarily beautiful woman. I was too shocked to do anything but stare.

'He's a werewolf?' The bobbing blonde threw her hands up in disgust, ignoring the splatter of flying blood that the movement created. 'Just my fucking luck.'

Monroe staggered backwards. I simply gaped. I had imagined many things that might be in the dark red pool but she wasn't one of them.

The woman flicked her eyes to me with a

22

disdainful toss of her head. 'What are you looking at?'

My jaw worked uselessly. She sighed and spun, her head disappearing into the gruesome depths. A half-second later there was a flash of silver and a large fish tail appeared, flicking at us like a middle finger.

I pinched my skin. Nope. I wasn't dreaming. I swivelled towards Monroe. 'Was that…?'

'A mermaid?' he grunted. 'I believe so. Yes.'

Chapter Two

We scrabbled up the muddy bank in a bid to regroup and steer clear of any further mermaid-style shenanigans.

'She's not exactly what Disney envisaged, is she?' I whispered half to myself. I turned to Monroe. 'Why didn't you tell me mermaids existed?'

He was looking as disturbed as I felt. 'I didn't know.' He gazed out across the expanse of blood. 'She must have been enticed here by the magic.' He tapped his mouth thoughtfully. 'And she obviously has powers.'

I snorted. 'Seductive powers.' At Monroe's sidelong look, I jabbed him on the arm. 'You were all but ready to climb into that reservoir along with her. What the hell happened?'

He seemed annoyed, although more with himself than with me. 'I don't know what I was thinking. I heard her song beckoning to me and…' His voice drifted away and he frowned, unable to account for his own actions even to himself.

Personally, I wouldn't have called that weird buzzing sound a song but each to their own. 'I thought it was Sirens who were known for doing that. Singing, I mean.'

Monroe scratched his chin. 'Legends often get mixed up in the re-telling. You've heard the human version, which has no doubt been warped over generations. From what we've just experienced, mermaids and Sirens are one and the same.'

'She wasn't wearing a shell bikini. And she didn't have any singing crabs with her.' I cast a quick look around the seemingly empty reservoir.

'What?' Monroe asked.

'I'm checking to see whether Tom Hanks is about to show up.'

He tsked. 'I think you can forget what Hollywood has told you.' He frowned. 'If you think about what the old stories say, though, mermaids are tough cookies. Very tough cookies.'

'Walking on knives,' I said, suddenly remembering. 'When the Little Mermaid was transformed into a human to win the love of the prince, every step felt like she was walking on knives.'

Monroe nodded grimly. 'Exactly. We can surmise that not only does her kind have a high pain threshold but also that they'll go to any lengths to get what they want.'

I pointed at the reservoir. 'What she apparently wants is you.'

'No. She lost interest when she realised I was a werewolf. She wants a man.'

I shivered. 'To mate with?' I asked. 'Or to eat?'

He folded his arms. 'There's only one way to find out.' He raised his chin and called out across the lake of blood. 'All we want is to talk!'

There was no response. Big surprise: Monroe's shout was hardly the invitation of the year.

My brow furrowed and I tried to think. I didn't know squat about mermaids but I possessed a whole wealth of information that I'd garnered throughout my gambling career. I had laid bets on all manner of things over the years and the most successful ones had been where I'd used my knowledge and hard facts to predict the outcomes.

One thing I knew for sure was that sound travelled faster in water than in air. The mermaid seemed to be on her own and there certainly wasn't much in the way of action going on out here. Given the choice between swimming around a pool of blood and ignoring the only visitors who'd shown up for weeks or earwigging on their conversation, I knew which option I'd plump for.

I also doubted that even if mermaids did eat humans, our flesh was their sole source of food. Drowned bodies washed up on shore and they didn't all disappear into the hungry mouths of mermaids. Our little tailed temptress probably ate fish most of the time. I doubted there were many of those in the reservoir, certainly not now it was tainted. She was probably bored and definitely hungry. Now that I could work with.

I touched Monroe's arm and raised my eyebrows meaningfully. 'Put yourself in her shoes. It can't be easy for her being here. I don't know why she'd choose this place to live when there are so many other good spots with the same, if not better, concentration of magic. Some of my lot were out fishing in the canal and caught some tasty carp. Surely there are other places where she could get a reliable food source and potential company.'

I glanced at the surface of the reservoir and spotted the faintest undulations that didn't look entirely natural. Yeah. She was listening.

Monroe's expression cleared as he caught on. 'You know, I once heard Madrona chatting about just such a place. It doesn't only have fish, it's got ducks too.'

'Aw,' I said. 'I like ducks. Where is this place?'

'Boggart Hole. Traditionally it was a magical spot even before the apocalypse. I don't know where it is because I don't know Manchester all that well, but...'

'I know Boggart Hole,' I interrupted. 'The lake there is large and it's fed by various streams and rivers so you wouldn't feel trapped if you had to stay in water to survive. If I were a mermaid,' I said pointedly, 'I'd be somewhere like that instead of somewhere concrete and dull like here.'

The corners of Monroe's mouth tugged upwards. 'But you're not a mermaid. Neither am I.'

'Obviously.'

His smile grew. 'Obviously. Maybe that lass down there prefers it here. We can't speak for the preferences of mermaids.'

'I guess not. Shame though.'

'Indeed.' He pushed back his hair. 'It doesn't look like she'll come out and talk to us. We should probably just go.'

'Yeah.' I sighed. 'I wish she'd let us help her but you can't force anything on anyone. It has to be her decision to chat.' I paused. 'She might be afraid that we'd hurt her. You *are* a werewolf, after all.'

'And you're an enchantress.' He grinned. '*The* enchantress.' His eyes held mine and, for an odd moment, I forgot entirely that we were putting on a performance. His gaze dropped to my mouth. I leaned in and…

'I'm not fucking scared of a werewolf!'

Monroe and I pulled away from each other and returned our attention to the reservoir. Bobbing there, and with an extraordinarily irate expression on her face, was the mermaid herself.

I gave my body a little shake and re-focused. 'Of course you're not,' I soothed with hopefully the right hint of patronising gentleness.

She glared at me. 'What's an enchantress anyway?'

I curtsied in her direction. 'I am. A baby enchantress, at least. I'm still learning.'

'Bully for you,' she sneered.

'I'm Charley,' I said. 'This is Monroe.' I tugged at his sleeve. 'It was nice to meet you. Don't worry.

We'll leave you in peace and put up warning signs so that no one else comes close.'

Monroe nodded in agreement and we both turned as if to depart.

'Oi!' the mermaid yelled. 'Where are you going?'

Monroe evinced surprise, glancing at her over his shoulder. 'You don't want to talk to us, so it seems better to leave you alone.'

She wrinkled her nose. 'I don't talk to wankers,' she said. 'But maybe you two aren't as annoying as I first thought.'

'You tried to get him to join you in … there,' I reminded her, narrowly avoiding calling the reservoir something hopelessly derogatory. 'He could have drowned.'

Various expressions flitted across her face as she searched for an appropriate answer. 'Well,' she said finally, 'he didn't, did he? He's perfectly fine. No harm done.'

'Guess not.' I flashed her a smile. 'Nice meeting you.' I turned away again.

'Wait!' There was a pleading note underlying her imperious command. 'You don't have to leave straight away. You can stay a while. I don't mind chatting for a bit.' She cleared her throat. 'My name is Nimue.'

Monroe started beside me. 'Lady of the Lake,' he murmured to me.

'That's right!' Nimue yelled. 'That's what I am.'

I took a moment to cast a quick, disparaging glance around her 'lake'. She caught it – just as I'd hoped she would. 'Beggars can't be choosers,' she muttered.

Taking the opportunity to angle in more real conversation than screeching shouts, I gave her an interested look. This time I wasn't even acting. 'How did you get here?'

'I felt the magic,' she said. 'It called to me. I was miles and miles away in the ocean but the magic tugged and yanked and...' She sighed. 'I didn't plan it. I didn't mean to end up here.'

'You swam here?' Monroe's disbelief was obvious and not surprising, given that Manchester wasn't on the coast. That would have been some miraculous kind of swim.

'No, you furry moron,' she snapped. 'The magic carried me here. I let myself feel it from the depths and, in doing so, it overtook me. Before I knew it, I was here in this *pit*.' She looked around in disgust. 'I can't explain how it happened. It just happened.'

Monroe and I exchanged looks. Maybe it had been some kind of bizarre osmosis. Maybe Nimue was part of the water cycle. Who the hell knew? If she didn't know, then we certainly couldn't work it out.

'We can't get you back to the sea,' I said, 'even if we wanted to. We're trapped here in the city too.' In a manner of speaking.

Nimue tossed her hair and sniffed. 'I don't want to return to the ocean.' She spread her arms wide. 'Here I have power. The magic is in the water and it's making me stronger by the day.' She licked her lips in a disturbingly predatorial fashion. 'But somewhere other than this grey bathtub would be better.'

I was desperate to ask her how she knew what a bathtub was. Or a werewolf. But this wasn't the time for curiosity, so I managed to bite my tongue.

Nimue, it appeared, knew exactly what I was thinking. 'Do you think I'm stupid?' she spat. 'I know your kind. I've *eaten* your kind. And I can survive out of water for a time if need be. I've traversed the boards of your cruise ships and your yachts and your steamers.' Her face took on a dreamy quality. 'There were times when they were far easier to sink than they are now. *Good times.*'

I felt rather sick but Monroe was fascinated. 'You can transform your tail into legs?'

I glared at him. He raised his shoulders. 'I'm a shapeshifter,' he said. 'It's professional interest.'

Nimue blew air out impatiently. 'What do you think this is? A fucking fairy tale?' She swam towards us, cutting through the blood with frightening speed and ease. When she reached the edge of the reservoir and was terrifyingly close to Monroe and me, she raised herself off the surface with zero effort. Blood slid from her pale skin. Then she waddled out completely.

My mouth dropped open. As the blood dissipated and soaked into the ground, her tail became fully visible. She walked – if walking is what you could call her movements – towards us on her tail fins. She wasn't fast, and I reckoned a turtle could probably beat her in a race, but she could definitely move on solid earth. I swallowed my astonishment and gazed at the rest of her. Her tail was an extraordinary thing to behold. It was covered in shimmering scales of every hue and colour. She didn't appear to have any genitals; instead the scales melted into her flat stomach where fish gave way to skin. Standing like that, Nimue towered over both of us.

She cupped her naked breasts in both hands and purred in Monroe's direction. 'Do you like what you see?'

He met her challenge full on. 'You're not my type,' he murmured with a nonchalant air that I could only admire.

Something flashed in Nimue's eyes. 'I'm prettier than *her*.'

'No,' he said simply. 'You're not.'

He was wrong. I am completely, one hundred

percent heterosexual but even I found Nimue's form alluring. I nearly reached out to touch her, unable to help myself and desperately curious to know whether her tail was slimy to the touch. Then I pulled back. Despite her loneliness and her beauty Nimue was, beyond a shadow of a doubt, a predator. A predator who swam in blood.

Apparently unimpressed at Monroe's lack of immediate devotion, Nimue's lip curled. 'You're lying. But that's okay. Regardless of your foolish untruths and untrustworthy nature, you will take me to this place, this Boggart Hole. I command it.'

I shook off the last dregs of my amazement. 'I don't see why we should.'

She drew herself up and glared. 'Because I am telling you to.'

'*Quid pro quo*, sweetheart,' Monroe said. 'Return the reservoir to its natural state and we might consider helping you. I brought a car. We can transport you there if you do what we need first.'

The mermaid rolled her eyes then she snapped her fingers. As if a giant bottle of dye had been emptied, the liquid behind her changed colour, transforming from viscous red to murky blue. You'd think it would have taken a while to achieve but no; it was as easy as that. For Nimue, anyway.

'I only changed the water because I was bored,' she said. 'And,' she added with a smirk at me, 'it was fun watching you trying to change back it to its original state. I knew you'd keep returning if I kept changing it. The first time was an accident. The other times have just been for fun.' She opened her mouth, revealing jagged teeth that I suspected could tear through any kind of flesh in an instant.

I resisted the temptation to slap her. 'We all need a little entertainment in our lives,' I said.

If Nimue was disappointed that I didn't rise to her bait, she didn't show it. 'Well?' she demanded. 'Are we leaving now?'

Monroe looked at me. I didn't particularly like the idea of transporting her by car. Being in a small space with Nimue didn't bode well – and the odds of successfully knocking her out were stacked against us.

'Sure,' I said, hoping my voice didn't betray me. 'I guess we can manage that.'

Chapter Three

I used to have many daydreams where I fantasised about how my future might turn out, but I can guarantee that none of them ever involved being squashed into a little car with a werewolf and a mermaid.

The magic in the air meant that the more technologically advanced a vehicle was, the less likely it was to run reliably. It's the same reason why the small group of electricians I had working on small generators, which in theory could give us power, had yet to succeed. So far magic superseded just about everything else.

Monroe's car of choice was a virtual rust bucket with sunken seats and very little room inside. It screamed discomfort even before we piled in, and it didn't help that Nimue seemed to be going to particular lengths to draw attention to herself. She flicked her tail around as she tried to get comfortable and took up the entire back seat. When she couldn't squirm herself into the perfect position, she whipped her tail out so that it dangled over the passenger seat and draped down my torso. No, it wasn't slimy, but it did smell like putrid sardines.

'I have never been in one of these contraptions before,' she declared, while I did my best to shift away from the fishy reek.

'It's called a car,' I said, breathing through my mouth.

'I know what it is,' she sneered. She paused. 'So when does it start flying?'

I didn't answer. In truth, I should have trusted my instincts and stuck to cycling; I would have enjoyed seeing Nimue attempting to ride a bike. I smiled at the thought.

I was doing Monroe a favour by travelling with him and Nimue. Obviously it was purely out of concern that she might get peckish and decide to snack on him, and nothing to do with the fact that she was bare-breasted and gorgeous. I had no reason to be jealous if he got together with a fish. It wasn't like I had any claim on him. Hell, it wasn't like I'd seen him for weeks.

For Monroe's part, he appeared considerably more relaxed now that the reservoir water had returned to normal and there was an explanation for the bloody anomaly. Given his supernatural ethnicity, maybe he was used to this sort of thing. I wasn't feeling relaxed at all – but then I was half-covered in cold fish.

I reminded myself that Nimue's actions at the reservoir were probably a call for help and that she needed this 'rescue' far more than she was willing to admit, then I hunkered down for the journey.

'I don't think much of this place,' Nimue commented, peering out of the window at the passing buildings. 'I thought cities would be prettier. There aren't many people around. I need this Boggart place to have a steady stream of traffic so I can feed when I need to.'

'There will be no eating people,' Monroe said, his voice stern like that of a headmaster's. At the same moment, I hissed in exasperation at the flesh-eating mermaid.

'You two,' she declared with a sniff, 'are no fun at all.'

I started to count to ten in my head. No wonder Disney had altered the original storyline and character of *The Little Mermaid* if Nimue was anything to go by.

Fortunately for all of us, the journey to Boggart Hole was reasonably short and the route had been cleared of debris. I was surprised at that. There were a lot of trees in this area, and we passed a considerable number of houses and blocks of flats that were sprouting foliage. There were plenty of potholes and fissures in the cracked tarmac beneath the small car's wheels but there was nothing that actually impeded our progress.

'Someone has been here,' I murmured to Monroe when we finally pulled up in a small clearing in front of the little lake. 'Those roads didn't clear themselves.'

He shot me a sideways look. 'I assumed it was your people.'

I shook my head. 'We've been doing a lot to sort out the streets, but no one from my group has been out this way. I'm sure of it.'

'So you're saying there are others living out here?'

I nodded. 'It stands to reason. Whoever they are, they're certainly keeping themselves to themselves.' I bit my lip. 'They're probably not going to take kindly to Nimue showing up.'

'We all have our crosses to bear.' He seemed blithely unconcerned that the nearby inhabitants might have a problem with a ferocious creature who liked turning water into blood and luring unsuspecting males to join her in the depths.

'We'll have to find them and warn them.'

Monroe shrugged. 'If you say so.' His eyes gleamed. 'But they might get rather cross at her intrusion.'

I had the distinct impression he was hoping that was exactly what would happen. 'Are you spoiling for a fight?' I asked softly, and with genuine concern.

Before he could answer, Nimue leaned forward between our seats, her tail slapping me in the face as she shifted. 'What are you two muttering about?'

'Nothing,' I said. I pointed at the water shimmering ahead. 'Look,' I said brightly. 'Here's your new home.'

Nimue's gaze followed my finger. She wasn't as impressed as I'd thought she would be. 'I thought you said it was large.'

She was used to the ocean, I thought to stop myself from snapping at her. 'We're in a city,' I said evenly. 'This is the best we can manage. It's a step up from the little reservoir.'

Her bottom lip jutted out. 'Anything would be a step up from that hellhole.' She frowned. 'Are there any sharks? Or dolphins? Maybe a porpoise or two?'

Deciding that I couldn't absolutely deny the possibility of such creatures living in Boggart Hole, I shrugged. 'I couldn't say for sure,' I murmured. I should probably have managed her expectations, but all I really wanted was to get rid of her.

Aware that Monroe was watching me carefully, I slid out from underneath the weight of Nimue's heavy tail. 'There are definitely fish.' I opened the car door and hopped out.

I walked to the edge of the lake. The raft of ducks bobbing on the surface didn't so much as glance in my direction. They had to be loving this, I thought: peace and quiet to enjoy life and be a duck. No more pollution – unless you counted the magical kind – and no more pesky people to interrupt the tranquillity. I wondered whether they mourned the loss of bready titbits tossed in their direction before remembering that bread was supposed to be bad for ducks. I watched them for a moment, an odd longing for their simple life twisting at my insides. And at least they could fly away if Nimue became too annoying.

Hearing a heavy grunt, I turned round. Monroe

was heaving Nimue out of the car, her arms coiled round his neck. I rolled my eyes. 'You walked before. It's not far from the car to the lake. I'm sure you can manage it.'

She held the back of her hand up to her forehead in an almost perfect facsimile of a fainting nineteenth-century woman. 'I'm weak from having been out of the water for so long. I just need a little help.'

Didn't we all? I gave her an irritated, dismissive wave and ignored the glare emanating from Monroe. If he'd agreed to carry her, that was his look out. You shouldn't volunteer unless you are prepared to see your actions through.

Clearly Nimue was heavier than she looked. Monroe staggered over with a pained expression and eventually dropped her beside the lapping water. The mermaid flopped down on her belly, dropped her head and her face disappeared beneath the surface. She stayed like that for some time until I ambled round to her tail, hefted it up and used it as leverage to shove her into the water.

I wiped my hands on my jeans. Yuck. It would be a long time before I could eat fish for dinner again.

Nimue's head broke the surface. The water had to be shallow, but she was doing a good job of keeping most of her body submerged. Guilt traced through me; maybe she really had been suffering from being in the car for so long.

'How is it?' I asked.

Various expressions crossed her face and I waited for another snide remark. Instead, she settled for grudging acceptance. 'It's alright.'

Surprised, I smiled. Nimue smiled back. One of the brown female ducks separated from the rest and came to investigate the lake's new arrival. Nimue raised a dripping hand and stroked its head. It quacked softly in response and my smile widened. Then Nimue opened her jaws wide and her head snapped down. The duck didn't even have time to flinch.

Sickened, I looked away. 'Was that necessary?'

There was the sound of crunching bones – and possibly beak – as she munched. 'Sorry,' she mumbled through a mouthful. 'But I really am hungry. It's been a few weeks since I've eaten anything substantial. Are you vegetarian?'

No. I ate meat and I knew where it came from. I also understood that, as far as Mother Nature was concerned, there was a food chain. But that didn't mean I enjoyed that little display of death. I briefly acknowledged the hypocrite within me and changed the subject. 'Don't turn this water into blood. We won't come here to help you a second time. There's food here,' I said, avoiding looking at the rest of the ducks. 'There's no need to alter the entire ecosystem.'

Nimue looked at Monroe. 'Your girlfriend is very annoying.'

He didn't bother to correct her. 'Charlotte is right. We've helped you this time despite your attempts to push us to the contrary. You don't want to cross us a second time.'

Nimue tsked. 'Fine. I'll be good.' She pouted before throwing him a kiss.

I sighed. 'Let's get out of here.'

Monroe nodded and took my arm.

'Wait!' A high-pitched note entered Nimue's voice. We paused and looked at her. 'You're leaving already? You're not going to wait around to see if I behave?'

I tilted my head and looked at her. 'Whether you behave or not is your choice. If you don't, we'll come up with an alternative plan to deal with you. But in the meantime, it's up to you.'

'You'll have to come back and check up on me to know what I'm up to!' she yelled, a whine colouring every word.

Suddenly I understood. I grimaced, as much to myself as anyone else. 'Sure,' I said. 'We'll come back.'

'Every day.'

Too much. 'Every month.'

'Every week,' she countered.

I sighed. I supposed I could manage that much. 'Okay,' I conceded. 'We'll come every week.'

Nimue grinned, a fleeting expression that transformed her face. 'Thank you,' she said. 'For everything.' Her tail flicked out and her head vanished beneath the lake's surface.

I breathed out. 'I think she actually meant that,' I whispered.

Monroe gazed at me unblinkingly then he gently pulled me back towards the car.

'My little brother, Joshua, liked mermaids,' I murmured. 'He'd have been terribly disappointed to find out they're so nasty.'

Monroe's hand gave mine a tight squeeze. 'But lonely, too,' he added.

Yeah. I sighed and pulled away from him. We all had our problems.

I climbed into the car and huffed at the lingering fishy reek before clipping on my seatbelt. Monroe gripped the steering wheel but didn't turn on the engine.

I waved at him. 'Monroe? Hello?'

He dropped his hands and turned towards me. 'When the vampire came to see me about you, I thought it was part of some stupid plan to get me to pull myself together. But now I see you are struggling too.'

I stared at him. Heat rose through my skin,

flushing its way from my neck to my cheeks. 'I'm not sure where to start with that,' I said faintly. 'I thought you came to the reservoir because you wanted to see me.'

'I didn't lie,' he said. 'I did want to see you.'

'But Julie went to you and told you to come.' My voice was flat.

Monroe gave a humourless chuckle. 'I think you know my opinion of her well enough to realise that she couldn't make me do a single thing I didn't want to.'

All the same, I'd wring her bloody neck when I saw her next. She had no right to go to Monroe behind my back. 'What do you mean I'm struggling?' I demanded. 'I'm perfectly fine. Beyond feeling slightly sick at watching a mermaid decapitate a damned duck, that is.'

'You've lost your usual sheen of optimism,' he said mildly.

'I'd have thought that would make you happy,' I sniped. 'And, whether you recognise it or not, I'm still very optimistic, thank you very much.'

'You found Nimue irritating.'

'She's an irritating being,' I shot back.

'You're short-tempered.'

'I fucking am not.' I clenched my fists together. Then I realised what I was doing and slowly released them. 'Okay,' I conceded. 'Perhaps I have been a bit on edge recently.'

'The Charlotte I know would have bent over backwards to help Nimue.'

'I *did* bend over backwards to help her.'

'And,' Monroe added, ignoring my protest but with his blue eyes filled with concern, 'she'd have enjoyed helping.'

I looked away. I wasn't sure that anyone else would have noticed my change in temperament, even

Lizzy. I thought I'd been doing a good job masking the worst of my stress; somehow the knowledge that Monroe had seen through me annoyed me more. 'You can talk,' I said accusingly. 'You're covered in bruises. You've obviously been fighting. Or provoking fights.'

Monroe reached across, his hand covering mine. 'Maybe we're both in need of a break.'

I squeezed my eyes shut as Monroe's gentle tone finally caused something deep inside me to break. The growing well of tension inside my stomach split open and flooded everything. It took over everything and, before I knew it, I was blurting it all out.

'I didn't think it would be this hard. There's always someone who needs help, or someone who needs to complain, or some disaster that's happening. It's not the magical shit that causes most of the problems, it's the mundane stuff that takes up most of my time. I had to break up a fight yesterday because of two people arguing over the best way to plant late-season potatoes.' I flung my hands upwards. 'We're supposed to have a council but whenever we hold meetings it descends into arguments, and nothing ever gets done.'

'Have you been getting much rest?'

I'd been getting a lot of tossing and turning. Not much else. 'I need a week's package holiday to somewhere sunny with cocktails. That's all. I'll be alright. It's just…'

'It's hard.' Monroe's hand tightened on mine. 'I get it.'

I appreciated the sympathy. My head dropped. 'I'm waiting for you to say "I told you so". From the start you said my community wouldn't work.'

'Your community *is* working – but it's not working for *you* right now. Besides, I can't say "I told you so". I'm struggling too.'

I laughed feebly. 'Then we're both screwed.'

He leaned into me. 'Not by a long shot. We just need to allow time for self-care.'

'By getting into fights?'

He shuffled uncomfortably in his seat. 'I wouldn't recommend it.'

'Then what…'

There was a loud thump on the steamed-up window. I wound it down. 'Nimue, what do you want now?' I asked, letting my irritation get the better of me.

But it wasn't Nimue. An oddly green-skinned man was brandishing a sword in my face. 'I want,' he said with a nasty grin, 'for you both to get out of the vehicle and come with me.'

Chapter Four

Monroe would have quite happily shifted into his wolf form there and then but, despite the green man's unpleasant expression and threatening manner, I felt sure that this was the time for words and diplomacy rather than fighting. Escalation wouldn't help anyone. Apparently, there was hope for me yet.

I jumped out of the car before Monroe could turn furry and pasted on my best smile. 'Hi,' I said. 'I'm Charley.'

'I know who you are,' the stranger growled. He waved the sword at me. 'And if your buddy decides to change and grow big ears, you'll be one dead enchantress.'

Monroe got out of the other side of the car and snarled.

'Oooh, impressive,' Greenie drawled with full-blown sarcasm. Unfortunately I knew only too well that was not the way to woo a wolf.

Mentally taking a step back, I assessed our would-be attacker. Although his green skin was the most arresting thing about him, I put that out of my mind for now and focused on the rest of him, which actually seemed fairly normal. He was young, maybe early twenties or thereabouts. His clothes were casual but well kept, with a patch neatly sewn onto the thigh of his jeans, no doubt to cover a hole. He wore old trainers on his feet and there was the slightest tremor to his hand as he clutched the sword.

I slowly raised my hands to indicate submission

and shuffled over to Monroe. 'Let's do as the man says, shall we?' I murmured.

Monroe appeared to be in no mood to listen to me. 'Wave that blade at me once more and I'll rip out your throat.'

Greenie's hand tightened round the weapon. Uh oh. Despite that, I didn't think we were in immediate danger – unless Monroe made a move. Nervous people reacted badly, especially in life-or-death situations. A mere one percent of the population have malfunctioning amygdalas and won't resort to fight-or-flight reactions when in stressful situations. Greenie might not be human in the way that I was, but I reckoned he'd react in a similar fashion.

I cast a quick glance at the lake, wondering if Nimue was about to reappear and save the day. There was no sign of her. What happened next would be down to me. I gathered up the stress and tension inside me and pushed it all down. Calm would win the day.

I returned my gaze to Greenie's face. 'Take us to your leader.' My voice dropped. 'Before one of us does something we'll both regret and my friend here rips out your intestines.' Oops. That was less calm than I'd intended.

Greenie's mouth twisted. Before he could react, however, Monroe started to laugh. We both turned towards him. Greenie was confused; I was irritated.

'What?' I demanded. 'What's so funny?'

'He's a little green man.'

Greenie bristled.

'And you said take us to your leader.' A most un-wolf-like giggle escaped Monroe's lips. 'Maybe now we've got aliens to contend with on top of everything else.'

'Don't be silly,' I snapped. 'He's obviously not an

alien.'

'You don't know that. He could be.'

I folded my arms. 'He's not.'

'I'm not,' Greenie interjected.

I ignored him in favour of continuing to glare at Monroe. 'Just when we were finally having a sensible conversation and you were being thoughtful and nice, you start acting like a five year old. Are you on drugs?' I asked. 'Have you taken something?'

'No,' Monroe grinned. 'But if you've got something and you're offering, I won't say no.'

I tsked loudly.

Greenie coughed. 'You have to come with me.'

'See? He *is* taking us to his leader,' Monroe said.

'You're an idiot.'

Desperately trying to reassert control, Greenie lifted the sword until the very tip of the blade was brushing against my temple. Monroe's eyes flashed with anger before his bizarre sense of humour reasserted itself and he started to grin again.

'You'll walk in front of me. Twenty paces. And,' Greenie uttered with hard finality, 'you'll do exactly what I say.'

Monroe looped his arm round mine and pulled me with him. 'Yessir!' He dragged me with him, doing exactly as he'd been ordered. That was unexpected.

Once we were some distance ahead, Monroe dipped his head. 'I don't know who he is, but he's only a kid. He's more scared than anything.'

'Keep walking!' Greenie yelled from behind.

'I know that,' I hissed to Monroe.

'He's not a looter because his trainers are old. His clothes have been patched up, no doubt because there's someone out there who cares enough about him to spend hours bent over a needle and thread. He's probably from the community that cleared the roads around here and we probably want to get on their good side. I was trying to keep the situation calm and I think I succeeded. I was prepared to take him down but, once I started looking at him properly, I realised that we're not in any real danger. It's important to pay attention to the little details, Charlotte. It could save lives.'

'Turn left!' Greenie shouted at us.

We followed the path round while I tried my best not to punch Monroe in the arm. 'I know all that,' I whispered to him. 'I saw all those details.'

He let out a quiet snort of disbelief. 'You were making things worse, not better.'

'You were the one who was acting all threatening and scary. I'm not the big bad wolf here, Monroe. You are.'

He smiled. 'You're just annoyed that I'm taking control of the situation and avoiding a fight. He knows who we are and he's not approached us before now. That means his kind are more interested in peace than war. That's what we all want. We have to be careful to turn this situation to our advantage rather than cause further problems.'

The worst thing was that Monroe was one hundred percent right and his approach was what I was aiming for initially. He was explaining my own strategy to me – except that I hadn't done as good a job as I'd thought of locking away my own stress. My mouth had ruined my strategy before I even got started.

'I used humour to deflect the tension,' Monroe said proudly. 'I've still got it. I didn't rule my pack with authoritarian control, you know. I was a good leader.'

I sniffed. 'It was bad humour.'

He smirked. 'It was better than continuing with your suggestion that I yank out his insides. Diplomacy,

Charlotte. You should think about it some time. It has its place.'

Forget the green dude with the big sword, it was Monroe I was going to kill first. 'You threatened to rip out his throat!'

'Yes, but that was before I saw who he really was and used my wits and intelligence to get us out of this situation without bloodshed.'

'He's behind us waving a sword at our backs. Bloodshed could still ensue.' I had no idea why I was arguing because I agreed with Monroe's assessment of the situation.

'Not today.' And with another serene smile, he released my arm and put his hands in his pockets and started to whistle.

I sighed to myself. Yeah. I really did need a holiday.

***

Greenie marshalled us into a neat cul-de-sac. There was no doubt it was occupied. For a start, doors banged up and down the street, and there were worried calls as children were ushered inside from their gardens when we approached. Secondly, the entire place looked pretty much untouched by the magical apocalypse. There was evidence that things had been patched up, with darker spots on the road where potholes had been filled in and new tiles on the roofs of the houses where no doubt the fire rain that had attacked us had penetrated. Whoever had done these things had done a remarkably good job. I should know: I'd spent weeks overseeing the same sort of work in my own neighbourhood and it didn't look anything like as good as this.

We had walked about halfway down the road

when Greenie shouted at us to halt. I wondered if he would actually slice us with that blade if we ignored his command; for a moment, I was tempted to test him and see. Monroe was playing the role of good wolf, however, and slid to an easy stop. I had no good reason not to do the same.

A door opened to our right and another green face appeared. This one belonged to a woman. She had the sort of expression that I tended to associate with motherly types – exhausted but happy. All the same, when she walked towards us her shoulders belied her tension.

'Good afternoon,' she said. Her accent was Manchester through and through. I even spotted a tattoo on her wrist of a bee – the symbol of the city. Whatever manner of creature she really was, she was a part of Manchester as much as I was. Perhaps more so.

Greenie marched up behind us. I noted that he'd sheathed the sword; that suggested he trusted in the strength and power of the woman in front of us and no longer required weaponry to hold us in place.

'I caught these two out by Boggart Hole,' he said. 'It wasn't easy to bring them in but I managed it. The wolf is smart but the enchantress is a hothead.'

I normally prided myself on my poker face but Greenie's words provoked a reaction that I couldn't hide. My eyes widened and an irritated huff escaped my lips.

The woman smiled faintly. 'Thank you, Malbus,' she said. 'You may go now.'

Malbus twitched but remained where he was.

'You did a good job,' she told him. 'You should be proud of yourself.' She reached out and patted his arm.

He dropped his head, suddenly abashed, then he trotted off. I wondered if that sort of praise would work with my community – I needed some way of keeping my inhabitants at bay when the need arose.

'I am Alora,' she said. 'You are Monroe and you,' she nodded at me, 'are Charley.' She smiled at me. 'You've been having a hard time lately.'

'I...' Her gentleness was so unexpected that I suddenly found myself blinking back tears. 'I'm not a hothead,' I blurted out. Not normally anyway.

Her expression softened further. 'I know.' She took a step back and her demeanour altered, becoming businesslike and professional. I had the distinct impression of someone who was steel sheathed in marshmallow. We had to tread very carefully indeed. 'Tell me,' Alora said, 'what are you doing here?'

Monroe and I glanced at each other. He ran a hand through his hair and straightened his shoulders. 'We were helping someone out,' he said. 'Relocating them to the lake.'

'A water being, I assume?' she enquired. 'Because of the blood from the taps?'

Damn. This woman didn't miss a trick. 'Yes.'

'Thank you for sorting that out. It has saved us a job.' She knit her fingers together. 'What manner of being was it?'

I licked my lips. 'Uh, it was a mermaid. It *is* a mermaid. Her name is Nimue.'

I wanted to explain that she wasn't necessarily a friendly mermaid who would sing happy songs and befriend children, but Alora was ahead of me. She tutted. 'A mermaid? And you brought such a dangerous creature here? To this place?' She glared at both of us. 'We have children. Don't you know how dangerous mermaids are?'

I swallowed. 'She's not all that bad.' I had no idea why I was sticking up for Nimue. We were hardly bosom buddies.

Alora snorted. 'That's easy for you to say. She's not your new neighbour.'

Monroe interjected. 'We didn't know you were here. We wouldn't have brought the mermaid here if we'd known. To relocate her again might prove … difficult. If we could leave her for a couple of weeks and then reassess the situation…'

'Yes, yes.' Alora waved a hand in the air. 'I know what mermaids are like. We'll stay away from the lake and leave her in peace for the time being. If she causes problems, however, we will expect you to deal with them.'

This was going far better than I could have hoped. 'Yes.' I nodded vigorously. 'We will.'

'Good.' She gave a satisfied nod. 'You will tell no one about our existence here. We have no desire to get mixed up with your shenanigans.' Her eyes hardened. 'We've had enough trouble from other species as it is.'

'What—' I cleared my throat and hoped I wasn't being too forward. 'What species are you?'

Alora gave me a look to suggest I was particularly dim-witted. She might well have been right. 'Bogles, of course.'

'Of course.' What on earth was a bogle?

She seemed to recognise my confusion because she smiled slightly. 'We've been here for a long time. We were completely assimilated into Manchester, but before the apocalypse we had some trouble with the faeries.'

Monroe growled. 'Didn't we all?'

She shot him a look of sympathy, which made me think she knew exactly what had occurred with Monroe and his pack of werewolves. 'We mean you no harm. Leave us in peace to continue with our lives and we will do the same to you. That is why we would appreciate you keeping our presence a secret.'

'You're magical,' I began. 'You have knowledge that we don't. We have supplies and manpower. Perhaps we can trade or—'

'No.' Alora's tone brooked no argument. 'We are managing perfectly well on our own, thank you.' She looked me up and down. 'The tension you hold within you is palpable. We do not require those sorts of problems.' She held my eyes and grimaced. 'I do not wish to be impolite, and please understand that is not my intention. The world at large may have been saved from magic but in Manchester things remain difficult. We are only trying to survive as best we can. Maybe things will be different in the future.'

She appeared implacable and I knew there would be no changing her mind. All we could do was respect her wishes. The bogles had remained out of sight and unknown to all of us for this long. They had their reasons, even if I didn't fully understand them.

'Okay.' I touched Monroe's hand. 'We will do as you ask. If you are amenable, Monroe and I will return in a week's time. If the situation with Nimue, the mermaid, is untenable then we will try and move her again.'

Alora inclined her head. 'I appreciate that.' She smiled. 'Who knows? Maybe she's one of those rare mermaids who isn't a bloodthirsty bitch.'

I had my doubts about that. I forced a smile. 'We should go.'

'Charlotte.' Alora's use of my full name made my head jerk up. 'You have a lot of power within you. Magic can be a difficult thing to manage. Such a surge within a human body … it is no wonder that you are feeling ill effects. You should take care. Be kind to yourself.' She glanced at Monroe. 'Make sure others are kind to you also.'

I opened my mouth, desperate to ask her more. She seemed to know more about me than I knew about myself. But Alora had already turned on her heel and was walking up the path to her house.

Monroe shook his head, his words a low warning intended for my ears only. 'Leave it for now, Charlotte. There is pain in this community. In time we can approach them again but if we force the issue today we will only make things more difficult.'

The lupine bastard was right again. I stared longingly after Alora and sighed. 'Okay.' I pushed my hair out of my eyes. 'But we'll try again when we come back.' I met his gaze. 'We *will* come back.'

'Naturally,' he said lightly. 'We promised.'

Chapter Five

I'd hoped that Monroe would give me a lift to my neighbourhood or, at the very least, drop me at the reservoir so I could retrieve the bike. Instead he made a beeline for the centre of the city.

There was only one place that he could be aiming for. The last thing I wanted was another confrontation with Mike Timmons, the sole remaining faery in the city.

'Is this necessary?' I asked. 'What's there to say that's not been said already?'

'We're not going to the Travotel to pick a fight,' Monroe replied calmly. 'That time with the faery wanker has been and gone.'

'He's not really a wanker, you know. He's an alright guy.' I meant it, despite some of Timmons' more questionable actions. He had told Max, my human nemesis, where to find me. He'd only done it to avoid bloodshed on his own turf but he knew he'd erred and he'd made up for it since, dropping in to help out with all manner of projects and encouraging his long-term hotel guests to do the same.

'He's a faery,' Monroe answered. 'He'll always be a wanker.'

I sighed. Monroe could be obstructively stubborn when the mood took him. 'If you're not cruising for a faery bruising, then what?' I asked. 'Even if he's got further insights into mermaids, I think we've got Nimue covered for the time being. I don't think she'll be any more trouble.' I mentally crossed my fingers; I *hoped* she wasn't going to be any more trouble.

'That's the optimistic Charlotte I know and love,' Monroe grinned. He pulled the car into the Travotel car park and turned off the engine.

'Love?' I enquired.

He leaned across and gave me a light peck on the cheek. 'Of course,' he said easily. There was a dancing gleam in his blue eyes. 'Everyone loves the enchantress.' Then something darker and deeper flickered in his expression and he pulled back.

Feeling awkward, I got out of the car and shoved my hands in my pockets. 'If you cause any trouble, Monroe, I will have to intervene.'

'I won't cause any trouble.' He began striding towards the front door. 'Trust me.'

Hell, these days I couldn't trust myself. With a deep sense of foreboding, I trailed after him. All I wanted to do was put my feet up. Please, I whispered to myself, no more blood. I'd had enough of that today, even if it had only been of the magical variety.

Timmons was rearranging flowers on a small side table. Goodness only knows where he managed to get them at this time of year. I prided myself on my local knowledge but I'd be hard-pressed to come up with much more than a straggly, half-dead daffodil. Timmons had conjured up a bouquet of roses and lilies.

He straightened up as we entered, smiling until he registered who we were. There was a flash of taut fear in his face before his smooth, hotel-manager persona took over. 'Good day! And how are you two on this fine afternoon?'

'Fabulous,' Monroe murmured, sounding anything but.

Timmons looked at us and we looked at him, a moment's silence descending into something far more awkward. I had to give it to the faery, though – he stood his ground.

'What do you want?' he said finally, yielding to the inevitable and querying our intrusion. 'I don't want any trouble.' This last statement was addressed to Monroe. I couldn't be certain, but it seemed to me that it wasn't just old history that was making Timmons concerned. There seemed to be something fresh about his anxiety.

'I don't know why you think I'm here to cause havoc. There's only one reason we are here. It's obvious really. Why else would we come to a hotel?' Monroe said, almost purring. 'We want a room. Your *best* room.'

My mouth dropped open. I turned to Monroe, more surprised than Timmons was. 'Excuse me?'

'We need chocolate,' Monroe continued. 'And wine.' He pointed at the floral display. 'Some fresh flowers wouldn't go amiss either.'

I found my voice. 'What exactly do you think is going to happen here?' My eyes shot daggers at him. 'How dare you? If you want to get into my knickers, the least you could do is ask me first.'

Timmons coughed awkwardly. 'I'll go and check our availability,' he said. He skedaddled out of the way and into his back office as fast as his legs could carry him.

'I mean, seriously, Monroe?' I put my hands on my hips. 'Yes, sex is a great stress reliever. Yes, a screaming orgasm might help me put all the other shit out of my mind for a while. But you're assuming a great deal, a great fucking deal. I suppose you think I should be grateful that you're booking a room by the hour instead of leading me down some dreary back alley.' I drew in a sharp breath. 'And if you're about to suggest that you make use of *my* back alley, then I'll have more than harsh words for you. I thought by now that we'd worked out a decent working relationship, that we had respect for each other. Instead, you seem to think that you can crook your little finger and I'll throw myself backwards and spread my legs. You bastard of a werewolf.' I scrunched up my face in disgust. 'Just when I was starting to like you. You think that because you've got sexy blue eyes and a gorgeous body you can do what you want. Well, I'm here to tell that you can't. Not with this woman. No way.'

Monroe didn't react once during my tirade; he merely watched me without expression. Only when I paused to gather myself did he actually speak. 'Are you finished?' he asked.

'Oh, I'm only just getting going,' I told him in no uncertain terms.

'That's a shame. I thought you'd enjoy some relaxation time. I thought a couple of days here would give you the space and time you need to get your head together. I'm returning to the north – I've got things to sort out there – but I reckoned that some time alone would do you good. The room is for you, Charlotte. Not us.' He smiled faintly. 'Unless that offer of screaming orgasms really is on the table.' He leaned forward. 'But it wasn't what I was planning. And I appreciate that you think I have sexy blue eyes.'

My hands dropped to my sides. 'P–pardon?'

Monroe smiled again, the corners of his eyes crinkling. 'You need a break,' he said gently. 'You know, I know it. Even that green-skinned gatekeeper Alora seemed to know it. Stay here for a couple of days. More if you need it. Read books. Sleep. Chill out.'

I blinked rapidly. 'I can't,' I protested, focusing on logistics rather than my embarrassment at getting Monroe's intentions so very wrong. 'There are a hundred and one things I've got to do. There are people who need me. Today alone, I've got a council meeting to go to as soon as I get home. After that, I promised a family on the road across from me that I'd do something about the giant spider living in their basement. And when I say giant, I mean giant – it's the size of your damned car. And that's without the dozens of other complaints and requests and moans that I'll have to deal with before I can get to bed tonight. I don't have time for a break.'

'Yes, you do,' Monroe said. 'It's not a tropical island, and I'm not sure I'd trust any cocktails that the faery would make, but you need this, Charlotte. I'll tell Lizzy and Anna and the rest that you're taking a few days out. They'll manage without you. The world isn't going to stop turning because you're having a holiday.'

I opened my mouth to continue arguing but Monroe put his index finger to my lips to hush me. 'If you kill yourself in the process of sorting out your community, you'll be doing no one any favours. You need a rest.' His voice brooked no dissent. 'I'm ordering you to have a rest.'

'You can't order me to do that! You're not my boss.'

'In this,' he said simply, 'I am.'

Timmons nervously popped his head out of the door. 'Uh, it appears that we do have a room available.' He glanced from me to Monroe and back again. 'If you still want it, that is.'

'We do,' Monroe said cheerfully.

Timmons looked at me. 'Charley?'

A wave of exhaustion overtook me. It seemed too much effort to continue to protest. I answered before I could think about it too much and change my mind. 'Yes,' I said, in a near whisper. 'Yes. I'd like the room, please.'

***

I didn't order room service or thumb through the selection of books that Timmons had so thoughtfully provided. I didn't even really think properly. I stripped off my clothes, collapsed on the bed and slept for sixteen hours. Sixteen blissful hours with no dreams, no interruptions and no craziness. Although I have to admit that I slept so soundly that a herd of mammoth pink elephants could probably have stampeded past my room and I wouldn't have stirred. In fact, it was only when I woke up that I realised I had melted chocolate smeared across my cheek from the treat that Timmons had thoughtfully left on my pillow and I'd been too tired to notice. I peeled the foil wrapper away from my skin and dropped it onto the nightstand before absently grabbing a tissue and wiping at the chocolate. Then I stretched out starfish fashion and contemplated the ceiling with half-lidded eyes.

It shouldn't have come this, I thought, as I mentally traced a fissure of cracks barely concealed by the last coat of paint. I'd all but run myself into the ground. I'd pulled plenty of all-nighters before – it came with the territory of being a professional gambler – but I hadn't ever had to deal with these levels of stress and anxiety. It felt like I was responsible for several thousand lives. The simple truth was that it wasn't sustainable. Monroe was right: if I continued down this path, I'd burn out completely and be of no use to anyone.

I hoped everyone else would be able to see that too and would step up to help out more. In recent weeks that had seemed a very forlorn hope but, after the good sleep that I'd had, my effervescent optimism seemed to be reasserting itself. The others would see my plight once I took the time to explain it to them. Right?

I wiggled my fingers and toes with the deep

satisfaction of the newly refreshed then rolled out of bed. It was time to go in search of food.

I pulled on my wrinkled clothes, feeling slightly icky at having to put them on again. When I opened the door to my room, however, there was a neat pile of brand-new clothes sitting on the floor. I gazed at it for a moment, a lump in my throat at the unexpected kindness. Five minutes later, my old clothes were on the floor in a pile and yet again I was feeling a million times better.

Given that it was about five o'clock in the morning, the corridors were silent. I wondered how many people were staying here. The hotel had a lived-in and much-loved air about it, despite the lack of people around. Maybe that was because Timmons was a faery, or maybe it was because he was an incredibly good hotel manager. Either way, there was an ease to my steps as I wandered to the stairs, past the long-since out-of-order lift and made my way to the lobby.

Towards the back of the hotel there was a small restaurant cum café which, by the lingering smell, was definitely still in use for the hotel residents. It was dark and quiet now but I envisaged that it would be a bustling place in a few hours' time. I could find something to eat and then make my way home. Or I could find something to eat and go to my room to relax. It didn't take much internal debate to plump for the latter. Monroe had been right: the citizens of the south would last without me for another day.

I ambled to a swing door where I assumed the hotel kitchen was located. The fridges might be out of action but the pantry was reasonably well stocked given our post-apocalyptic world. As far as I could tell, the old wood-fired pizza oven had been appropriated to bake bread and I found more than enough leftovers, plus some very tasty-looking jam, to quiet the grumbles in my stomach. My last three meals had been cold beans eaten out of the tin to save time. Fresh bread and fruity jam right in front of me was utterly glorious.

I lifted a plate off one of the shadowed shelves, located a knife, then hopped onto a table and started to spread jam thickly onto one of the bread slices. It tasted so good that I crammed half of it into my mouth, murmuring with delight. I probably looked like a messy toddler with strawberry jam smeared round my mouth. I didn't care.

I was about to start on my third piece when the most godawful keening sound filled the air. It sounded vaguely akin to a tortured dog. I dropped the bread and froze. I couldn't work out where the sound was coming from. Under pre-apocalyptic circumstances I'd have assumed it was a fire alarm but under these circumstances – well, it could be anything.

With magic tingling at my fingertips, I leapt off the table and ran out to the lobby. Whatever it was, I'd deal with it.

From the stairwell, a dressing-gowned, flapping figure appeared. 'Whatever you are,' Timmons bellowed, 'begone!'

I blinked at him. 'Um…'

He swung wild eyes in my direction before relaxing. 'Oh,' he said. 'It's just you.'

I decided I preferred being told to begone. All the same, I injected a cheery note into my voice, speaking loudly enough to be heard over the continuing wail. 'Just me.' I waved a hand. 'What on earth is going on?'

Timmons ran a hand through his hair, which did absolutely nothing to smooth it down and only served to make him look more dishevelled. 'Magic alarm,' he muttered and then gave a loud curse. He screwed up his face, concentrating. A few seconds later, the screeching stopped. 'What did you do?' he asked. He sounded irritated. I didn't mind that; I'd be irritated at being woken up this early by a wailing banshee too.

'Nothing! I was hungry so I went looking for something to eat. I found some bread in the kitchen...'

He sighed. 'And some jam too, by the looks of it.'

I wiped my mouth. Yep. Some sweet strawberry goodness still clung there. Mmmm. 'I didn't think it would be a problem.'

'It's not.'

Uh oh. 'So if I didn't set off that alarm, what did?'

'It was you.' He tutted to himself.

'But...'

'Some of the residents are concerned about their safety. We had an invasion of snakes a while ago. Then there was your friend Max—'

'Hey! He was never my friend!'

Timmons nodded, distracted. 'Yes, alright. Anyway, everyone wanted assurances that I'd keep them safe so I used a bit of magic to set up an alarm system. Any time anyone does anything deemed to be a danger to the hotel, the alarm goes off.'

'Ah.' I pursed my lips and nodded gravely as if I understood what he was talking about. 'So making myself a jam butty was dangerous?'

Timmons grimaced. 'You'd be amazed at what the magic decides fits the definition of danger. The alarm went off when a vase of flowers was knocked over by accident. It went off when Phil in 204 snored so loudly that his neighbours were kept awake.' He ticked off his fingers. 'It even went off when there was something of a love tryst occurring between two of our older residents. It's not an exact spell. I've been adjusting it for weeks.'

'Is it a good idea,' I asked carefully, 'to be using

such magic all the time?' After all, it was magic usage that got Manchester into this mess in the first place. I'd been under the impression that I had to curb my own spells to avoid any further city-wide turbulence. Timmons himself had told me months ago that I couldn't make Manchester any worse more than it already was but I was still nervous about it. Who wouldn't be?

Despite my palpable concern, Timmons scoffed. 'What I do here is a drop in the proverbial ocean. It won't do any harm. Only a large group of magic wielders constantly making use of their skills will cause issues.' He gave me a clever look, obviously understanding where my concern was coming from. 'You don't have to worry, Charley. Things are settled here now. I might have been concerned in the initial aftermath but now I seriously doubt you could use enough magic to create problems.'

All the same, I wasn't sure it was wise to use magic unless the situation genuinely called for it. A magical alarm that was set off when someone spread some jam on a slice of bread struck me as a step too far.

From beyond the stairwell, a wide-eyed face appeared. 'Is it safe?'

'Yes, yes.' Timmons smiled. 'Don't worry, Jacob. It's all fine.'

A woman appeared behind the nervy Jacob. 'This isn't good enough! It's the middle of the night! That damned alarm goes off far too often.'

I sensed Timmons holding back. 'You asked for the alarm. You agreed to it.'

'I didn't know it would keep screaming at me all the time, did I? It's your magic. You have to sort it out.'

'I'm doing my best—'

'Do better!' she snapped.

I watched her. I wasn't the only person in

Manchester who was being put under pressure to make sure everything worked and everyone was safe. Timmons appeared less aggrieved than I was but there was a tightening in my stomach at the woman's tirade, which was all too familiar to my ears these days.

Timmons inhaled deeply and offered a benign smile. 'I'm working on it.'

I cleared my throat. 'It was my fault,' I said. 'I didn't realise the alarm was in place.'

The woman scowled at me. I might never have met her before but I'd encountered that same facial expression many times in recent weeks.

'I'm sorry,' I said. 'It won't happen…' There was a thunderous clatter of footsteps from the stairwell.

'Help! Someone help!'

My blood froze. Whoever was yelling, there was no mistaking the note of pure fear in their voice. Timmons heard it too. He pushed past the couple and glanced upwards.

'Mr Timmons! You have to help! Valerie has been murdered! She's … she's … dead!'

And right then and there I knew that my short-lived-but-very-welcome holiday was well and truly over.

Chapter Six

It didn't help that I knew Valerie, and not just from the apocalyptic madness. Our paths had crossed many times on the poker circuit. We never got on that well but I'd like to think there was a sort of mutual respect. Occasionally. The old adage that you shouldn't speak ill of the dead rang true for me more than it probably should have done.

Until I entered her room, following on Timmons' heels, I'd kept my fingers crossed that she'd passed away from natural causes. In these turbulent times it would be easy to jump to conclusions. Valerie wasn't exactly decrepit but she was old and she hadn't lived a particularly healthy lifestyle. I could well imagine that she'd had a heart attack or a stroke. Maybe such a swift death would be a blessing, given our lack of trained doctors and working hospitals. All these thoughts were running through my head right up to the point where I saw her body. In that moment everything changed.

'Shit.'

She lay on her bed, one arm draped over the side and dangling lifelessly while her fingers trailed on the floor. Her fingernails, which were always immaculately manicured, were cracked and broken. Her hair looked matted and in knots, like someone had deliberately scrunched it up. If I were honest, I'd have struggled to recognise her as Valerie but little details referenced her, from the delicate filigree bracelet on her wrist to the beauty spot on her cheek. As a whole, however, the sunken look to her skin and her skull-like appearance made it difficult to equate her corpse with the living being who had once occupied it.

'How long…' My voice cracked. I swallowed and tried again. 'When was the last time anyone saw her?'

'I can ask around,' Timmons said. He looked as pale as Valerie did. 'I saw her at breakfast yesterday.'

I am no forensic scientist or mortician but even I knew that a body couldn't shrivel like this in less than twenty-four hours. She was practically a husk. I dredged up the word for myself. Exsanguination: that was it. Valerie's entire body had been drained of all its blood. I shuddered.

Steeling myself, I edged over to get a closer look. There was only the faintest odour of death emanating from her; most of what I smelled was talcum powder. I stared into her glazed eyes, willing her to blink and giggle and tell us all this was nothing more than a tasteless joke. That wasn't going to happen. We all knew it.

Her head was tilted slightly to the side and her neck was arched. Something caught my eye and, holding my breath, I leaned down for a closer look. When I saw what it was, I stiffened and pulled back.

'What?' Timmons asked. 'What do you see?'

I gave him a grim look. 'Puncture wounds,' I said. 'Right by her jugular.'

We gazed at each other for a moment – let's face it, it was better than looking at Valerie's corpse. The identical thought was mirrored in our expressions. The shit was well and truly about to hit the fan.

***

I couldn't tell you for sure how many vampires were now living in Manchester. Great numbers had flocked here in the immediate aftermath of the apocalypse, drawn by the magic that strengthened their powers and by the idea that, finally, they could be free to live their lives without worrying about secrecy. For a long time their numbers had been depleted, hunted down by a small cabal of hunters who knew of their existence. As vampires are born and not made, their population had dwindled to near extinction.

Despite their woes, they had few fans. Julie, a vampire herself, had come close to triggering the end of the world rather than simply the end of Manchester. To make matters worse, as they enjoyed the magic atmosphere of this newly-born city the vampires grew more arrogant and predatorial. Still, as far as I was aware, none of them had actually killed anyone.

'I knew we should have worked harder on that census,' I muttered to myself as much as to Timmons while we waited for Anna to arrive. 'At least then we'd have a proper pool of suspects.'

He offered me a helpless shrug. 'How on earth would you have enforced it? Anyway, from what I've heard you've been more than busy with other matters.'

He was right but it didn't stop me thinking yet again that I should have done more. I should have been better. For the briefest moment the face of my long-since-dead little brother flashed into my mind. I should have done more to save him back then; I should be doing more to save my city now. Then maybe whichever vampire had drained Valerie of all her blood would have thought twice about it.

I curled my fingers into tight fists. Whatever I'd thought of the woman, I wouldn't let Valerie's killer get away. I didn't care who had ended her life; no one was allowed to act like that. Not in my city. Not under my watch.

———

It seemed to take an age but it was probably little more than an hour before Anna strode through the door, kitted out in her full police regalia. Lizzy, Julie, Cath and the runner who Timmons had sent to fetch them all trailed behind her; they'd now been seconded to the cause.

In our southern side of Manchester, Anna had taken it upon herself to become the police commissioner, dealing with everything from stolen goods to the odd neighbourly fist-fight. She investigated the problems and left it to me to mete out justice. I crossed my fingers and hoped she was ready to deal with murder as well as petty crime. After seeing Valerie's body, I was ready to mete out an entirely different kind of justice.

Fortunately, Anna didn't waste any time. 'Right,' she said briskly. 'I take it all the hotel residents are still here?'

Timmons nodded. 'Some wanted to leave but we've told them to stay in their rooms.'

'Good. We need statements from each of them. What they saw or heard during the night, what they knew of the victim and her plans for yesterday, and when the last time was that they saw her.' Her expression was stony but there was a professional air about her that was immediately reassuring. 'In over eighty-five percent of murders, the victim already knows their killer. Everyone here is a suspect.'

Timmons fidgeted. 'Uh, the manner of her death…'

Anna swung her eyes onto him and I could swear he cowered. 'Yes?'

He cleared his throat. 'It looks like it was a…' He shuffled and dropped his gaze.

'A vampire,' I finished for him. Out of the corner of my eye, I noted Julie stiffening. Good. Her reaction suggested that she was shocked by the information; that meant it was unlikely that she'd had anything to do with it. The last thing I needed was for her to be on anyone's hit list.

'I was not informed of that,' Anna frowned. 'But it doesn't change anything. Our initial investigations will remain the same.'

Timmons coughed.

'What?' Anna snapped.

'Well,' he started, shuffling slightly. I grimaced. I knew exactly what he was going to say. The witch hunt was about to begin and it would apparently start with him. Bugger. 'The thing is, if all my residents are considered suspects then shouldn't all vampires be too? They're the ones who should be held to account.' He didn't look at Julie. 'She should immediately be placed under…'

I interrupted him before he could complete the sentence. 'I think it would be extraordinarily helpful if Julie could examine the body first, before we start with the interrogations.'

Anna flicked me a look. 'I'd prefer to call them interviews,' she said. 'Before we get to the thumbscrews and water-boarding, that is.'

'Interviews, yes,' I agreed hastily. 'Anyway, as a vampire, Julie might have some insights into Valerie's … death.' I nudged Timmons. 'That's what you were about to suggest, right?'

It wasn't. He knew and I knew it but he wasn't prepared to argue about it, not with Julie standing in front of him with her arms folded and her fangs a mere foot away. 'Sure,' he said. 'Yes. That's what I was going to say.'

Julie looked unimpressed.

'I'll lead the way,' I said, before she could be the

one to start the trouble. I grabbed her elbow and steered her towards the stairs. 'This way!'

As soon as the stairwell door clanged shut behind us, Julie wrested her arm away from me. 'He was about to say that I had to get out of his hotel. He was about to say that, because I'm a vampire, I'm a suspect too and I should be under lock and key.'

'I don't think he was planning to say that at all,' I demurred, lying through my teeth.

'Don't bluff me, darling. I'm not stupid.'

I sighed. 'Okay. Yes, he probably was about to say all that, but once we start down that road chaos will ensue. The last thing any of us need is for every vampire in the city to be placed under suspicion. We need to work on a presumption of innocence, not guilt, otherwise I can imagine what the other vampires will do when they're accused by anyone who passes them by. We don't need that kind of hassle. Relations across species are fragile enough without entire ethnic populations being accused of murder.'

Her eyes narrowed but she didn't argue. I breathed out.

'Anyway,' I said, moving the subject to slightly safer ground, 'I have a bone to pick with you in private. What the hell did you think you were doing going to Monroe and telling him I needed his help?'

'You did need his help, darling.' She glanced at me critically. 'You still do. In fact, he should be here now. This affects him as well as us. All those vampires you're so keen to protect live in his part of the city, not ours.'

I opened my mouth to tell her that I'd go in search of Monroe as soon as things were wrapped up here but, before I could, the door behind us opened again and a voice called out. 'Wait up!' Cath bounded up the stairs towards us. 'I'm coming too!'

I was well aware of the teenager's bloodthirsty nature. 'I'm not sure that's a good idea,' I said.

'I'm the only one here who knows anything about medicine.'

'Darling,' Julie drawled, 'I don't think you'll be able to bring a corpse back to life, no matter how well trained you may be in first aid.' In the absence of any qualified doctors or nurses, Cath was our best option at stitching up wounds and doling out medication. She didn't have a lot of experience but she had more than the rest of us. Unfortunately that wasn't saying much.

Cath paused to give Julie a glare. 'Unless you can find us an expert in post-mortems, I'm the best person you have to help you investigate.' She turned to me. 'Tell her, Charley.'

I raised my eyes heavenward. Just think, a few hours ago I was sleeping blissfully without a care in the world. 'We're all here now,' I said. 'Let's see what our combined brains can work out from Valerie's body and the crime scene.' Of course, the odds were that we'd discover absolutely nothing but we had to try.

We emerged at the third floor where Valerie's room was located. At least the proximity to the place of her death meant that Cath and Julie lapsed into a respectful silence. I led the way to the room, although I was fairly certain that the scent of death was already in Julie's nostrils and she knew exactly where we were going.

'The fire door,' Julie said. 'Has it been open all this time?'

I glanced round and realised she was right. At the end of the hallway, close to the other staircase at the opposite end of the hotel, the fire exit leading to the outside world was ajar. I thought about it. 'Yes,' I said finally. 'It was open when I came up here the first time.' It was the perfect escape route for any intruder – vampire or otherwise.

'Mmm,' Julie murmured. 'You can't open those doors from the other side.' She looked at me meaningfully. 'If the murderer isn't from inside the hotel, your corpse must have invited her killer in.'

I sighed. It did make sense, otherwise Timmons' magic alarm would have gone off earlier. Unfortunately all that information did was widen our pool of suspects from several dozen to several thousand.

I steeled myself and walked into Valerie's room, while Julie and Cath hesitated at the door. Cath let out a gasp. Julie remained more stoical but even her skin looked paler than normal.

We wouldn't do Valerie any good by wringing our hands and retching. I swallowed and strode over to her body. 'Don't touch anything until Anna gives us the say so.'

'Sure,' Cath murmured. 'We wouldn't want to disturb the scene before the fingerprint technicians get here.'

I tutted at her. 'We might not have the resources but that doesn't mean we need to be stupid.' I pointed at Valerie. 'There are the puncture wounds. Julie, come here and tell me what you think.'

The vampire actress edged in with considerable reluctance. She moved round to my right side and peered at Valerie's body. Cath came over and did the same.

'Maybe,' the teen said, sounding nervous for the first time, 'I should check to make sure she's really dead.'

'She's really dead,' Julie snapped. 'How many alive people do you know who look like *that*?'

I placed a warning hand on her shoulder. Cath was only trying to be useful in the face of a terrifying sight.

Julie shrugged me off but she did at least subside. 'Yeah,' she said finally. 'Those puncture marks look vampire-like to me.'

'You told me once,' I said, 'that you could never drink all the blood in a human's body in one go. That there's just too much. Was that the truth?'

'Yes,' she answered. 'It's a lot of liquid to chug down.'

I winced slightly at her choice of words but I didn't interrupt.

'Whoever did this,' Julie continued, 'must have spent quite some time with her.' She shuffled round the other side of the bed and squatted down beside Valerie's trailing hand. 'You see the way her fingernails are cracked? She put up a fight. Our perpetrator is probably covered in scratches.'

'How quickly do vampires heal?' I asked.

Julie's mouth flattened into a thin line. 'These days? With all the magic floating in the air? Hours, at best. If you're using attack wounds to find her killer, you'll have to move quickly. Unless your Valerie here managed to score a life-threatening hit, whoever did this will have healed their scratches and cuts by noon.' She paused. 'And it's light outside. Most vampires will be sleeping away the day by now.'

I absorbed this information with a sinking sensation. This was not going to be easy. 'Do you know how many vampires there are in Manchester, Julie?'

She shook her head. 'No.' She looked away from me and towards Cath. 'What are you staring at?'

Cath didn't appear in the slightest bit intimidated. 'I was checking you over,' she said. 'For scratches.'

Julie bared her teeth at the teen but without any real malice. She grabbed her blouse and started to unbutton it. 'Would you like to check all over?' she enquired. 'I didn't do this,' she said. 'I *couldn't* do this. Frankly I don't know of any vampire who could.' She glanced at me. 'If there were more puncture wounds, I'd have said there must have been more than one attacker.'

'Unless,' Cath said thoughtfully, 'they were *really* hungry.'

'Darling,' Julie replied, 'no one is *that* hungry.'

I twisted my fingers together and sighed. Pointless as it seemed, I'd have to go to the north as quickly as possible to see if I could find any vampires with tell-tale wounds who were wandering about in the morning sun without a care in the world.

'Are there any other signs I should look out for?' I asked. 'With the vampire –or even vampires – who did this?'

Julie considered. 'We do tend to become lethargic after a big, um, meal,' she said. 'And happy.'

So I was looking for a bloated, sleepy vamp with a cheesy grin and bloody scratches. And I only had about three hours to find them before their wounds healed. Great. I'd seen better odds on Pamela Anderson becoming the next James Bond.

I squared my shoulders and reminded myself that sometimes long shots paid off. I cast a last look at Valerie. 'I've got this,' I promised her quietly. 'I'll find the bastard who did this.'

Chapter Seven

I hadn't visited the northern part of the city since Monroe and his supernatural cronies had settled in. It wasn't out of a lack of desire to go there, it had simply been a matter of logistics and time. Even so, I'd heard enough about what was going on to have a good idea about the situation. I had an odd idea that it would look like a scene out of *Blade Runner*. It didn't: it just looked like Manchester.

The streets in the newly developed enclave were surprisingly clean. As I entered the first boundary, receiving a grave nod from the two guys who were positioned at the entrance and who obviously knew who I was, I spotted several others sweeping away bits of debris. The windows were sparkling and there was little sign of any damage. For some reason I couldn't identify, I felt a sour tug at the realisation that Monroe's community was managing the challenges of the apocalypse better than mine was.

Much like in the south, there was a row of neat little shops that had been commandeered by enterprising folk. Most of them offered similar items – household goods and the like. One or two had artfully-penned signs indicating that they sold weapons, from crossbows to guns. This was more like the sort of vigilantism I'd expected – until I noted the other sign stating that 'all purchases were to be logged and identification produced'. It appeared they weren't taking any chances that anyone would go off gung-ho or battle royale style.

I crossed a quiet square, noting what appeared to

be the headquarters at its eastern side – a grand old building with large stone columns and weathered carved gargoyles on its front. I couldn't remember what it was used for originally but now there was a group of what were presumably werewolves gathered outside. A man stood at the head of them, passing out sheets of paper.

'You need to check on the Canal Monster, Derek. Make sure it's staying to its territory and check on its current attitude.' There was a pause as another sheet was passed out. 'Rick and Jo, the ration shops need stocking up with these goods. Check the outlying supermarkets first for any items. The updated map is attached to your orders. Make sure you mark where you've been and what the state of play is in terms of supplies.'

The words 'well-oiled machine' sprang to my mind. Yes, I did something similar in the south but I had fewer eager volunteers and more complaints to put up with.

Monroe had once told me that serious punishments were never needed for werewolves because they always followed pack orders. At the time I'd scoffed at the idea that they always fell into line and did as they were told, but now I was starting to think that he was right. I made a mental note to talk to him about sending a group of my less community-spirited individuals over here for a fact-finding mission. They could certainly learn a few things about pulling together as a team.

Tempting as it was to hang around and see what else was going on, I didn't have time. I picked up my pace, aware that eyes were following my progress across the square. I thought I could get past without being stopped but, right before I turned into the first street on the left, a voice hailed me. 'Enchantress!'

I grimaced and turned, unwilling to waste more time than was necessary. Julian strode over to me. He was smiling, but I had the distinct impression he'd have preferred me not to be there.

'I go by Charley,' I said drily.

'I wasn't sure of the correct protocol,' he said. 'I apologise that I wasn't here to greet you earlier. I was unaware that you were visiting us. The border guards got the news to me quickly enough, but next time you should let us know in advance and we can make proper preparations.'

He was making it sound as if I were a visiting dignitary – who also needed my passport checked at the same time. 'This is only a brief visit,' I told him. 'I'm … looking for someone.'

An intelligent light gleamed in his eyes. 'Monroe is back that way.' He pointed behind him.

I shook my head. 'It's not Monroe I'm looking for.' I heaved in a breath and wondered how much I should say, then I remembered that neither Julian nor anyone else here was actually my enemy. We were all in this together, whether we lived separately or not. 'There's been a murder,' I told him. 'At the Travotel. All signs indicate it was a vampire.'

Julian stiffened. He turned his head and snapped his fingers. 'I need a patrol here now!'

At once six figures trotted over. None of them were holding weapons but each one had an air of danger; to a person, they were primed and ready for any kind of trouble.

'You will escort the enchantress to the vampires. Rouse them all.' Julian glanced at me. 'Do you have some idea who you are looking for, or is this a fishing expedition?' There was no judgment in his tone: Julian certainly didn't betray his thoughts or his emotions. As someone who prided herself on reading expressions and tells, I could only be impressed. He'd make an excellent poker player.

'Scratch marks. Superficial wounds.' I shrugged. 'That kind of thing.' I was starting to feel that, instead of this being a hunt for a needle in a haystack, I'd find Valerie's killer before lunch with ease. I met Julian's eyes. 'Thank you.'

He didn't smile. 'Security and safety are our priority. We will find the vampire responsible and bring him to justice.'

I wondered briefly what it would be like to live your life with such unerring certainty that things would go the way you wanted them to. I also wondered why Julian wasn't the one in charge around here. Then again, there was still no sign of Monroe. Maybe Julian was the boss and Monroe had neglected to mention it.

The nearest woman to me nodded her head. 'This way, ma'am. We will show you where the vampires bed down and help you catch the culprit.'

I licked my lips. 'Uh, sure.' I hesitated. 'Thank you.'

'Felicity, make sure the vampires do what you need. Tell them that if they don't cooperate, there will be serious consequences.' There was something worryingly ominous about the way Julian said that. The werewolf nodded grimly.

'I don't want to cause trouble with the vampires,' I said hastily. 'One bad apple doesn't mean the barrel is rotten.'

'Oh, it's rotten enough,' I heard another werewolf mutter.

Julian's eyes narrowed and the snarky wolf subsided. 'Caution is advised,' he said, although I wasn't sure whether that statement was directed at me or at his wolves. He inclined his head and strode away. I watched him for a moment; he certainly acted more like the part of absolute leader than Monroe did.

I turned away. It wasn't my problem.

It was something of a struggle to keep up with my new buddies because they marched at a tremendous pace. It was just as well that we only had to travel a few streets or I'd have started to feel seriously embarrassed by my short legs and comparatively slow movements. I was out of breath by the time we arrived at what appeared to be another barricade made out of water barrels and steel panels. The werewolves looked like they were merely out for a Sunday stroll.

'Who do these idiots think they're kidding?' muttered the female werewolf who'd led the way. 'This shit wouldn't stop a toddler.' She kicked at the nearest steel panel, causing a loud clang to reverberate around the now nearly empty street.

A moment later a hooded figure appeared and peered over the makeshift barrier. The hood wasn't merely a trendy sweatshirt of the sort favoured by teenagers, it was a proper cloak fashioned out of what looked like dark velvet. It all but covered the figure's face. This, then, would be a vampire, hiding from the sun's rays and looking for all the world like he was about to attend a Halloween party. I squinted at him. When I concentrated, I could see the blue aura surrounding his body that set him apart as a magical creature. It gave me a headache to do it too often, though, suggesting that looking directly at magic was bad for my eyesight.

'We've been through this,' the vampire said, in a surprisingly high-pitched voice. 'Do not bother us until dusk.' He disappeared behind the barricade as if that were the end of the matter.

The werewolf rolled her eyes and kicked the barrier again. Then, without waiting for an answer, she leapt over it. The others behind her followed suit. I stood there for a moment, not sure what I should do. A moment later there was the sound of a brief scuffle and a large section of the barrier tumbled forward.

'Enchantress,' said one of my new werewolf buddies. 'Please, come on through.'

'Charley,' I told him. 'Please.'

He grinned suddenly. 'I'm Billy.'

I declined Billy's offer of a hand and gingerly stepped through the gap in the barricade. At one side, two of the other werewolves were holding the hooded vampire in place.

'That's Kate and Sal,' Billy said. They nodded in unison. 'Then Steven, Guy and Felicity.'

Each werewolf waved at me in turn. I did my best to memorise their names but it was difficult to focus, given the angry vampire they'd grabbed hold of. 'You can't do this,' he spat. 'The terms of our agreement state that you can't! Get your grubby paws off of me!'

'This issue is time sensitive,' Kate said. Or maybe it was Felicity. 'Every vampire needs to get out here now.'

'We are sleeping! When you will you stupid animals get it through your thick skull that we are nocturnal? It's not fucking rocket science. Sun bad. Night good. Jeez.'

Uneasiness slid through me. It was clear that, despite the orderly scenes I'd witnessed, things were not all rosy in Monroe's north. Taking a deep breath, I stepped forward. This was my doing; maybe I could smooth things over and still get the answers I needed. 'Don't blame them,' I said. 'Coming here was my call.'

The shadowed face of the vampire turned towards me. 'Yeah?' he sneered. 'Who are you?'

'Idiot,' hissed the nearest werewolf. 'She's the enchantress.'

'She doesn't look like the enchantress.'

'She's got blue hair, hasn't she?'

The vampire shrugged. 'It's so cold out here that I've got blue balls. It doesn't make me an all-powerful magical being.'

I gritted my teeth. This wasn't helping. I cleared my throat. I most definitely did not have time to deal with vamp-versus-wolf fisticuffs. 'A human has been murdered at the Travotel.'

'The one run by the faery?'

There was only one hotel open in the whole of Manchester. Yes, it was the one run by the damned faery. I smiled. 'Yes.'

The vampire tutted. He jerked his arms against the werewolves' grasp. 'Let me go,' he said. 'Your restraint is completely unnecessary.'

'We're not…'

'Let him go,' I said.

The werewolves released him. Nice. At least some people did what I said.

The vampire inclined his head and stepped back into the shaded part of the street before finally drawing back his hood.

Despite his squeaky voice, he looked younger than I expected. I still couldn't always separate a vampire's appearance from their actual age. Julie, for instance, looked like she was in her forties when she was more like two or three hundred years old. That meant this guy was probably … seventy or eighty? His hair was slicked back, as if he'd just come out of the shower, and he had a pencil-thin dark moustache that added to the effect of a young teenager trying to look older than his years. I gave up judging him by his looks and met his eyes.

'It was a vampire who killed her,' I said. 'By all

accounts.'

'How did she die?' His question was casually worded but there was no denying the serious intent in his gaze.

'Her death is still fresh,' I told him. 'And we've only done a cursory examination of her body. She put up a fight. Her fingernails are broken. I didn't notice any bruising but there could well be some. Her body is all sunken and,' I swallowed, 'there are puncture wounds on her neck. There's no other indication of trauma.'

He blinked at me slowly then he threw back his head and laughed. 'So of course you thought it was a vampire who did it? Puncture wounds? How terribly trite! Even a young vampire wouldn't kill a human simply by drinking from them.' He continued to chuckle to himself while I stared at him.

Felicity growled. 'Maybe she had a heart attack when one of your bastards sank his fangs in.'

If only. 'Maybe she did but the way her body was … shrivelled into itself suggests all her blood was drained.' I sharpened my voice and addressed the vampire again. 'My source indicates that it looks like a vampire was responsible.'

He wiped the tears from his eyes. 'Your source? You mean the actress?'

I responded stiffly. 'Yes.'

'She knows nothing. She's a troublemaker who lies for a living. Nothing she says can be trusted.' As he spoke, his nostrils flared slightly. Ah ha. That was his tell, then. Whether Julie was a liar or not, so was he.

I stilled and kept talking, hoping to draw him out further. Suddenly I felt on surer ground. 'All the same,' I said, 'if we could see all the vampires here for ourselves and check them out for scratch marks, we can eliminate them from our enquiries.'

He bared his white teeth in a supposed smile. 'They're sleeping right now. You're welcome to come back when the sun falls.'

Several of the werewolves hissed in annoyance. I kept my cool. 'By which time, any such superficial injuries will have healed.'

The vampire waved towards the rows upon rows of terraced houses. 'There are almost a thousand of us here. How exactly do you propose to wake everyone up? It'll only antagonise us. We're obviously being fingered for the crime. Terrible as murder is, you are jumping to conclusions.' His voice hardened. 'And no one is being woken up so you can check them over. What happened to presumption of innocence?'

'Look, you undead piece of shit—' Felicity began.

I put a hand on her arm. 'I've got this,' I told her. 'Don't worry.'

'You can't deal sensibly with these bastards. They're tricksy and slippery and always up to no good. They—'

'Enough.' I turned and faced her and the others. 'Thank you so much for your help up. I will take things from here.'

'Wait a minute,' she protested. 'Julian told us to help you. We can't just walk away. You can't deal with this lot on your own.'

'You can just walk away,' I replied firmly. 'And you will.' I forced a smile. 'Bye now.'

She wanted to refuse, it was there in every quivering muscle. I forestalled her. 'I'm the enchantress,' I reminded her. 'I will take things from here.'

She drew in a deep breath as if counting to ten. 'Very well,' she snapped. 'On your own head be it.' She whirled round and stalked through the broken barricade, the other wolves following her with narrowed eyes and closed expressions. I wouldn't hear the last of this but it was for the best.

Once the wolves had gone, the vampire opened his mouth and ran his very red tongue over his teeth. Those fangs looked decidedly sharp and lethal and I suppressed a shudder. 'Nicely done,' he said. 'Werewolves are so prone to violence. It's much easier when they're out of the way.' His eyes gleamed and there was the definite suggestion of a predatory leer as he looked me over. 'I'm still not waking anyone up.'

'Perhaps you'd be prepared to answer a few questions yourself,' I said, maintaining a light tone. I was tempted to shoot off some magic to make my will and power known, but I'd hold off until it was necessary. There were other ways to skin a cat. 'How long have you been posted out here?' I asked. 'By which I mean, when did your post begin?'

'Midnight.' He watched me, both amused and wary about where I was going with this line of questioning.

'Is this the main entrance to your area?'

'You mean are vampires likely to enter or leave via another route?'

I nodded.

He frowned. 'Anything is possible but, as far as I know, everyone uses this way.' He pointed behind me to a small desk with a clipboard on top. 'We keep a tally of who comes in and out. After all,' he added with a tight grin, 'one never knows what the werewolves – or the enchantress herself – might accuse us of.'

'Has anyone come in with any visible wounds in the last twelve hours? Any scratch marks? Anything at all?'

He leaned forward, pausing long enough to build

up anticipation. It worked for me – it meant I could get a clearer view of his flaring nostrils. 'No.'

Damn it. He was telling the truth. 'Can I have a look at your tally?'

He gestured at it again. 'Be my guest.'

I walked over, picked it up and scanned down the list. A lot of vampires had left and a lot had returned but, as far as I could tell, nine men and women who had gone out the previous night still hadn't returned. I yanked off the sheet of paper. 'I'm going to take this.'

The vampire folded his arms. 'I can't let you do that.'

I faced him. 'If I hadn't stepped in when I did, those werewolves would have broken down every bloodsucking door here, whether you liked it or not. If any of your lot fought back, you and I both know what could have happened next. I think you'll agree that my way is definitely the best way. Unless you want me to call the wolves back.'

He didn't move for a long moment other than tapping his foot. Another nervous twitch, I supposed. 'Fine,' he said eventually. 'You may take the sheet.' He said it as if were granting me a great, personal boon rather than yielding to my lupine threat. Whatever. As long as I got what I needed.

'Thank you.' For the first time, I let myself smile. 'What's your name?'

'Do you want to know so you can eliminate me from your enquiries?' he mocked.

'No,' I shot. 'I want to know because it's polite to know who you're talking to.'

He smirked at me. 'In that case,' he said with a bow, 'I am Theo.'

'I'm Charley.'

His smile grew. 'I know.' He permitted me one

last flash of his fangs. 'I'll be seeing you around, Charley.'

'I can't wait.' With slow, measured steps so as not to give away my anxiety, I walked away from the vampire barricade. Unsurprisingly, the werewolves were still waiting for me just beyond.

'Oh, and Charley?' Theo called out. 'A vampire didn't do this. Not in the way that you think, anyway. It would be far too difficult to suck dry an entire human body. Your killer is someone entirely different.'

I wasn't convinced by that, even though Julie had already suggested the same thing. But I would keep an open mind. For now.

Chapter Eight

'You should have gone to see all the vampires with your own eyes,' Felicity said. 'It's the only way to be sure.'

'Sure of what?' I enquired. 'The perpetrator could have sneaked out before I reached him. He could be living elsewhere. He could be hiding in a hole somewhere. Hell, he could already have healed. There are hundreds of vampires living there and realistically we can't wake them all. Besides, I believe Theo when he says no one passed him with any scratches on their face. We won't find the culprit that way.' I waved the piece of paper in her face. 'I'm more interested in the names of the nine vampires who haven't returned home yet.' And indeed whether Valerie's murder had been carried out for no other reason than to give the vampires an even worse reputation than they already possessed.

'They need to learn their place,' she said. 'If they want to be part of this community, they need to toe the line.'

I gaped at her. In that moment, I wasn't capable of anything else.

'What?' she asked.

'You're talking about them like they're second-class citizens.'

'They're not second-class citizens.'

'Good,' I said, 'because—'

'They're undead. They don't count as citizens.'

Good grief. I passed a hand over my face. 'They're not undead.' I had been through all this with Julie and she'd explained it to me very clearly. 'That's propaganda put about by the sort of people who hunted their kind to near extinction.'

'Who told you that?' she enquired. 'A vampire?' She rolled her eyes. 'They drink blood. Human blood. They killed that woman. I'm not saying we should throw them out on their ear, I'm just saying that they need to play ball.'

'And do things the werewolf way?'

'If it ain't broke…' She moved away and started muttering to the rest of the group, flicking the odd glance in my direction to suggest that I was a derisible creature who belonged with the vampires because I'd dared to suggest that they weren't necessarily all evil.

I watched her. No wonder the vamps had shut themselves away with their own guards and their own barriers. This was not a good situation. Felicity's beliefs were deeply embedded. I wasn't going to change any hearts and minds on my own – I needed a werewolf to sort things out because, as far as I could tell, the only person a werewolf would listen to was another werewolf.

While the group continued to gab about what to tell Julian and how to find the nine missing vampires, I whirled round and marched away. Julian had told me I could find Monroe over to the east of the square. Somehow, I suspected I'd have more leverage with him than with Julian. Besides, it wasn't yet noon: I reckoned there was still the teeniest tiny chance I could stumble across a vampire with the marks of Valerie's fingernails across his face. The longer the culprit ran free, the worse things would get for the vamps.

Although I walked quickly, I still half expected Felicity and the rest of the werewolves to catch up and continue their escort. Apparently, however, they'd decided I was no longer worth the effort because I was left in peace. Relatively speaking.

I passed various people of all manner of ethnicities – and all of them stared at me. I suppose it was the blue hair that gave me away. It was an odd sensation being a minor celebrity; maybe I should have offered to hand out autographs. I wondered if this was how Julie felt, given her career as a soap actress.

There was something ego-boosting about the attention, I reflected as I trotted on. If you are treated as special, you start to believe that you are; it's a self-fulfilling prophecy. I wondered if the reverse could also be true: if everyone believed that vampires were stone-cold killers, would they *become* stone-cold killers? I pondered and then discarded the idea. As a gambler, I was well aware that the smallest, weakest players could rise up against all odds and defeat expectations to win the day. I grinned to myself. At the end of the day, gambling had an answer for everything.

I veered round a corner, suddenly aware of a loud babble of voices nearby. Where there were people, there would be vampires – and maybe even Monroe. I adjusted my course slightly until a large group, which appeared to have arranged itself into a circle, came into view. So what on earth was going on here?

I walked over to the crowd and pushed myself onto my tiptoes to peer over the tops of various heads. Unfortunately for me, I appeared to be very short in comparison to other supernatural beings and I couldn't see much except for a flying fist somewhere deep within the circle. I edged round to get a better view but, before I could see much, a werewolf sidled up to me with glinting brown eyes.

'Hundred to one he slams all three of them to the ground,' he said in an undertone.

I couldn't suppress the thrill that ran through me at the prospect of my first real bet in months. Obviously I wasn't going to take it until I knew more about what was going on, and such high odds immediately made me wary. All the same, this was the life I loved. I didn't want to be the *de facto* leader of a bedraggled, whining community in an almost abandoned city that was suffused with dangerous magic; I wanted to be a fun-loving gambler who took unnecessary risks and didn't worry too much about the consequences.

'I can't see much to make a judgment,' I admitted to my new buddy.

'There's three of them,' the wolf purred. 'Young, strong, agile wolves the lot of them. He's got the experience. They've got the enthusiasm.'

On my other side there was a derisive snort. 'Enthusiasm is something he's definitely lacking. He's been beaten in every fight he's had since Halloween because he's got no enthusiasm. He *wants* to be beaten.'

'Yeah,' another interrupted, 'but I heard he's on borrowed time. A little birdie told me that Julian wants him out. In fact…'

I moved away. I suddenly knew exactly who they were talking about and I was not a happy little enchantress at all. So this was why Monroe was covered in bruises and too busy to hang around the Travotel with me. I grimaced. I had to see this with my own eyes.

Ignoring the tightly bunched spectators, I nudged my way through. Some lanky guy aimed an elbow at my face as I disturbed him. I didn't think: I zapped out a bolt of magic and sent him stumbling back into others. They shoved him, yelling expletives. The scuffle gave me enough room to squeeze through to the front. What I saw there made me want to retch.

Monroe was facing off against three others who seemed to be working as a team to attack him. They were grunting and hissing, darting forward with jabs and kicks.

Blood was streaming from a cut above his eye and his right ear had swollen to the size of a golf ball. I couldn't call Monroe a fighter because he wasn't fighting. He was barely defending himself, he just let them continue taking shot after shot. Every time another punch landed, the crowd cheered. Only a few people seemed to be on his side.

I stared, aghast. How could anyone allow this to happen? I knew that Monroe was in self-destructive mode as a result of his guilt-driven grief, but this was far worse than anything I could have imagined. This wasn't a fight. This was torture.

When the dark-haired werewolf nearest to me kicked Monroe in the ribs brutally enough to make his legs give way, I couldn't take it any more. I stepped forward as Monroe fell to his knees. Someone grabbed at my shirt, ready to haul me back. Monroe's pain-glazed eyes registered the movement and he raised his head, shock appearing on his face when he saw me.

I brushed off the annoyance from behind and opened my mouth but Monroe shook his head. Screw him: I wasn't about to stand by and let him be beaten to a pulp. It would have been one thing if he was actually participating but he wasn't. He wasn't trying to win; all he wanted was to get hurt to hide the real pain he was feeling inside.

I tilted my chin and raised my voice. 'You have to stop!'

My words were immediately drowned out by the roar of the watching crowd. As soon as I started to speak, Monroe staggered back up to his feet. He deliberately moved to rejoin the fray to make sure that I wasn't heard. His eyes held mine for a second, imploring me to keep out of the fight and keep my mouth shut. No chance. I'd use my magic to scream my way through this, if need be.

This shouldn't be happening.

Monroe blinked, as if recognising what I was about to do. It wasn't resignation in his face, however: it was determination. He spun round, his leg kicking out at the three young pups. In the time it took me to draw breath, all three of them had collapsed. The middle wolf groaned and rose to meet Monroe once again. All he received for his efforts was a punch to the side of his head.

I hissed through my teeth, still sickened at what was going on. Monroe had let himself be used as a punchbag and was only fighting back because he knew I was going to interrupt. I watched for another short moment, then I turned away and pushed my way through the nauseating, voyeuristic spectators.

Julian was standing against a wall, his arms folded and his expression closed. I stalked up to him and jabbed him in the chest. 'What kind of fucking place are you lot running here? How can you let this sort of thing go on?' My fury was transcending just about every other coherent thought.

'I'm not in charge here,' he answered.

'It looks to me like you're in fucking charge!'

'You'd be surprised.' A muscle throbbed in his jaw. 'Even with Monroe in the state that he's in, people around here will still flock to his cause before they'll flock to mine.'

'The only thing people are flocking to is his demise! If he carries on like this, he'll end up being killed! He's *grieving*, Julian. He *wants* to be hurt. He needs help, not a fucking fist in his face!

'Charlotte,' Monroe drawled, his Scottish accent lilting through the air as he suddenly appeared next to us, 'don't blame Julian. He's been trying to stop me fighting. He's threatened to throw me out.' He hawked up bloody phlegm and spat it on the ground. 'Not that he could.'

Julian pushed himself off the wall. 'Listen to her,' he said. 'You're on a collision course with hell. This is not sustainable.' He started to walk away. 'And I *will* throw you out if it's for the good of the community.'

'He won't,' Monroe said to me, wiping the last of the blood from his mouth. 'He can't.'

'You fucking idiot,' I told him. 'You absolute piece of shit.'

If Monroe was taken aback by my language, he didn't show it. 'What? I won the fight. I won it for you, Charlotte. Isn't that what you wanted?'

I shook my head in despair. 'I knew you'd been fighting, I just didn't think it was like this.' My voice dropped to a whisper. 'What are you doing to yourself, Monroe?'

He stepped forward, leaning down until we were virtually nose to nose. 'This is who I am, Charlotte. I'm a wolf. A predator.' He bared his teeth. 'And I'm fucked up. You'd do better to stay away from me.'

I drew myself up and eyeballed him. Monroe was not going to intimidate me; I wasn't going to let him. 'You're the one who keeps coming to me, not the other way around. You need to pull yourself together.'

'Do I?' he asked, his tone dangerously silky. 'Do I really, Charlotte?'

I stared at him. He was still high on adrenaline from the fight. This wasn't the real Monroe. This wasn't the guy I knew. Not deep down. I inhaled and pulled away slightly. 'You're hurting,' I said, more gently. 'But you're not a bad person, Monroe. You don't deserve this. You don't deserve to be hurt.'

His response was flat. 'I'm an arsehole.'

'Right now,' I answered, 'you're *acting* like an arsehole. But you're not really like that. Arseholes don't force the people they know to take a holiday before they collapse. Arseholes don't help vicious mermaids to relocate. You have to stop punishing yourself for things that aren't your fault and that can't be changed.'

I'd been expecting Monroe to argue or to storm off. What I didn't expect was the sudden sheen of tears in his eyes. 'Charlotte,' he said, 'I—'

A hooded figure collided with him, stumbling against him and interrupting whatever he'd been about to say. Monroe snarled and snatched at the figure's arm. 'Watch where you're going!'

There wasn't any answer. The man – or woman – staggered off, drawing away from Monroe's grip before spinning round. 'Vampires,' Monroe hissed. 'They shouldn't be out at this time of day. Not with the sun as high as it is.'

Damn it, I hadn't got a glimpse of the vamp's face. Was it one of the nine who'd not returned home this morning? Or was it simply a stray vampire who'd wanted to watch Monroe's fight and lay a bet or two? I twisted my head, trying to make out its shadowed features.

'Charlotte?' Monroe's voice was different now. 'What is it?'

I looked at him then I looked at the retreating vampire. I gritted my teeth. 'Sorry,' I murmured. 'This won't take long.' I jogged away from Monroe towards the vamp, who saw me coming and picked up the pace.

'Wait!' I shouted. 'I just want to see your face!'

The vampire started to run. I cursed. Feeling my fingers tingle, I used my left hand to send a tiny zigzag of magic towards the ground, making the vampire stumble and trip. I scurried forward and used my right hand to pull back the creature's hood. She howled in pain, immediately throwing up her hands to protect her face from the sun. Her unblemished, unscratched face. I slammed my palm against the nearby wall, ignoring the pain it gave me, then I reached down and helped the vampire up to her feet.

'Sorry,' I muttered. 'I'm looking for someone else.'

She didn't answer; all she did was turn and run away from me as fast as her legs would carry her.

Monroe appeared by my side. He tilted his head towards me and raised his eyebrows. 'I think there's something you need to tell me,' he said.

Chapter Nine

For reasons that didn't entirely make sense, other than ego coupled with the joy of having something else to focus on, Monroe was incredibly pissed off that I'd not come to him first.

'I could have immediately set up a task force to find this vampire,' he said.

I tapped my foot. 'A task force? You're not the President of the United States.' At the moment, he wasn't really even the leader of the north. To all intents and purposes, that appeared to be Julian. 'Besides, time was of the essence. I needed to move and find him as quickly as possible. I couldn't worry about finding you at the same time.'

'Except,' Monroe pointed out, his earlier pain locked away again where I couldn't see it, 'you did find me. And you've not yet found the murdering vamp responsible for Valerie's death.'

I gazed heavenward. Enough already. 'Not to mention that I'm wasting time having this argument with you.'

He looked at me calmly. 'Then let's get a move on. Let me see the list.'

I handed it over, pointing at the nine names. 'These are the ones who didn't clock back into the vampire ghetto after last night. That doesn't necessarily mean they have anything to do with Valerie's murder but…'

'But they're a good place to start.' He nodded. 'As a minor point to be aware of, though, we don't call it a ghetto.'

It was a ghetto as far as I could see. All the same, I just shrugged; semantics weren't worth arguing over. Not right now.

Monroe jabbed at one of the names. 'You can rule this one out. You accosted her five minutes ago.' His finger trailed down the list. 'These two will be in the Blood and Bones. It's only round the corner.'

'Blood and Bones?'

'One of the pubs.'

'Charming name.' I paused. 'How do you know they'll be there? And how do you know them in the first place?'

There was a beat before he answered. 'I might be falling apart with far more drama than you've managed, but I still know who lives here and what their proclivities are.'

I blinked. 'What? Everyone?' How many residents were there in the north? It had to be several thousand at least.

'It seems prudent to know the people here and who they are, considering the safety measures that are important to keep us all breathing in this new world.'

Of course it did. Monroe had set up here in the north with the proviso that everyone who came with him followed his rules. It made a sort of sense that he'd take time to get to know them all, but it was still a remarkable feat. I knew the faces of many of my community members but I couldn't have confidently stated their names or what they liked to do in their spare time. And I was aware that I didn't know everyone. 'You realise,' I told him, 'that makes you some kind of eidetic genius?' A gambler like me would love to have that sort of skill.

'Genius is far more to do with hard work than brain cells,' he told me.

I gave a small smile. We did have some things in common then: I felt exactly the same about Lady Luck. 'Well,' I said. 'Let's put that hard work to the test. To the Blood and Bones it is.'

It wasn't far. That was one good thing about these new communities that Monroe and I had set up: it didn't take long to travel from one end of them to the other. In two proverbial shakes of a lamb's tail we were standing outside the pub, which advertised itself by a swinging sign overhead that depicted a bone dripping with blood. Lovely.

I could hear raucous cheering inside. I guessed that the vampires would be there for the day, downing pint after pint while they avoided the sun's glare. That little fact already told me a great deal about them – but it wasn't quite enough.

'What else do you know about these two?' I asked quietly.

'You mean, are they likely to cause much trouble when we ask them if they've recently sucked a woman dry?'

I raised my shoulders. 'I guess.'

Monroe put his hands in his pockets and considered. 'As vampires go, I think they're alright.'

Damned by faint praise. I sighed. It wasn't a lot of information to go on but there were six more suspects to track down after these two and not much time left to do it in. 'Are you alright?' I asked him. 'I can do this on my own if—'

'I'm fine,' he interrupted with a dark expression. 'I don't need your mollycoddling.'

I suspected he was wrong. I'd have to set aside my mollycoddles for now, but I'd do what I could for him later. Monroe and I were inextricably linked, whether we liked it or not. And, truth be told, I did like it.

'Come on then,' I said. I shot him a glance. 'I'll do the talking.'

I pushed open the door. Almost at once I was virtually bowled over by the cloud of blue smoke that engulfed me. For a moment, my imagination got the better of me and I actually thought I was under attack. I choked and wheezed and flailed my arms around to clear the air so I could see. It was only then that I realised the smoke was coming from the pipes of the bleary-eyed patrons of the Blood and Bones rather than some bizarre smoke monster.

Something else we had the apocalypse to blame for – the loss of the smoking ban.

Coughing one last time, I entered with Monroe so close behind me that I thought he was about to tread on my heels. Rather than his close proximity making me claustrophobic, it was very welcome – there was something about this pub that set my teeth on edge. Maybe it was the glares of suspicion I received from the dozen or so people inside. Maybe it was the annoying music floating over from the far corner that was being strummed by an ancient-looking bloke on a lute, of all things. Or maybe it was the three semi-conscious people who currently had fangs embedded in their wrists.

'Ladies and gentlemen!' the rotund bartender bellowed. 'The Joyless Brigade has arrived!'

A range of mutters reached my ears, mostly consisting of 'werewolf', 'bastard' and 'enchantress bitch'. How lovely it was to be welcomed so warmly. I tutted and strode up to the bar. Including the three who were feeding, the idiots they were feeding upon, the bartender and the irritating lute player, there were four vampires, five werewolves and three humans. I congratulated myself on being able to pinpoint each of their ethnicities. I was getting better at this identification malarkey. Unfortunately, it only took one sweeping gaze to register the lack of obvious facial wounds on any of the vamps. That was frustrating – but I could hardly have expected it to be so easy to catch a cold-blooded murderer.

'You all know who I am,' I said, my voice ringing out.

Every face turned to me. Annoyingly, the would-be musician continued to strum aimlessly on the lute. I slowly turned in his direction and dripped an icy stare over his seated body. His fingers ceased their incessant plucking and he laid down his instrument. Just as well, it was definitely out of tune. I didn't think I was the only one who was pleased at the loss of the so-called music; every shoulder in the pub appeared to sag in relief.

Monroe took advantage of the sudden silence to push in. Great. So much for me doing all the talking.

'Who are these humans?' he asked. His voice was dangerously low. 'Have they agreed to this?'

The nearest vampire, a blond-haired man who looked like he wouldn't say boo to a goose normally, sniffed and detached himself from the human he was feeding from. 'Of course. We know the rules.'

'Yeah,' sneered the woman next to him. 'Besides, it's not as if we're monsters.'

'I'll be the judge of that,' Monroe replied. He drew nearer. Satisfyingly, all three vampires flinched. Blondie carefully pulled away from his breakfast – no mean feat considering the human had draped herself over his legs and was moaning in an obsequious, fawning manner. I had to admit she certainly didn't look like she was being forced into this situation.

The final vampire patron was continuing to suck from the wrist of a young man. Monroe grabbed the back of the man's head and, with more force than was necessary, lifted it up and looked into his eyes. The man smiled dreamily. 'Don't stop,' he murmured. 'I like this.'

'See?' Blondie said. 'They're here of their own volition. They like it.' He leered at me. 'Want to try?'

Monroe snarled softly, fur popping out across his cheekbones.

'Oooooh. I don't think the wolf likes that very much. What do you think, Carter? Have we offended your delicate sensibilities, *Lord* Monroe?'

I reckoned it was the 'Lord' that did it. Monroe drew himself up, revealing every arrogant inch of the werewolf alpha he used to be. The other wolves in the bar cowered.

'Get out,' he said, so quietly that his words were barely audible.

The five wolves collided with each other in their haste to do Monroe's bidding. It was comical to watch them squeezing out of the door to escape, though the barman didn't find it funny. He glared. 'They still have tabs open. You'd better hope they come back to pay up or I'll be billing you.'

Monroe ignored him. 'You are here in this community under my sufferance. If you can't follow the laws, then you have no place here.'

'We were all vetted when we entered,' Blondie said. 'And we are breaking no laws. No one is in any danger here. No one is in pain.' He gave Monroe a pointed look. 'Apart from you, that is. Your agony screams from your pores. I don't normally enjoy lupine blood but I can be persuaded to drink from you to ease your hurt.' He smiled slowly. 'I can offer oblivion.'

Okay-dokey. Time to step in. 'Funnily enough,' I said, 'we are here for that very reason. One of your kind has imposed oblivion on a human by killing them. We are trying to find the person responsible.'

Blondie shrugged, suggesting that he couldn't care less, but the expression in his eyes told a different story. He was putting on a good show but he was discomfited by my news. 'Accidents happen,' he said. 'Some people have weak hearts and underlying medical conditions.' He pointed at the bartender. 'Carter?'

Carter nodded and reached under the bar. Monroe stiffened as if half-expecting him to pull out a shotgun but I didn't feel any threat. I moved to my right, brushing against Monroe to offer brief reassurance. Carter produced a clipboard and waved it in our direction.

'Waivers,' he grunted. 'All legal and above board. We ran them by Julian when we first got here. He agreed them.'

If Monroe was surprised by this, he didn't react. He took the clipboard and started to read. I scanned it over his shoulder. *All feedings are undertaken with an element of risk. While all vampires will undertake to protect their meals and to limit their blood intake, they are not liable for any deaths caused by underlying health conditions. Blah blah blah.* Each waiver was signed at the bottom.

Blondie's human smiled at me. 'That's my one. We all know what we're getting into.'

'Then why get into it?' I asked. 'Why risk yourself like this?'

She sighed happily. 'The euphoria,' she whispered. 'It's like nothing else you've ever imagined. It's better than the most potent drug.'

Blondie leaned forward, looking serious. 'We don't harm our meals,' he said. 'Not deliberately. It wouldn't make any sense.' He stroked the woman's head. 'We want them to return. Warm bodies with a pulse are the gift that keeps on giving. Dead bodies are worthless. You should be happy that we're not using up your other food supplies. Whatever happened to your human, it was either an accident or it wasn't a vampire. Heart attack. Betcha.'

My stomach turned. He certainly didn't mince his words. 'It wasn't a heart attack,' I said. 'She was drained dry.'

He whitened. 'That's not possible.'

'Apparently it is,' Monroe growled. 'I should never have allowed Julian to persuade me to let the vampires join us here. It was a mistake from the start.'

Carter took a step backwards. 'The death happened here? In the north?'

'No,' I said. 'At the Travotel.'

Blondie looked surprised. 'Under the faery's nose?' He exchanged looks with the others.

His human 'meal' raised her head. 'Wait. Wasn't Philip going there last night?'

Blondie's teeth clenched and he nodded. 'He was.' He looked at Monroe and me. 'But he wouldn't have done this. He *couldn't* have. Philip is a sensitive sort. He only drinks the minimum, even when his meals ask him to take more. He's the kind of guy who writes poetry and walks around with his head in the clouds. He wouldn't kill anyone. And he doesn't spend a lot of time with the other vampires. He lives on his own, away from the rest of us.'

'Where?' I asked urgently. We were getting somewhere. We didn't have a motive but it certainly seemed like we had opportunity. A loner? Philip sounded like he could be our man.

Carter glared. 'He wouldn't have done this. He's an annoying guy but he's not the type to hurt someone. Even by accident.'

'We have to find him,' I said. 'Valerie, the woman who was killed, put up a fight. If he attacked her, there will be evidence – if we can find it before it heals.' I registered the growing panic in the vampires' eyes. 'This isn't a witch hunt. We're not looking to blame the nearest vampire, we're looking to find the person who did this. It'll be better for all of us if we can eliminate Philip – or identify him as the perpetrator. You lot don't want this to become a lengthy investigation.'

Blondie met my eyes. 'You already seem to think we're evil bastards. What difference is it going to make?'

Monroe glared. Carter's shoulders dropped and he grabbed a pen, scribbling down an address on a scrap of paper. 'Here,' he said. 'He lives here.'

I glanced at it. It wasn't far off and we could get there in minutes. There was still time. 'Thank you,' I said quietly.

'Just remember that we helped.'

The human woman next to Blondie nodded. 'All of us helped.'

I nodded. Vampires weren't so bad. 'We'll remember. And,' I added, 'for what it's worth, I don't think you're evil bastards.' I jerked my chin at the lute player. 'Apart from him maybe. Anyone who can produce music like that must be soul-less.'

I'd intended it as a joke but nobody laughed. The display of bravado that had confronted us when we entered had vanished completely.

'Make it quick,' Blondie said suddenly. 'If it was Philip who did this, at least make it quick.'

Chapter Ten

As soon as we were outside, Monroe lifted his head and howled. It was brief but it was filled with anguish. Then he turned and slammed his fist into the wall. When he raised it again, I leapt in front to stop him.

'What the hell is wrong?' I demanded. 'We've got a lead. A decent lead. This is good!'

'This is not what I wanted,' he spat. 'A dive bar filled with vampires feeding off humans? This isn't the community I planned! I should have been paying more attention. I should have never allowed this to happen! It was supposed to be safe here, it was supposed to be a place where things like this wouldn't happen. Otherwise what was the point of setting up away from you?'

I suddenly understood. 'Those humans want to be there,' I said. 'Unpleasant as we might find the idea, they've chosen to do this. And those vampires need to drink. They won't survive if they don't have access to blood. At the end of the day, they're not doing any harm. They're not hiding. It's out in the open. It's better this way.'

'It's not right, Charlotte,' he snapped. '*They're* not right.'

'Didn't you see what was going on in there?' I asked. 'They were scared of us. That's what the show was for when we entered. Those vampires have spent their lives hiding from the world. Now they don't have to hide but they're still not treated like real people. They're shut away behind their own barricades. The wolves treat them like some kind of sub-species. The vampires are half expecting to get their heads kicked in at any moment.'

'My wolves do *not* treat them like that.'

I took his hands in mine. 'You've not been paying attention,' I told him. 'And that's not your fault. You've been mired in your pain and your grief. Let's face it, things still aren't great for the vamps. Yes, their powers are enhanced because of the magic in the air but so are their vulnerabilities. They can barely spend any time outside because of the sun. They're loathed by just about everyone else in Manchester. Maybe this will turn out to be a good thing,' I said. 'Maybe it'll highlight their plight, stop this place from being a powder keg and turn it into somewhere everyone can be welcome. Maybe we all needed this to open our eyes to what's really going on.'

Monroe gazed at me for a long moment. 'Unless,' he said eventually, 'deep down they're all like this Philip, and they're all capable of killing at any time. No matter what the vampires are feeling, Valerie is still a corpse. And, if you're right, a vampire killed her.'

I swallowed. Despite my sympathy for the vampires and their plight, I couldn't lose sight of what had happened. 'Valerie's killer deserves to be brought to justice.' My voice hardened. 'It will happen, make no mistake about it. But the people in there think we'll kill Philip if he's the culprit. That's why they said to make it quick. If we do that, we're the ones who are monsters.' I looked away. 'Maybe we are all monsters in the end.'

'I've always been a monster.' Monroe laughed harshly. 'Whatever. If Philip did this, we can't shove him out of the city and let him loose on the rest of the world. He's our problem and we'll have to deal with him. We exiled Max. But a stone-cold killer who's also a vampire? That's an entirely different scenario.'

I breathed out. 'Then we'll cross that bridge when

we get to it. But we can't let every vampire be tarred with the same brush.' I smiled sadly. 'Besides, this community is safer than you think. Valerie wasn't killed here. And Philip, if he is our killer, doesn't live here either.'

Monroe looked away. 'Maybe you were right,' he said distantly. 'Maybe isolation from others was the worst possible thing I could have encouraged.'

'Not everything is your fault, Monroe. You made the best decision you could with the information and feelings you had at the time. We'll find Valerie's killer and then we'll deal with everything else. We've got this.'

For a moment he didn't react then his hands squeezed mine tightly. 'It looks like that break in the Travotel worked for you,' he said gruffly. 'You've made a sudden return to blind optimism and care for the whole community.'

I grinned. 'I can highly recommend a day or two away.' And, I added silently to myself, it was amazing what a big problem could do to provide focus and clarity. There wasn't time to feel stressed about other worries and issues. Perhaps every cloud did have a silver lining.

Like he'd read my mind, Monroe tilted his head and offered me a crooked grin. 'I could do with more sunshine in my life,' he admitted.

A thrill ran through me. If that didn't brighten me up, nothing would.

***

'Go on then,' Monroe said, gazing up at the red-brick house where Philip, the potential murderer, was supposedly staying. 'What are the odds that he is the killer we're looking for?'

'I'm not a police investigator,' I said.

'No,' he conceded. 'But you worked for the police

and I bet you picked up a lot from them. You're too curious and too nosy not to have rifled through their papers and paid attention to their procedures when you were cleaning for them. Anyway, I know you'll have already calculated the odds in your head.' He leaned towards me. 'From what I know of you, you'll be spot on.'

'Three to one,' I told him. 'It's not looking good for him.'

Monroe nodded. 'But it *is* looking good for us.'

I could only agree. As long as Philip the vampire had scratches on his skin, we could prove we had our man. I hoped so. It would be great to think that Monroe and I had solved a murder in a mere morning. It would certainly deter anyone else from thinking about doing something similar – and it wouldn't lead to further misery and accusations for the rest of the vampires.

'Shall we knock?' I asked.

Monroe shrugged. 'Sure.' He walked up to the front door but it wasn't a fist he raised to it. He threw out a powerful kick, splintering the wood and causing the door to crash open. He turned and grinned. 'Knock, knock.'

I rolled my eyes, but secretly I was pleased to see that Monroe was acting more like the wolf that I knew. Yes, he was mercurial and still suffering badly but it was good to know that the old, arrogant Monroe lurked behind those blue eyes.

If we'd been expecting Philip to storm down the hallway at the sound of our intrusion, we were disappointed. The only response that greeted Monroe's battering ram of an entrance was silence. In theory that should have been a good thing but it filled me with foreboding.

'How good is your magic these days?' Monroe

asked as we continued to hover on the porch. 'Can you use it to tell whether anyone is inside?'

I pursed my lips. 'Potentially, but I don't want to over-use it.' I told him about my fears that I might cause more magic to flood the atmosphere and lead to further problems across the city.

'There's only one of you,' he pointed out. 'There were loads of faeries here for decades who caused the magic build-up.'

'All the same,' I said, 'I'm still uneasy about it. I'll use magic when it's the best option but when we can go down the old-fashioned route…'

'In that case,' he replied, 'ladies first.' He gestured at the door.

I smiled and walked past him into the house.

At first nothing appeared to be out of the ordinary. True, the place felt empty but that didn't mean our potential killer wasn't curled up in bed somewhere upstairs until the sun went down. Ignoring the ground floor for now, I tiptoed upwards. The stairs were creaky but there was still no sign of anyone living and breathing. And yes, no matter what some werewolves might think, vampires are both living and breathing.

It wasn't a grand place. Upstairs there was a small bathroom, filled with all manner of masculine accoutrements from shaving cream to anti-perspirant. Our Philip took care of his appearance, if nothing else. There were two bedrooms, one that didn't appear lived in and one which was clearly where he slept. The bed was neatly made with the duvet smoothed over.

There was an open book on the nightstand. I picked it up and examined it: William Butler Yeats. So ol' Philip really was a poetic soul. Although if I dredged through my memories, there were more facts to consider. I'd once gambled on a national competition where people could vote on their favourite poet. It didn't take much to work out that Kipling would be the winner – Brits are a predictable bunch – but I took my research seriously. Even though Yeats was Irish rather than British, I'd given him the attention his poetry deserved. From what I could recall, Yeats was an interesting man. He'd been part of a secret society that conducted ritual magic. I tapped my mouth thoughtfully. Maybe Fangy Phil just enjoyed the poems – or maybe there was more to it than iambic pentameter.

I glanced at the scrap of paper he'd been using as a bookmark. It was an outline drawing of a man with a swirly pattern where his head was. A few words were scribbled underneath it: *Therapy For Survivors.* Well, Valerie certainly hadn't survived.

From downstairs, Monroe called up. 'He's not there, is he?' There was an odd note to his voice.

'No,' I shouted. I turned on my heel and clattered down the stairs to join him.

Monroe was standing in the living room. I paused at the doorway, sweeping my gaze around. Well, shit.

It looked like a whirlwind had torn through the place. Chairs and tables were upended. One painting was hanging haphazardly off the wall and two others were on the floor. There was broken glass, scattered papers and splattered blood. A considerable amount of splattered blood. I let out a low whistle.

'What do things look like upstairs?' Monroe asked.

I gazed at him grimly. 'Philip is a neat guy. Everything has a place. It's clean and tidy and…' I waved a hand around the devastation in the living room '…not like this.'

Monroe turned slowly, examining the room with a critical eye. 'Is it possible,' he enquired, 'that after a struggle he killed Valerie here and then took her dead body back to the Travotel to leave it there?'

'It seems unlikely. What would be the point?'

He glanced at me. 'To make her death appear to be an accident.'

'Her body was drained of all its blood,' I said, still feeling somewhat ill at the thought. 'That was no accident.'

'Something happened here, though,' Monroe said. 'Something violent.'

I swallowed and nodded. 'Could someone have got here ahead of us? Some bright spark might have worked out Philip's culpability and come here to take their revenge.'

Monroe frowned and crouched down, his fingertips touching one of the blood splatters. 'This isn't very fresh,' he said. 'Whatever happened here, it was at least a day ago. Most of the blood is already dry.' He flipped over one of the fallen paintings. It was an old portrait of Yeats. Him again. That didn't bode well.

I sucked on my bottom lip. 'Whatever happened to Philip, he's obviously not here. We should go back to the Travotel. Anna will have combed through the murder scene. If there's any more useful information or evidence, she'll have it.'

Monroe agreed. 'Let's vamoose. This place is giving me the creeps.'

Him and me both.

Chapter Eleven

'None of the other hotel residents saw or heard anything useful,' Anna said. Her frustration was obvious, although I thought I caught a glimmer of something else too. Horrific as Valerie's death was, Anna was in her element. She had been a police officer before the apocalypse after all; investigating a murder probably felt like normal to her. 'We can't even be sure if it was your jam-sandwich eating that set off Timmons' alarm or if it was our vampire's actions. Timmons said the system has been faulty from the start. It could have been a delayed reaction or it could have nothing whatsoever to do with Valerie's murder.'

I'd have been seriously concerned about any magical alarm that thought purloining a breakfast butty was worse than killing someone, but the unfortunate truth was that we were all still fumbling about in the dark where magic was concerned. Even Timmons, who was supposedly the most experienced of us all.

I told Anna what we'd discovered about Philip and his house. 'He could have killed Valerie there and brought her back here in the middle of the night.'

She didn't appear convinced. 'There are all sorts of beasties out there,' she said, 'especially when the sun is down. I find it hard to believe that someone could drag a corpse through the streets and avoid the apocalyptic creatures that roam around at night.'

Anna had a point. Even during the day you had to keep your wits about when you were crossing areas that were unoccupied by either of our communities. Nimue was only the start; all sorts of nasties had appeared as a result of the apocalypse. Maybe they'd been created by it. If they smelled a whiff of death, they'd descend in an instant; transporting a corpse would be nigh on impossible.

'Have you checked the cars?' Monroe asked. 'He could have driven her body here. It would have been the safest bet if he wanted to stay away from other magical predators.'

'Timmons already did that. He's confident that no new vehicles have been left in front of the hotel or nearby for weeks. Not many people drive any more, and those who do don't tend to leave their cars here for long.'

Anna pointed at the long-since-defunct security camera. 'There's CCTV everywhere,' she said irritably. 'And none of it does us any good. None of it works – like everything else in this damned city.' She aimed a kick at a nearby chair.

I suddenly realised that all of us were suffering under the pressure of this new life. It wasn't just Monroe and me; we all had a lot of adjusting to do. It didn't help that there were constant reminders everywhere of what used to be.

For a fleeting moment, I let the crushing maw of depression open up and suck me in into a spiralling pit of black despair. Then Monroe's hand brushed against mine and I remembered to breathe again. It was okay. I had this.

I made a deliberate effort to relax my muscles and zoned in on Anna. 'Was there anything about Valerie's body that indicated it wasn't a vampire who killed her?'

'Nope. The only wound was the one on her neck. Some fangy piece of shit sank his teeth into her and drank her dry.'

I glanced at Julie who was doing a good job of

looking casual but whose rigid neck betrayed her. 'You're adamant that's not possible?'

'Darling,' she said, 'I told you before that it is *possible*. But it's pointless. A couple of pints of blood will sustain a vampire – any vampire – for a week. There's no need to take it all.'

'No need,' I said grimly. 'But perhaps plenty of desire and bloodlust. You said before that if you drink too much, you become bloated and happy. Is there anything else we could be looking for? Any clue as to what our killer might do after such a meal?'

'What happens to you when you eat too much? We've covered bloat. You might also be sick. Goodness, drink all the blood in one human and you'd definitely be sick.'

'Could there have been more than one vamp?'

She shook her head. 'There would have been more bruising. I checked and double-checked. There are only two puncture wounds. I just...' She muttered a delicate curse. 'I just can't see the point in drinking all of it.'

The answer was right in front of us but it took Monroe to voice it. 'To kill,' he said flatly. 'The point wasn't to feed, it was to kill. This was no accident, much as we might want it to be.'

We were all silent. We'd been through a great deal in the last few months – that was a given. To have struggled and made a life for ourselves, despite our disparate communities, and then have someone swing along and ruin our work because they had murder on their mind was horrible to think about. It was almost impossible to fathom. It was, however, the stark truth.

'We searched Valerie's room,' Anna said, finally breaking the uncomfortable silence. 'She had a lot of cash scattered around. Given that this is a cashless society, that doesn't make a whole lot of sense.'

I cleared my throat. 'She was a gambler and old habits die hard. She kept inviting me to her poker nights.'

Everyone looked at me. 'Did you go?' Anna asked. 'If Valerie had a group of regulars that she played cards with, they would be a good place to start. The other hotel residents said they joined her for a while but she abandoned them when she found others who were more skilful and more … interesting. We don't know who they were, though.'

'That sounds like the Valerie I knew,' I admitted. 'She was always on the lookout for the next best thing.' I picked at a hangnail. 'We don't know who these new people were?'

'Not a clue,' Anna said, shaking her head. 'But we did find this.' She held up a leather-bound book. 'It's a diary. If what she's written here is true, Valerie was quite, uh, generous with her attentions.'

I motioned towards it. 'Can I have a look?'

She passed it over. I flipped open the first pages and scanned through. There were a lot of random sketches and scribbles, many of which were rather lewd. Despite her advanced years, Valerie had clearly enjoyed an active sex life. As far as I could tell, the drawings were her way of capturing her own experiences. There were little comments etched by the side, such as *Worth a second go* or *Doesn't wash often enough*. Unfortunately, none of the drawings or notes gave identities. It was also impossible to tell whether any of Valerie's lovers were vampires: fangs were not mentioned.

'Is this real?' Monroe asked. 'It could be her imagination getting the better of her.'

'The Valerie I knew pre-apocalypse,' I said, 'flitted from one young man to another. She enjoyed the chase and she wanted men she could control. She was always wealthy and she seduced them with promises of a better life.' I shrugged. 'When she got bored with them, she dumped them back where she'd found them.'

Anna looked interested. 'So there could be a plenty of men who held a grudge against her,' she said. 'That helps.'

Monroe nodded. 'This Philip guy we're looking for is a loner. She could have targeted him as a lover and then tried to get rid of him when it suited her. Except it didn't suit him and he got his revenge by bleeding her dry. After he'd had a tantrum and destroyed his own house, of course.'

It was certainly possible but I couldn't help feeling we were missing something crucial, and Monroe's conjecture didn't help with the most pressing issue. 'Having a motive doesn't help us locate him,' I pointed out.

'Honestly, Charley,' Anna told me, 'I'm not sure we *can* locate him. He could be anywhere. This is a big city with a lot of empty buildings. He could be hiding in any of them.'

I bit my lip and nodded. Hiding out – but bloated and maybe ill from such a big meal. I turned to Julie, who was still draped languidly over her chair. 'Do you get indigestion?' I asked.

'Me personally, darling?'

'Vampires. Do vampires get indigestion?'

She wrinkled her nose. 'Yes.'

'Can I assume that your bodies work the same as ours?'

An expression of faint disgust crossed her face. 'If you're about to ask me about my defecation habits then—'

'No,' I interrupted. 'I'm asking you if indigestion tablets affect your kind in the same way that they affect human kind.'

Julie shrugged. 'Yes, I suppose so.'

My eyes met Monroe's. 'All the shops around here were cleared of their contents weeks ago. I doubt there's anything useful in the pharmacies nearby but Philip might not know that. If he stumbled out of here after his … meal … in the middle of the night and didn't feel well, he might have tried to get some sort of medicine.'

Monroe ran a hand through his hair. 'In the absence of any other leads, we might as well check out the pharmacies. If there's any kind of trail, I might be able to pick something up.'

I nodded. It wasn't much of a plan but it beat standing around and wringing our hands. 'We need to tell everyone to be on the alert in case Philip shows up. Timmons can put the hotel on shutdown. Cath and Anna, you go home and make sure everyone knows to keep a look out and to keep away from anyone strange. And ask around to see if anyone attended Valerie's poker nights. Julie,' I paused and looked at her hopefully. 'You spend time with Monroe's lot. Can you go to the north and warn them?'

'Julian,' Monroe interjected. 'Speak to Julian.'

She didn't look very enthusiastic but she nodded. 'Very well, darling. But this Philip person won't be able to do anything but sleep, quite possibly for days.'

'All the more reason not to let the grass grow under our feet,' I said firmly. I let my fingers brush against Monroe's hand again. 'The two of us will go vampire hunting.' Maybe, just maybe, we'd find Philip before any more tragedies occurred.

Monroe smiled at me and bowed. 'As you wish, sunshine.' He leaned towards me. 'I know you only want my company for a little longer. But I do offer excellent protection as well.'

'Durex?' Julie enquired.

Anna began to choke with laughter.

'No!' I protested. I shot Monroe an irritated look while he blew me a kiss and winked. I knew what he was trying to do: he didn't want the others to think he wasn't still the arrogant alpha werewolf he'd first presented himself to be. It didn't mean he had to draw me into his shenanigans too. 'It's not like that!'

Julie sniffed. 'It should be.'

***

Monroe and I moved quickly and quietly through the streets surrounding the Travotel. The first pharmacy we came across already had its windows smashed in. It seemed empty but even so I stepped carefully inside to check. This might be like looking for a needle in a haystack but I wasn't going to quit. I'd made a promise to Valerie that I was determined to keep.

The pharmacy was a mess. Cheap, non-prescription reading glasses were scattered across the floor from a fallen stand and there were empty boxes everywhere. Glass crunched under my feet as I went to check out the store room behind the main desk.

Monroe raised his head and sniffed the air. 'I can't scent anything,' he called out to me. 'This place hasn't had a living soul in it for weeks. Our little vampire psycho killer hasn't been here.'

I scanned the empty shelves. I wasn't sure if it was my lot or Monroe's who had emptied this shop but, whoever it was, they'd certainly done a good job. Virtually everything had been taken.

'Yeah,' I agreed, unwilling to waste time. 'Let's move on to the next place.'

I was ready to leave. I'd just lifted up my leg to step through the window when Monroe yanked me back. 'Wait,' he said under his breath. He curved an arm round my ribcage and held me against him.

'You don't have to grab me,' I said. 'If you're telling me to wait, I'll wait.'

'I'm not sure you always trust my words, sunshine,' he murmured in my ear. 'Sometimes action is required.' A half beat later, a shadow fell across the street outside. I flinched and pressed against Monroe. I heard him give a soft chuckle then we both waited to see what manner of beastie had decided to show itself.

Prevailing post-apocalyptic wisdom suggested that it was far better to stay away from the creatures that now abounded across the city than to confront them, even when you had magic like I did or an animal form like Monroe's. We'd lost several citizens in those first days and weeks. It was a while since anyone had died that way, but now most people travelled in groups when they left the safety of their little enclaves. That was less to do with the fact that we were scared and more because of a healthy respect for our new neighbours. Not all of the beasts were carnivorous, not all were aggressive, and it also helped that most chose to venture out only after the sun was down. Even so, it was prudent to take care when out and about. Even the most theoretically innocuous creatures such as mermaids could be vicious.

There was a loud huffing sound, followed by a strange scraping noise, and a white-furred body appeared, moving on all fours. It swung its heavy head towards our motionless figures inside the pharmacy and blinked wide red eyes in our direction. Then it huffed again and shuffled past. I couldn't tell what it was or what it wanted – but I caught enough of a glimpse of its sharp claws to want to stay the hell away from it.

Monroe and I stayed where we were for several moments after the beast disappeared, thumping its way down the main street to wherever it was going. I didn't try to pull away until Monroe's head dipped down and he murmured, 'You see? You do want my protection after all.'

I hissed under my breath. 'We're alone now, you know. You don't have to play the tough guy.'

'It's in my DNA,' he responded calmly.

I stepped back and examined his face. 'No, it's not.'

'I'm not lying to you, Charlotte,' he said. 'And I'm not playing. You might think I'm being an overbearing male who's never heard of equal rights, but I am an alpha wolf. I can't always help myself.' He put his hands in his pockets and looked away. 'Old habits die hard, no matter what else is going on.'

I softened my tone. 'I'm saying that you don't have to put on a show for my sake. I can look after myself and I see you more clearly than you think.'

'Do you?' His mouth tightened. 'A couple of days ago you seemed to think I was coercing you into sleeping with me.'

'I didn't think that!' I protested. 'Not really anyway. I just…' Damn it. I grimaced. 'I was tired. I wasn't thinking straight.'

'I'm the guy who let his entire pack die, Charlotte. I'm the guy who lets himself get beaten up for fun. I'm also the guy who will pull you to safety when a furry white monster happens by.'

I crossed my arms. 'I'm the woman who ended up with magic by default, not design,' I told him. 'I'm the woman who is barely holding it together and who has taken on so much more than she can handle that she needs a werewolf to tell her when to have a break before she bites off someone's head or collapses into a puddle of melty stress. And, yes, I'm also the woman who sometimes mistakes intentions and desires. None of us is perfect, Monroe!'

He gazed at me and I gazed back at him, frustration reflecting like a mirror. 'You didn't mistake my desire, Charlotte,' he said eventually. 'It wasn't the time to act on it. That's all.'

I blinked. Did he mean…?

'But please,' he added, 'explain to me. What on earth is melty stress?'

I laughed suddenly, a brief release of tension that did us both good. We smiled at each other, the flare-up already forgotten and our shaky emotions pushed beneath the surface again. At least for now.

'We're a mess,' I whispered. 'Both of us.'

'You got that right,' he replied.

We exchanged a look of mutual understanding – and perhaps something more. In the end I dropped my eyes. 'Do you think we'll find him?' I asked quietly. 'Philip, I mean? Trawling through abandoned pharmacies seems like a waste of time.'

Monroe raised his shoulders. 'Maybe it is. But yes, we'll find him before anyone else is hurt.' He grinned. 'I'm Monroe the werewolf and you're the enchantress. How can we not find him?'

Sometimes, just sometimes, a bit of overconfidence was needed. Besides, Monroe was right. We were powerful beings in our own right, despite whatever else was going on in our psyche. I thought about that for a second, then I threw out my arms in sudden, exasperated realisation.

'What?' he asked.

I rolled my eyes at my own stupidity. 'I'm the enchantress,' I said. 'I know exactly how we can find him.'

Chapter Twelve

'I can sense magic,' I told Monroe, with the air of someone who was both superior and knowledgeable. Yeah; I'd have been annoyed with me, too.

'What on earth do you mean?'

I waved a hand around. 'Magic is blue,' I informed him. 'I can see it.'

His forehead creased. 'I still don't…'

'When the explosion happened and all the faeries vanished, I saw a cloud of blue appear.'

'Yes, I saw that too. I was half-unconscious but I registered that. I think just about everyone did, no matter who they are.'

'But I bet,' I said, 'neither you nor they can see that same blue now.'

Monroe stared at me. I tried to explain. 'It's everywhere,' I said. 'Everything has a blue aura. It clings to the city like,' I searched for the right word, 'like a kind of mist. I'm so used to it that I don't pay it much attention but it's definitely there. When that furry monster thing wandered past, it was swathed in blue. You have it too. The more magical something is, the more blue I see attached to it. It gives me a headache to focus on it too much when it surrounds people so I don't try too often, but it's definitely there.'

'You never thought to mention this before?'

I shifted uncomfortably. I had mentioned it to Lizzy and Cath once and they'd looked at me like I was mad. I had enough trouble adjusting to my new status without dwelling on all the things that made me … other.

'It didn't seem important,' I mumbled. 'But it can help us. The Arndale Centre is near here. It's like a beacon of flashing blue. That's because…'

'The faeries directed the worst of the escaped magic into the wishing well there.' Monroe nodded. 'I remember.' He fixed me with a serious look. 'So you think that you can track Philip the vampire by following the blue ether stuff that you can see?'

'Yeah.' I grinned enthusiastically. 'He's pumped full of blood. Every magical being, whether it's a werewolf or vampire or mermaid or canal monster, has more blue hanging over its head than a normal human. I bet Philip has loads of blue. Whether he's dozing off his feast or not, the magical by-product from what he's done will be seeping from his pores. I just need to look for the brightest spots of blue in the city and,' I snapped my fingers, '*voilà!*'

'Easier said than done,' Monroe grunted.

'Ye of little faith.' My smile grew. 'We need to find a vantage point then, through a process of elimination, I reckon we can narrow down all the places he could be. We'll find him before the sun sets.'

Monroe watched me with warmth in his eyes.

'What?' I asked.

He leaned down and brushed my lips with his. 'It's good to see your sunny side returning.'

'Then,' I replied primly, 'let's not allow it to disappear again. Let's get a move on.'

'As my lady desires.' He bowed. 'Lead the way.'

I skipped out of the pharmacy and glanced up and down the street. 'City Tower,' I said decisively. 'It's closest.' I beamed at him. 'Come on. The faster we move, the faster we'll find him.'

Monroe winked at me – then he exploded in front of my eyes, buttons and scraps of fabric flying in all directions. I took a step back and frowned at the gigantic wolf who had taken his place. 'Was that really necessary?'

He swung his head round, indicating his back, then he wagged his tail. Since when did wolves wag their tails?

I shook my head. 'I can walk. Or run.'

He padded forward, opened his mouth and ever so gently snagged my wrist with his teeth and pulled me towards him.

'Monroe,' I sighed. 'I know you're a big wolf but I'm a fully-grown woman.'

He let out a tiny growl and tugged at my wrist a little harder.

I sighed. We would get there a lot quicker, I supposed. And it was Monroe's call. I nodded reluctantly and he released me. I walked round and clambered onto his broad, furry back, curling my fingers into his red curls. For a wolf, he actually smelled pretty good. Not that I'd ever been this up close and personal with any other werewolf, not while they were in animal form.

I squeezed my thighs round his large frame and closed my eyes, hoping I could hang on. I felt his muscles bunching underneath me. Taking a deep breath, I held on tight. A second later, we were off.

I don't suppose you've ever given much thought to what it's like to ride bareback on a werewolf. Funnily enough, neither had I. All the same, I was surprised by how smooth it was. Monroe's gait was neither juddering nor awkward. Wind whipped past us until it felt like we were actually flying through the streets. Before long, I stopped being terrified that I was going to fall off and started enjoying myself.

I managed to stop gripping his fur quite so tightly and let my arms drop round his neck to hang loosely there for balance. I gave a loud whoop when we swung round a corner without slowing down. Why did Monroe bother taking a car when he could travel like this?

By the time we reached the foot of the massive City Tower building, I was panting – and with pure exhilaration rather than exertion. When I slid off Monroe's back and checked to make sure my weight hadn't damaged him in any way, he gave me a wolfy grin. Then he sprang forward and licked my cheek.

'Ew! Was that necessary?'

In the blink of an eye, his fur melted into skin. He stood there, stark naked, right in front of me, and continued to grin. 'It seemed appropriate,' he purred.

'You're naked.' Talk about stating the obvious.

'It's not an invitation,' he told me. He paused and his blue eyes danced. 'Unless you want it to be.'

All of a sudden my mouth was dry. 'Let's find Philip first, shall we?' But later... I swallowed.

Fortunately, Monroe removed his flirtatious gaze and nodded. 'Fair enough. It's a long way up to the top and you know the lifts won't be working.'

I stretched back my head. This seemed like one of those occasions when it was worth expending a bit of not-entirely-necessary magic. The faster we found our psycho vampire killer, the better. 'In that case,' I said, 'it's your turn to hold on.' If he could do it, so could I.

Monroe took less persuading than me and he moved closer. 'Like this?' he asked, putting one arm tightly round my waist.

'I'd use both arms if I were you.' The last thing I wanted was to lose him halfway up.

'If you insist, Charlotte,' he murmured as he wrapped his other arm round me.

I breathed out. It was probably just as well this part of the city was almost deserted. I couldn't imagine what anyone would think if they saw me with a naked man with more sex appeal than should be legal clinging onto me.

'Are you comfortable?' I asked. 'You still have a lot of bruises.'

'I wouldn't call this comfortable.' Monroe's voice was a low husk. 'But it's not the bruises that are making it difficult to relax.'

I should have called him out again for continuing with his alpha-wolf mask but I was enjoying every sexy insinuation. Business, Charley, I reminded myself; we were here on business.

'Hang on,' I told him. I tilted my head to focus on the roof of the tower and visualised the path upwards and the thread of magic I would need to get us there in one piece. I let my fingers tingle and the magic surge forth.

A heartbeat later, we were flying through the air. I caught glimpses of office furniture and abandoned coffee mugs and family pictures sitting on desks before they blurred and we sped up, zipping straight up as if in an invisible lift. I thought that Monroe's weight might slow me down but we moved at a terrific speed. In seconds, we were stumbling onto the flat roof, thirty storeys above the ground.

Monroe released his grip and staggered to the side. I lost my footing but the adrenaline surging through me helped me to spring up again. With sparkling eyes, I spun round and flashed him a brilliant smile.

'That was amazing!' I tossed my hair. 'I wasn't sure it would work but it did. From sea level to above the city in less than thirty seconds! Maybe I really can fly!' I flapped my arms in a bird-like manner. 'Next time, I'll aim to go further. What do you think, Monroe?'

He raised his head and looked at me blearily. 'You weren't sure it was going to work?' He turned away and promptly threw up. Uh oh.

I grimaced. 'Heights aren't your thing, then,' I said.

'Flying isn't my thing,' he muttered. A gust of wind blew and he shivered. I yanked off my jacket and handed it to him.

'I'm not wearing that. I'm not a damsel in distress.'

'Save us all the arrogance, Monroe, and put it on.'

He shivered again and gave in. First he attempted to squeeze his arms into the sleeves; when that didn't work, he shrugged it round his shoulders. It looked ridiculous but it was better than nothing.

'If you were anyone else…' he murmured.

I smiled then I mentally slapped myself. Business. Find Valerie's killer, Charley. You can play with Monroe later.

I walked to the eastern edge of the building and narrowed my eyes. It was good that it was a clear day because visibility from up here was excellent. For a brief moment, I gazed out beyond the city limits to the normal world. I didn't honestly wish to be there. I loved my city and, despite the stresses of my life now, I was glad I'd made the decision to stay. But it would certainly have been a far easier choice to leave. I shook myself and turned slowly. It was time to find the blue.

From this angle, I couldn't see the Arndale Centre, although the area where it was located definitely had a stream of blue light surrounding it. I ignored it and scanned the horizon. To the left there was an area where the blue light seemed more concentrated. I squinted, realising what it was. I spun round and looked in the opposite direction.

'What is it?' Monroe called from the centre of the tower's roof, as far away from any of the edges as he was likely to get.

'It doesn't make sense,' I muttered to myself.

'What is it?'

I registered the urgency in his tone and explained. 'The magic hanging over your community to the north is not that much stronger than the magic hanging over my community to the south.' Monroe's enclave included all types of magical beings. It should have emitted a far brighter hue than the humans from my place did. I scratched my head. It was weird – but it wasn't why we were here.

I kept peering. When I concentrated like this, the cloud of blue that clung to every part of Manchester was unmissable. There were patches and flares where the magic was stronger, from the canal to the odd building here and there. One or two of the spots were moving as magical beasts moved from one street to another. I walked round the edge of the building, ignoring the strong breeze that whipped at my exposed face and bare arms. There were more pockets of strong magic than I'd anticipated.

'Do you see anything that might show where our man is holed up?' Monroe asked.

I frowned. 'I'm not sure. I'm looking for anything out of place.' I had a good database locked inside my brain from all the reports that people had given me. I knew that the suburbs to the west housed all manner of shadowy monsters. I'd been told that the pink mammoth elephant, which still roamed the streets from time to time, tended to hang around the university, and that there were ghostly beings clumped together in the vicinity of the Lowry. I ignored those spots and focused on what was close by. It stood to reason that Philip would have been feeling too unwell after drinking every ounce of Valerie's blood to travel far, so I scanned the buildings nearby. A patch of blue was moving just to my right – but that was heading in the same direction as the white furry thing that had passed the pharmacy. I reckoned I was looking for something static.

Then I saw it. When I did, I let out a crow of delight.

'Winner winner chicken dinner!' I beamed. 'Come look!'

Monroe was very reluctant but clearly he didn't want to look like a scaredy-wolf. He slunk in my direction but kept away from the edge.

I pointed. 'That building there. There's a strong pulse of blue. That's the place. I know it.'

'You seem very sure.'

I fixed my gaze on the stone building. It looked abandoned but I knew deep down that it wasn't. Not entirely. 'I've been there before,' I told him. 'Many times. In fact, it's where I first met Valerie.' I smiled; it wasn't an expression of pleasure or glee but satisfaction that I'd found my mark. 'It's the oldest casino in the city.'

'The poker nights she set up,' Monroe murmured.

I nodded. 'You can bet your sweet naked arse that she held a lot of them there. Maybe she met Philip there and he's returned to the scene not only to recover but to relive those times. The magic is certainly strong enough over that building.' I swivelled round and looked at Monroe. 'That's where the bastard is.'

Chapter Thirteen

I'd have headed down to the ground in the same manner in which we'd left it but Monroe was still looking green around the gills so I took pity on him and agreed to take the stairs. Shame though. Now that I'd discovered I could fly – sort of – I wanted to try it again.

I reckon Monroe sensed my mild dismay at using a normal method to get down to ground floor and mistook it for haste. He offered to shift into wolf form again but it seemed prudent to conserve his strength for whatever lay ahead. Instead we jogged down, pausing only for him to grab a navy-blue boiler suit from a janitor's cupboard. I shouldn't have been surprised that it looked good on him. Everything looked good on him.

There was something very eerie about tripping down the stairs of an empty high-rise building. Our footsteps echoed, clattering in a way that made me think no one had been inside City Tower since the first days of the apocalypse. Here and there plant roots had broken through the plaster and there were a few gaping holes through which I could have stuck my hand and waved it around in the cool air outside. The wind whistled through these gaps and did nothing to detract from the ghostly atmosphere.

I was certain that the building was also groaning in the wind and shifting slightly from side to side. I wondered how long it would remain standing. Even now, mere months since Manchester had been abandoned to magic, it felt like it already had an expiration date. Perhaps everything in the city did. Oddly, that thought didn't make me feel melancholy or nostalgic. This was the natural order of things – just like bringing Valerie's killer to justice was part of the natural order.

'You're thinking too hard again,' Monroe remarked when we only had a few flights of stairs left to go down. He already knew me too well.

'I've been doing a lot of that lately,' I admitted. 'Normally I don't have time to dwell on things. There's always another problem or issue or complaint that takes up my brain space. I miss having a chance to take my time and ponder things.' I was quiet for a moment. 'When I'm with you,' I continued, 'it feels like the noise in my head is less bothersome. I get the chance to think properly about…' I waved a hand around '…the bigger picture.'

Monroe grunted. 'Thinking is over-rated.'

I smiled. I didn't think he meant that. And there was the faintest indication of a blush high on his cheekbones from my acknowledgment that being with him made me feel more at peace. When he wasn't being a total dickhead, of course.

When we reached the ground floor and the doors leading into the city streets, Monroe stopped and turned to me. 'I don't talk about my feelings very often,' he said stiffly. 'But, for what it's worth, you make the noise in my head quiet too.' Then, before I could say or do anything, he pivoted, pushed open the doors and walked out.

I remained where I was for a moment, gaping after him. Monroe had been so quick to pull away from me in the early days of the apocalypse. He hadn't wanted what I stood for – and I hadn't agreed with his vision of the future. But perhaps we were growing closer to each other as a result of being so far apart. I chewed on my lip. If that idea didn't make me think too hard about this new life and our place in it, then nothing would.

***

If I'd expected Monroe and I to continue a deep and meaningful conversation as we went towards the casino, I was sadly mistaken. We jogged in silence, both of us alert to any movement from either the ground level or the buildings around us. Even though the day was drawing to a close and the time when the beasties started coming out in force would soon be upon us, our journey remained event- and monster-free. In fact, there was barely a whisper until we reached the steps in front of the casino.

When we came to a halt Monroe said, 'I appreciate that your magic is incredibly powerful and you're capable of things that I can barely imagine, but I have more experience than you in confrontations like this. I'm not trying to sideline you or to exert my authority – I'm just suggesting that it would be a good idea if you let me deal with the vampire.' He folded his arms across his chest and glared at me as I were about to start arguing.

Naturally that's exactly what I did. 'You'll bulldoze your way in,' I told him, 'catch sight of Philip, see red and attack.'

Monroe's expression didn't flicker. 'What would be so wrong with that?'

I started to tick off on my fingers. 'First of all, we know from Julie that he's likely to be curled up in a corner sleeping. He's had too much blood to drink to be anything other barely conscious. He's not going to put up a fight, Monroe.'

'You don't know that for sure. Assuming we can trust what Julie told us, she made it perfectly clear that she's never taken that much blood in one sitting.

Therefore,' he pointed out implacably, 'she can't really know how it's affected Philip. In fact, the one thing we know for sure is that he's emanating vast amounts of magic because of what he's done. That makes him both unstable and very dangerous.'

'I hadn't finished,' I answered. 'Secondly, right now your headspace is telling you to fight first and ask questions later. You could very well end up killing him.'

He stared at me. 'Why would that be a bad thing?'

'Because things are bad enough already between the wolves and the vampires. I spent all of two hours in your neighbourhood, Monroe, and even I could tell you're sitting on a powder keg.'

'The vampires are free to leave at any point.'

I gave him a stony look. 'So the werewolves can live alone? A pure society untainted by other ethnicities? Do you know what that sounds like, Monroe?'

He winced. 'I do. And I don't mean it like that. There are plenty of werewolves I'd happily get rid of too but somehow, when I was busy doing other things, they all showed up and settled in. It was not what I wanted.'

'It's called free will. People have to be allowed to make their own choices. If those choices adversely affect others then they have to be held accountable – but you can't tell everyone how to live their lives.'

'Yes, I can.' He blinked slowly. 'Philip used his free will when he slurped every drop of blood from Valerie. And I'm not sure why we're suddenly getting into a philosophical argument about morality when I should be in there sorting out fucking Philip for killing *your* friend.'

'You can't kill him,' I insisted. 'You can't even hurt him unless it's absolutely necessary. He deserves to be allowed to speak about what he may or may not have done first.'

Monroe sighed heavily. 'I will agree to that if you agree to stay out—'

He was interrupted by a loud crash. We froze and stared at each other. 'So much for sleeping it off in a corner,' he hissed at me. 'Stay here.' He turned and barrelled into the door. Unfortunately, instead of going through it he bounced back and ended up sprawled on the pavement. He growled and got to his feet.

'Oh, did I forget to mention that the casino doors are steel reinforced?' I asked innocently.

He shot me an irritated look and tried again. 'They must be bolted shut from the other side. I'll have to find another way in.'

I nodded. 'Go on then.' I raised my hands and concentrated, allowing magic to spurt forth. A second later the doors sprang open. 'Look,' I murmured, holding my hands up in sarcastic awe. 'Maybe you do need me after all.'

Monroe hissed something under his breath. 'Just don't get hurt,' he said. 'That's the last thing I need.'

I would take that as evidence that he cared for me. I flashed him a quick grin before squaring my shoulders. 'Let's get this bastard. Without hurting him.'

Monroe rolled his eyes then he stalked into the casino with me hot on his heels.

Whatever – or whoever – had caused the crash had fallen silent again. The casino interior was very dark and very silent. In one corner close to the doors stood a smiling, life-size, cardboard cut-out of a scantily clad waitress holding up a wad of cash. Whoever she had been pre-apocalypse, she certainly wasn't here now. I gave her a wave and debated whether to bring her along to make it look like there were more of us.

Monroe clearly wasn't concerned with numbers. He marched forward past several empty tables and scattered playing cards and chips. I abandoned the smiley cut-out and followed, unwilling to let him out of my sight – until my foot slipped and I realised I'd trodden on a playing card. The ace of spades. I shivered. I wasn't usually superstitious and I didn't believe in luck or lack thereof; I made my own luck. All the same, something about that card gave me the willies.

I shook myself. It was only a card. It didn't actually mean anything. I looked up and realised that Monroe had also stopped. His head was tilted up and he was sniffing the air. It was difficult to tell through the gloom but to me he looked very confused and very unhappy.

I sidled up to him. When he didn't immediately respond, I nudged him. 'What's wrong?' I whispered.

His nose twitched and his hands curled into fists. 'Wolf,' he answered.

Now I was the one who was puzzled. I frowned at him. 'What…'

'There's a wolf here,' he said in an undertone. 'Young. Female.'

My heart sank. So I'd been wrong. Yet again, I'd fallen victim to my self- belief. It wasn't Philip the vampire whose magic signature had been broadcasting from this place, it was just a werewolf who wanted to play roulette. I cursed to myself. I'd been so sure this was where we'd find Valerie's killer.

'And blood,' Monroe added as an afterthought. 'There's a shitload of blood.' He unfastened his boiler suit and stepped out of it, taking his time, then turned to me in all his naked glory and placed a finger to his lips. It wasn't his lips I was looking at but I nodded anyway. A second later, his body expanded and shifted. I stepped out of the way just in time. Then he was on all fours, his fur bristling and those same lips pulled back over his teeth.

He sniffed again and, with a final warning look in my direction, padded forward silently.

I was unsure what to do. Monroe's nose was clearly telling him where to go, but should I follow? Despite my words a few moments earlier, I didn't want to get in his way. If there was a werewolf here, my presence wouldn't help matters. Shapeshifter hierarchy meant that any wolf would automatically do Monroe's bidding, regardless of what I did to intervene. But Monroe's certainty about the presence of blood... I gritted my teeth. I'd have to go after him and I'd also have to steel myself for what we might find.

Unfortunately my indecision had cost me because I could no longer see Monroe's wolf form. He'd disappeared among the poker tables and silent bandit machines. Neither could I move as quietly as he could; I took a few steps forward and, even walking on my tiptoes on the soft carpet, all I could hear was my own movement.

I stopped again. I was tempted to call out and ask Monroe to wait for me but I didn't want to draw attention to myself. We weren't alone here. Although I knew this casino well, the shadowy corners and almost impenetrable darkness ahead were making me nervous.

I could feel my magic pushing against my fingertips, eager to be set free again but I had to stay in control. It was the only way to gain the upper hand. I leaned forward, peering through the gloom. Where had Monroe gone? I glared, as if I could call him back to my side with dirty looks alone. Then there was a strange bristling sensation on the back of my neck and I knew that someone, or something, was watching me.

I tensed. I wasn't used to being stalked and I didn't like it in the slightest. I breathed deeply and tried to think. Whether my watcher was Philip the vampire, a werewolf or some other scary predator, I wouldn't win the day by letting my fear get the better of me. Instead of thinking like Charley the potential lunch dish, I needed to remember Charley the gambler. I had to act normally and bluff like my life depended on it. It probably did.

If whoever was out there believed that I was unaware of them, they might drop their guard in the mistaken belief that they were going to take me by surprise. All I had to do was maintain a poker face and work out exactly where my attacker was then I could keep myself safe. I had the magical defences I needed; I just had to know where and when to use them.

I started forward once again, more slowly this time. To my left, if I had my bearings right, there was a long bar with a mirrored back which had the potential to help me enormously. I tiptoed forward, giving the impression that I was wary but not unduly afraid. When I drew level with the bar, I turned to face it. I reached down to a blackjack table nearby, trailing my fingers distractedly across the scattered chips on the green felt. I kept one eye on the mirror, however, and a few seconds later my strategy was rewarded.

There was the faintest flicker of movement reflected from behind me just to my right. I couldn't tell what it was but, now that I had pinpointed it, I felt slightly less anxious. Gotcha. Sort of.

I abandoned the blackjack table and went deeper into the casino. There was still no sign of Monroe but that was okay. I had to draw my tracker further down where there were more tables. Any furniture between me and them would slow their progress and give me more time to react if I needed it. If my stalker thought I was trapping myself, they would be sorely disappointed.

Not far from me, a shaft of light cascaded down from a skylight. I wanted to avoid that area if possible;

the last thing I needed was to illuminate myself and make it harder for me to see who was stalking me. I slowed my steps, trying not to make it look too obvious. A loose blue curl fell across my forehead and into my eyes and I raised a hand to brush it away. That was when I felt the rush of air behind me.

I spun, just in time to see a gigantic shape flying through the air towards me with its jaws wide. A dark liquid dripped from its teeth. Wolf, I thought. Definitely another wolf. I jerked my palms up and out; magic bolts flew into the air but before they could smack into the wolf there was another flurry of movement to my left. Monroe leapt through the air and collided with my would-be attacker. My magic slammed into the wall behind while the lupine pair slammed onto the floor.

Monroe rolled to his feet and snarled; the other wolf growled in response, yellow eyes flashing. Monroe took one step towards her and her shoulders and tail dropped. In less time than it had taken me to brush my hair from my eyes, he'd cowed the other wolf into submission.

I tried not to look too impressed. A large chunk of plaster fell from the wall from my attempt at defence, and all three of us flinched. Monroe kept his gaze trained on the wolf in front of him and shifted, his spine clicking as he stood upright once again.

'And you were the one who cautioned against violence, sunshine,' he murmured. He smiled, seemingly unfazed by what had just occurred.

I stared at him. How had he appeared out of nowhere like that? My eyes narrowed. Hang on a minute. 'You used me as bait!' I accused. 'You deliberately left me there on my own because you knew that wolf was behind me.'

He shrugged but at least he didn't try to deny it.

'You were adamant that you could take care of yourself. Don't worry, I'd have never let you be harmed.' He said it so dismissively that I wasn't sure whether to be pleased or irritated. Either way, this probably wasn't the time for yet another spat.

Monroe still hadn't taken his blue eyes off the wolf in front of him. Although she was unnaturally large, she wasn't a match for him. Her belly was almost touching the ground and her head remained lowered. When Monroe knelt down and reached over to touch her muzzle, she whimpered.

He pulled back and examined his fingers grimly. 'Blood,' he said. 'Vampire blood.'

I stopped breathing. 'Philip?' I whispered.

Monroe's expression was hard. 'Let's find out.' He stared at the wolf. 'Take us to him.'

She didn't hesitate. With her body still low to the ground, she slunk forward like a whipped cur. Monroe and I followed. Nothing about this was making any sense to me, not yet. It didn't help that by the time we reached the back of the casino even I could smell the tang of blood in the air.

The werewolf continued to whine. Her whole body was shaking, I assumed from fear of Monroe. But when we came to the dim shapes of some squashy sofas, designed for those taking a break from gambling, her whimpers grew more fearful and high-pitched.

Monroe's spoke evenly. 'Charlotte, can you perhaps raise some light on this situation?'

I didn't want to do it because I already had a good idea what I would see. The outline was visible; were the details really necessary? I grimaced and squeezed my eyes shut, then flicked out the magic I knew would cast enough light to illuminate what I didn't want to see.

I heard Monroe suck in a sharp breath. The female

werewolf howled. I slowly opened one eye, confident I was going to regret it. I was right. Three seconds later I was throwing up onto a roulette wheel.

It was definitely Philip the vampire. And from his torn flesh and the ragged wound in his side, he'd virtually been ripped apart. Whatever he'd done to Valerie – and why – he wouldn't be able to tell us about it now.

Chapter Fourteen

Monroe had suggested that I head to the Travotel while he escorted the werewolf to the north. The hotel was closer to the casino and staying there would give me the chance to get some proper rest again. Truth be told, however, not only did I want to avoid the place of Valerie's death, I was also looking forward to getting home. I missed my own bed and I'd been away from my people for too long. Unfortunately, bedraggled, exhausted and traumatised as I was, I couldn't even turn the corner of my street before I was accosted. It's never a good thing when people run at you.

'I've been looking for you for days!' Elsie Jones, who lived out on Morecambe Road, barrelled towards me. For a moment I thought she was going to give me a hug and tell me how relieved she was that I was alright but that was a foolish hope.

'There's no gluten-free produce left anywhere in the city apart from the last of the cereal bars, and Alex at number fifty-seven took all of them! He knows I'm gluten intolerant! He can't be allowed them all, Charley. It's not fair! You have to talk to him straight away. We're all being rationed and he's having more than his fair share. It's not right!'

I blew air out slowly and tried to smile, hoping the smell of torn-apart vampire wasn't clinging to me. 'Well,' I said, 'obviously things will get more difficult as time goes on. We don't have an endless supply of…'

'I know that!' she bellowed in my face. 'That's exactly my point! But that's not all, not by a long shot.

He's not been disposing of his rubbish properly. We're supposed to leave it out for collection so that we keep disease and rats down to a minimum. Two weeks on the trot and he's not done it! If there's another infestation of rats, it will be his fault. Just because he's in a wheelchair, he thinks he should get special treatment.'

'I will investigate the matter and talk to him,' I promised.

'He's in the square at the moment. You can talk to him now.'

'I'll talk to him when I get the chance,' I said. 'Excuse me.' I managed another weak smile and walked past her. Her complaints had been loud enough for other people to appear. From their expressions, they all had something to say to me. My body sagged. I could do with half an hour's peace to get my head together.

I strode forward, hoping I could get to my house through sheer will power.

'Charley!'

I waved at the Entwhistles and picked up my pace to scoot past them without engaging in conversation.

'Charley!'

'I'm busy right now,' I called to Professor MacTavish, who wasn't a professor at all but insisted on being called one. 'I'll speak to you later!'

I sighed. I couldn't avoid everyone forever but I'd hoped for a longer period of grace than this.

By ducking and diving and smiling firmly at anyone who approached, I made it to my front door without too many interruptions. Alas, the door was wide open and I could already see Julie in the hallway, trying to usher out Albert. 'When she returns,' she was saying, 'I'll tell her you're looking for her.'

There was no way to sidle past the pair of them without being noticed. I steeled myself and stepped inside. 'Hi, Julie. Hi, Albert.'

They both turned towards me. 'You made it!' Julie exclaimed. 'Is everything alright? What happened?'

'I'll explain later,' I said tiredly. I didn't think old Albert would want to hear the gory details.

'What happened with the blood?' he asked.

'I avoided getting too much on me,' I answered, without really thinking.

He stared at me. 'From the taps?'

Oh. I'd forgotten about that, even though it was the reason why I'd left two days earlier. 'That's sorted,' I told him. 'We shouldn't have any more problems. It was a mermaid in the little reservoir. She was bored and unhappy and trying to get attention. I've relocated her to Boggart Hole so the mains water should be fine from now on.'

Even Julie appeared surprised at that. 'A mermaid?' she enquired. 'Are you sure, darling?'

'Well,' I said, 'she has a fishy tail and she lives underwater. Yeah,' I nodded, 'I'm pretty sure she's a mermaid.'

'Blimey. Just when you think you've heard it all.'

'Indeed.' I pushed back my hair. 'I'm sorry, guys,' I said. 'I need a cup of tea and a bit of time to relax then I'll sort out everything that's been building up while I was away.'

Julie's eyes widened fractionally. 'Of course.' She reached out to put her hand on Albert's arm. He flinched away. 'You should go now, love,' she said kindly. 'Everything is sorted.'

'Until the next thing happens,' he sniped, bunching his eyebrows together. He let out a huff and pushed past me, heading into the street.

Lizzy appeared at the top of the stairs. When she caught sight of me, she came bowling down. To begin with I almost cowered, but thankfully she just wanted a hug. She wrapped her arms tightly round me and beamed. 'I'm so glad you're back,' she said. 'It's been a madhouse here! I don't know how you do it. We need you here to keep the peace to stop everyone killing each other.'

'Hmm.' Julie wrinkled her nose. 'Let's allow Charley some breathing space, shall we? And instead of tea, perhaps some gin and tonic.'

Lizzy tutted but at that moment a proper drink sounded perfect. I smiled weakly at the pair of them and sniffed. 'That'd be really good.'

***

Lizzy looked aghast; in fact, everyone looked aghast. Cath was particularly wide-eyed. 'But why did that werewolf kill the vampire?'

'I don't know.'

'Was she a friend of Valerie's? Was she tracking this Philip guy?'

I shrugged. 'I don't know.'

Cath opened her mouth to ask another question. I held up my hands. 'She didn't shift back. Monroe told her to and she didn't. To be honest, it seemed like she couldn't.'

Lizzy's horror grew. 'She was trapped in that form?' She clasped her throat. As a type of shapeshifter herself – and very new to it – it was her greatest fear that she'd transform into her furry, horned, bunyip shape and wouldn't be able to change back to her human form again.

'I don't know that either,' I admitted. 'She did everything else Monroe told her to do. When he commanded that she shift, she looked like she was trying.' In truth, she'd looked like she was in terrible pain but I wasn't going to tell Lizzy that.

'That's awful.'

Julie snorted. 'She had just ripped a vampire apart. I don't think she needs much sympathy.'

'A vampire who deserved it! He murdered Valerie for no good reason,' Lizzie protested.

'Probably,' I interjected. 'He probably murdered Valerie.'

'An eye for an eye,' Lizzy declared.

Julie crossed her arms. 'Innocent until proven guilty,' she shot back.

I passed a hand over my forehead. Lizzy and Julie usually got on alright. The fact that they were arguing about what had happened did not bode well. I reached across, grabbed the bottle of gin and started glugging it neat. The pair of them slowly swivelled towards me then exchanged glances.

'Maybe you should go lie down, Charley,' Lizzy suggested.

Julie nodded. 'I think that's a good idea.'

At least we finally agreed on something. I yawned. Then I thought of all the people outside who wanted to talk to me; I had other responsibilities beyond killer vampires, insane werewolves and glorious sleep to deal with.

'In a while,' I said. 'Give me a rundown of what's been happening for the last couple of days while I've been away first.' I wanted to see what I could delegate and what I really had to deal with myself. I managed a tired smile and pretended I didn't see the worry in my friends' eyes. 'No rest for the wicked.'

***

The next morning, when I stumbled downstairs in the

search of something that could wake me up now that coffee was so scarce and only being kept for special occasions, I realised that yet again we had visitors. When one of those visitors spoke with a soft Scottish brogue, I stopped on the bottom step to eavesdrop.

'You need to do more to pick up the slack,' Monroe was saying. 'It's not fair.'

'I've been telling them that for weeks, darling.'

He snorted. 'What have you done to help Charlotte, then?'

'I came to find you, didn't I?'

I didn't need to see him to know that he was rolling his eyes. 'You're supposed to have a council that runs things. This isn't a one-woman show. In any case, Charlotte needs to come with me. We still have to find out what happened to Valerie – and why. I think murder takes precedence over your other business.'

'I'm a busy person too, darling. There are plenty of other people who can help Charley.' Julie paused. 'Most people don't like me all that much.'

There was a loud snort, which could only have come from Jodie. 'That's hardly the newsflash of the century. Look, Monroe,' she added, 'we do try to help. We don't just leave Charley to sort everything on her own. The trouble is that she's so...'

Her voice trailed off. I narrowed my eyes. I was so what?

'Capable,' Lizzy finished for her.

'Exactly,' Jodie said.

Capable? That was the last thing I was. Certainly these days.

'Well,' Monroe said, with a steely edge, 'the rest of you are going to have to become more capable too. I need Charlotte with me.' There was a beat. 'You can come out now,' he called.

I winced. Darn it. I walked down the final step and into the kitchen. 'Hey.'

Jodie, Julie and Lizzy stared at me guiltily.

'How much of that did you hear?' Lizzy asked.

'Enough,' I said. I fiddled with the buttons on my cuffs and drew in a deep breath. 'This isn't just about needing to help Monroe with the investigation,' I told them. 'I'm not coping very well right now. There's so much to deal with and there's never a break. I'm not saying I want to bow out or hand everything over to someone else.' I raised my head and looked at them all. 'But I need more help.'

Lizzy and Jodie looked even more guilty; Monroe and Julie just smiled. I glanced round. Well, hey: I'd asked for help and admitted I was struggling and the sky hadn't fallen in and the walls were still standing. Maybe there was hope for me yet.

'They don't listen to us,' Jodie said. 'The people out there. We'd do a lot more but they all want you. They believe in you.' She tugged nervously at her collar. 'Anna's a police officer. Shouldn't she be the one investigating the murder instead of you?'

'She is,' Julie said. 'She's also keeping the peace on a whole host of other matters.' She nodded decisively. 'We'll convene the council and see what we can come up with. Not everything should be on your shoulders, Charley.' She offered an airy smile and strolled out.

Jodie rolled her eyes. 'She's very good at telling other people what to do and avoiding any responsibility herself.' She sighed. 'But we'll do what she says and see how we can change things a bit.'

Lizzy nodded. 'I'm sorry, Charley. I knew you were finding things tough but I didn't realise quite how bad things were. And I didn't realise how much you had to deal with until you weren't here. As much as I like everyone in our little community, they do complain a lot, don't they?'

I permitted myself a small smile. 'They do.' I hesitated. 'Can I have a hug?'

Lizzy beamed and bounced over to me. She beckoned Jodie and Monroe. The former joined in; the latter grimaced awkwardly.

From the doorway, Anna cleared her throat. 'Am I interrupting something?'

'Come and join the group hug!' Lizzy sang.

'Come and save us from the group hug,' Monroe muttered.

'Hmm.' Anna didn't seem to know what to say. She watched us for a moment then shrugged as if deciding we were all crazy. I felt a giggle threatening to burst out of me at her expression. 'Is this a good time?' she asked. 'I've got some updates to discuss with you.'

Instantly, I sobered up. 'To do with Valerie?'

'Yes.'

I stepped back, reverting from Charley who had friends and knew how to enjoy herself to Charley the accidental leader of a group of post-apocalyptic survivors. You couldn't make this shit up.

'Take a seat,' I said grimly. 'Let's hear what you've got.'

Chapter Fifteen

Lizzy and Jodie made their excuses and beat a hasty retreat. I didn't blame them; it wasn't much fun poring over the gruesome details of a vicious murder, or examining the detritus of the life the victim had left behind.

'So,' Anna said, knitting her fingers under her chin, 'I understand that our working theory is that this vampire, Philip Someone, killed Valerie by drinking all of her blood and then the werewolf, Maggie, killed him.'

'Maggie?' I asked. 'That's her name?'

Monroe nodded.

It didn't sound like the name of someone who would hunt down a killer and rip them to pieces; it sounded like the name of someone who would dispense tea and hugs and the occasional chocolate biscuit.

'She's not still not shifted back,' Monroe said, his mouth in a thin line. 'We've tried everything but she's not budging. Until she does…'

'She can't answer any questions.' I frowned. 'I get it.' I glanced at him. Just the thought of her was turning his eyes a stormier shade of blue. It didn't surprise me. I'd seen him in action, using his own will to get Lizzy to transform from bunyip into human again. I knew what he was capable of – under normal circumstances. 'Is it clear yet whether she is refusing to transform, or is it something else?' I asked, echoing Lizzy's concerns.

He drummed his fingers on the table. 'It's impossible to tell. Once we're done here, I was hoping you could come with me to see her. You might be able to conjure up some magic to force her to shift.'

That seemed an unlikely scenario. I still didn't know all that my magic was capable of and I'd be worried about hurting her – or worse – if I forced the matter. Let's face it, if Monroe and all his fellow wolves couldn't command her to shift back, how on earth would I? All the same, I nodded agreement. It was better than staying around here and dealing with missing gluten-free cereal bars. I reminded myself that I was supposed to be the optimistic one. 'I'll find a way to change her,' I said. 'I'm sure it won't be that hard.'

At least Monroe had the grace to remain silent in the face of my over-confidence.

'The thing is,' Anna said, 'I've been through all of Valerie's stuff and read her diary from cover to cover. There is no evidence that she had anything to do with vampires, or werewolves for that matter. In fact, from the interviews I've conducted, she despised them. There was an incident at one of her poker sessions where a vampire tried to gain access and she refused them. Rather vocally from what I was told.'

'Sometimes,' I said thoughtfully, 'the one who protests the loudest is the one who has the most to hide. If Philip was one of her lovers, or merely a potential lover, and she was embarrassed by that fact, she might have tried to conceal it from others around her.'

'True,' Anna conceded. 'However, there were various anti-vampire objects in her room.'

I raised an eyebrow. 'Such as?'

'A crucifix. Garlic. That kind of thing.'

'That stuff doesn't work. It was made up by people who wanted to discredit vampires.'

Monroe shrugged. 'It doesn't matter if it works or not. What matters is that she *believed* it worked. She was clearly afraid of vampires and what they might do to her.' His eyes hardened. 'Or afraid of one particular vampire.'

Anna didn't look convinced. 'I'd have said the same,' she said. 'But most of this stuff was shoved away in drawers. She didn't have it within easy reach. It was as if she'd got hold of such things as an afterthought in case she needed them one day, but it wasn't a pressing issue. I don't believe there's anything more sinister here than the fact that she didn't like vampires very much.'

I wrinkled my nose. 'And if she didn't like vampires, she wouldn't be shagging one.'

She nodded. 'Indeed.'

'I don't like that word,' Monroe said.

I blinked at him. Eh?

'Shagging,' he explained.

Yeah, yeah. 'You're more of a fucking guy, aren't you?' I'd heard him use that term before. That wasn't my favourite euphemism either. If you could call it a euphemism.

His eyes held mine. 'Making love is better.'

My mouth suddenly felt uncomfortably dry. Anna's gaze flicked from Monroe to me and back again. 'Okay,' she said slowly. 'Getting back to the matter in hand...'

I coughed. 'Yes.' I turned to her. 'What about the men Valerie did recently sha— erm, have affairs with? Do you have a list of them? They might have engaged Philip's services.' I raised my shoulders in a vague shrug. 'Outsourcing murder. It could happen.'

'As far as I can tell,' Anna said, with an approving smile at my suggestion, 'there are three potential candidates. There aren't names for any of these three but Valerie did write down quite a few other details about them. If you two are focusing on the werewolf and anything else you can dig up about Philip, then I'd like to see whether I can identify Valerie's men. Whatever else is going on here, it started with her.'

The last thing I was going to do was disagree with Anna's proposal. She was the only one here who had any real experience in investigating crime, even if she was used to doing it with the aid of an entire police force, not to mention a database of criminals, DNA and fingerprints. 'It sounds like a good plan,' I said.

Monroe stood up. 'Definitely. And you're right about Philip. Once Charlotte and I have finished with Maggie, we should go and talk to the other vampires about him. They should have more reason to answer our questions honestly than before.' He glanced at me. 'Much as I hate to admit it, you're right about the way things are in the north. The vampires can't afford to be tainted with the suggestion of a murderer hiding in their midst. And, regardless of the motive, neither can the werewolves.'

'There's no place for murder in either the south or the north,' Anna said.

'Or anywhere in Manchester,' I added. They both nodded at me in grim agreement. 'Group hug?' I asked hopefully.

Anna actually looked slightly afraid. 'Let's settle for a firm handshake.'

I grinned and shook her hand, then Monroe did the same. It was oddly formal but it also felt right. Weird. Next thing, I'd probably be carrying around a clipboard and wearing a suit. What a thought.

Once Anna had departed, Monroe walked over to me. His expression was strange, intent but also doubtful. His hands reached up and he cupped my face. 'I don't want a hug,' he said softly. 'And it would be inappropriate right now, given everything that's going on. But what I do want more than anything is to kiss you. Properly. When you came downstairs, with your daft blue hair tousled and the look in your eyes so vulnerable…' He growled softly. 'I'm normally better at this sort of stuff. I simply wanted to let you know what I was really thinking and state my intent before a better offer comes along.'

I swallowed. Of everything I'd been expecting him to say, this wasn't it. My surprise must have registered because he stepped back and dropped his hands. 'Sorry,' he muttered. 'I shouldn't have said that.'

Whoa. 'No!' I interjected hastily. 'I mean, yes!' I wasn't making any sense. I cursed to myself then closed the distance between us and reached up for his face in the same manner that he'd reached up to mine. 'We've been doing this dance for a while, Monroe.' I licked my lips nervously.

His gaze darted downwards and it occurred to me that this might appear to be a calculated move on my part. Whatever you might think of me, I'm not the seductress type, much as a secret part of myself might want to be.

I yanked my tongue back and tried to explain before the moment was lost. My words tripped over themselves. 'Even when I didn't see you for weeks, you were what I thought about. A better offer isn't going to come along. You're the best there is. I want the kiss too. And more afterwards.'

His eyes darkened. 'I'm still fucked up, Charlotte. I'm a mess. You'd do better to stay away from me.'

I laughed lightly. 'Probably. But I'm not sure I can. And whatever mess you are, whatever front you put on for everyone else, you still show the real you to me. I see the real you and I know you see the real me.' I pushed myself onto my tiptoes and dropped my voice to a whisper. 'And, in case you've not noticed, I'm pretty fucked up too.'

'You just need more help from your friends.' He

tapped the side of his head. 'I need help up here.'

'Your entire pack was killed, Monroe.'

He snarled quietly. 'And it was my fault.'

'No.' I glared at him. 'It wasn't. It was a tragedy and awful, and you still need to allow yourself to grieve properly, but it wasn't your fault.'

'You weren't there, Charlotte.'

'I didn't have to be,' I answered simply. 'I know you. I *see* you. We're as vulnerable as each other. You hide it better.'

'I'm not vulnerable.'

'You are.'

'I'm not…' Monroe cursed. 'Fuck it.' He took hold of my shoulders and pushed me gently against the wall. At the same time, I pulled his face down towards me. His lips descended on mine, hot and insistent. Heat flooded through me. It wasn't only my body that was responding; the magic inside me reacted too, tingling up and down and making me shiver, despite the searing heat of Monroe's body pressed against mine.

'Charlotte,' he groaned.

'I know,' I whispered. 'I know.'

His breath was coming fast and heavy. His mouth found mine while his hands moved away from my face and down my body. I couldn't think straight. Nothing else existed apart from Monroe. Nothing else mattered. It was just me and him and…

There was the sound of a very loud cough. Barely registering it, my eyes flicked open then I jerked when I saw Cath, leaning against the doorframe and fanning herself. 'I have one word for you both,' she said. She raised her voice and crowed to the ceiling, 'Hawwwwt!'

Monroe slowly pulled away from me. 'Doesn't anyone ever knock around here?'

I sighed. 'Tell me about it.'

'Honestly,' Cath said, 'I've been shipping you two for like ever. It's about time you got it on.'

Monroe looked at me blankly. 'Shipping?'

I shook my head. 'Is there something you need, Cath?'

She grinned. 'I can wait.'

I folded my arms across my chest then realised that half my shirt buttons were undone. Cheeks flushing, I fumbled to fasten them. 'We're done.' I sneaked at look at Monroe.

'For now,' he murmured.

I blushed harder. 'What is it, Cath?'

'Anna told me you were heading north. I want to come along. The vampire's body is there, right? I want to take a look.'

I swear she grew more bloodthirsty by the day. 'I'm not sure that's a good idea.'

'I want to learn!' she protested. 'I examined Valerie's body and I learned tonnes from that! I want to examine the vampire's too. It's all in the interests of medicine. It's all very well stitching up the odd wound or handing out painkillers, but things aren't always going to be so simple. I'm the only person with any kind of medical experience and I barely know a thing. I'm not being voyeuristic. I'm trying to better myself. I thought you'd appreciate that.'

'You're not the only person. We have two doctors in the north,' Monroe said.

I started. 'You do?'

'Just because we're werewolves doesn't mean we can't hold down a job,' he said mildly. 'Although there's also a vampire who's a cardiac nurse. I have no idea how *that* works.'

Cath jumped up and down. 'O. M. G. I have to be there. Let me come with you!'

I frowned at Monroe. 'How did I not know you had real doctors?' We could have used them. Several times.

He looked apologetic. 'I guess I thought you knew. It appears I'm only just starting to learn how important communication is.'

And then some. 'What else do you have that we don't?' I enquired, still annoyed.

'You'll have to spend more time with me and find out.' His eyes glinted.

'Are you guys about to start snogging again?' Cath asked. 'Should I step outside?'

'No.' I sniffed. 'We're going to the north. We still have a murder to solve.'

'So can I…?'

'You can come.' I gave Monroe a long look. Three months and only now I was learning there were real doctors? 'Have you been holding out on me?' I asked.

'Not deliberately.' He caught my hand and squeezed it. 'I really am sorry, Charlotte.'

'I bet they don't have engineers,' Cath said. She looked at Monroe. 'Do you?'

He shook his head. 'No.'

'Ours are collecting generators from around the city,' she chirped. 'Before too long, we'll have enough electricity for the whole community. If the magic doesn't interrupt it, that is.'

He raised an eyebrow. 'Is that right? We could do with some of that ourselves. You didn't mention electricity before, Charlotte.'

'We don't have any yet. It's a work in progress.' I looked away. But, yeah, okay, I supposed we both had to work on our communication. And spend more time together in the process. I could live with that.

Chapter Sixteen

In the end, I was secretly glad of Cath's presence as we journeyed to the north of the city. It meant that there wasn't the opportunity for more awkward conversations with Monroe. Or distractions. My love life had to come second to Valerie's murder; it wasn't fair to her memory to spend my time being distracted by hearts and flowers. Or by how good Monroe smelled when he was pressed up against me. People died and life went on as it should. But there was still a time and a place, and this wasn't it.

We dropped Cath off at the building earmarked as both a hospital and a morgue. I made a bet with myself as to the likelihood that her approach to blood and gore would make even the werewolf docs appear squeamish in comparison. Then Monroe and I strode towards the community's centre, the imposing building in front of the square that served as the main hub, where Maggie was being kept.

It wasn't just werewolves who were out on the northern streets now. With dusk falling, more and more vampires were visible. Their presence made it patently clear that they didn't want to be locked away in their little enclave; they wanted to be out and about and involved in the world. They'd settled with the wolves rather than separating themselves away because they wanted to be part of things. I wondered how long that would last if the current climate of suspicion continued.

The vampires' nervousness was amplified by the fact that they steered away from Monroe and me. There were a lot of side glances and under-the-breath comments. From what I could tell, none of them was complimentary.

Despite the attention, our progress was unimpeded until we reached the square. Monroe took my hand as we crossed and, warmed by the small but affectionate gesture, I stopped paying attention to the people around us. Until the shouting began.

'Oi!'

The shout rang out across the cobbled street. There was no doubt that it was directed at us, especially when a hooded figure started to march our way. 'Oi!' he yelled again. 'I want to talk to you!'

A couple of days ago, Monroe would probably have ignored the bellowing vampire completely and continued blithely on his way. Now he came to a halt and waited, with me by his side. I was pretty sure what words would be said – but then the vampire flipped open his hood and exposed his head. I recognised him immediately.

'I gave you that list in good faith,' Theo said, speaking to me, his voice shaking with fury. 'I was trying to help you.'

I dropped Monroe's hand and faced Theo. 'You did help,' I told him, keeping calm. 'The list was useful, even if it didn't contain Philip's name. It led us to him, after all. Without your help we'd never have found him so quickly.'

Two high spots of colour appeared on Theo's cheeks. 'You didn't find him quickly enough, did you? It's one thing to dispense justice, it's quite another to rip someone apart. In the old world we had to hide to stay safe, and it doesn't appear that anything has changed. When that human tried to take over and hurt people, you banished him. When a vampire is accused of something, you kill them. I've seen his body. That was not an easy death. He was tortured.' He hawked up a ball of spit and shot it at the ground in front of my feet.

Monroe growled but I shook my head at him. Theo had the right to be angry; all the vampires did. 'It wasn't us who did that to him,' I began.

'No, but it was a fucking werewolf, wasn't it?' He jerked his chin at Monroe. 'You're obviously working with them. I thought you were independent but he's leading you around on a leash.'

Monroe drew himself up. 'Enough.'

'Is it though?' Theo was quivering. 'Because as far as I can tell, it won't be enough until you've got rid of every single last one of us. We know you never wanted us here in the first place and now you've hit on the perfect way to get rid of us all. Falsely accuse us of murder and you bastards can get away with whatever you want!'

Monroe's muscles bunched up. Any moment now Theo was liable to end up with a punch to his face and, if that happened, all hell would break loose. All around us, werewolves and vampires had frozen, watching the action and waiting to see if they had to get involved. Some clearly wanted to, but others appeared more reluctant. Either way, I knew in the depths of my soul that this was the moment that could make or break Monroe's fragile society.

'Why,' I asked carefully, angling myself so part of my body was between the vampire and the wolf, 'do you think he was falsely accused?'

Theo was struggling to contain himself. I shifted an inch or two to my right, forcing him to look at me. Be calm, I projected towards him. This still might be alright.

He took several short breaths before speaking. 'I could have mentioned him to you when you came looking but I didn't because Philip was the most unlikely suspect I could have thought of. Yes, he was a loner but he was a gentle soul. He would never have taken more blood than he needed. He barely drank enough to survive. He came to Manchester with us because he wanted the chance to be free like the rest of us. For Philip, freedom meant peace, it meant quiet. It did not mean killing little old ladies!'

I thought about the WB Yeats' poems and the portrait we'd come across in Philip's house. Yes, murder took all sorts but I had to agree with Theo that, even without ever meeting the man, Philip seemed an unlikely killer. Enjoying Irish poetry and guzzling blood were two activities that didn't quite seem to gel. Then again, Yeats had written a poem about the end of the world.

'"Things fall apart,"' I quoted softly, '"the centre cannot hold."'

Monroe and Theo gave me strange looks. I expelled the breath in my lungs. Poetry would only defuse a situation so far.

'I understand you're upset,' Monroe said to Theo.

'Do you?' he spat. 'Do you really?'

'Yes.' Monroe nodded at me. 'Charlotte and I are going to talk to the werewolf responsible for Philip's death. She has not yet transformed back so she can speak, but I am hoping that Charlotte will assist in that. As soon as she's in her human form, we can question her. You can come with us and help. It will be useful to have you along as a representative.'

I gaped at Monroe. He had been a very capable authority figure, who inspired confidence and awe; I would do well not to forget that. He didn't just flip between being arrogance personified and a grief-stricken mess. He was also an experienced leader, and good leaders didn't yell out orders. They soothed ruffled feathers and kept the peace.

'I tried that already,' Theo said, his eyes narrowing. 'Julian wouldn't let me talk to her.'

Monroe's gaze was steady. 'It's not up to Julian. Come with us,' he insisted.

Theo pulled back his shoulders and glared. 'Fine,' he spat. 'But I'm warning you, if you try and manipulate her answers or pull the wool over my eyes…'

'There will be no wool,' I said. 'Promise.'

Theo gave a minute nod and the atmosphere around us altered. The tension from the other vampires and werewolves who were watching us seemed to dissipate, and the pressure building in my chest eased. In the space of a minute, we'd gone from potential war to a temporary truce. I breathed out. Now all we needed was for Maggie to cooperate. Unfortunately, that could be easier said than done.

∗

Maggie, the werewolf in question, was still very furry. She was chained up in a small room and there was a glint of madness reflected in her yellow eyes. Her lips pulled back over her teeth as we entered, but I thought that most of the fight had gone out of her. She wanted this to be over as much as we did.

Monroe folded his arms and loomed over her, alpha wolf virtually seeping out of his tanned pores. He stared Maggie down and she whimpered and lowered her belly to the floor. She didn't, however, transform back to human in any way.

'Change,' he ordered. Her fur bristled but that was all it did. Monroe hissed in frustration and gestured at me.

I swallowed and stepped up. It was all very well having lots of magic at my fingertips but it didn't mean I knew what to do with it. There wasn't a manual for this sort of shit.

I rubbed my sweaty palms on my jeans and gave Maggie a small smile. 'I'm going to try a bit of magic,' I said. She whined and drew back, her eyes widening in fear. 'It's to try and help you shift. I won't hurt you.' I hoped.

Magic buzzed beneath my skin, eager to be put to use. Feeling more terrified than Maggie probably was, I lifted my right hand and pointed at her. A single plume of magic spouted forth, hitting her on her muzzle. It hissed as it made contact but nothing else happened.

'Is there a magic word?' Theo asked.

How the hell did I know? I gritted my teeth and tried again, using slightly more magic this time. I willed Maggie to change with every fibre of my being. Again, not a single thing happened.

Monroe cursed. 'Something is there,' he said. 'Something is preventing her from making the change.'

'Let me try,' Theo interjected.

Both of us stiffened but Theo's expression didn't change. 'What's the worst that could happen?' he asked.

He probably didn't want me to answer that. After a moment's indecision, Monroe nodded reluctantly.

Theo stepped forward – and Maggie's reaction was completely unexpected. She rose up and tried to back away, her chains jangling violently and her backside slamming into the wall. When she realised she had nowhere to go, she opened her mouth and snarled. Saliva bubbled up in the corners of her mouth as if she were a rabid dog.

'Stop that!' Monroe ordered, his words imbued with imperious command. They didn't make any difference: Maggie continued to snarl and froth.

'She's been like this ever since she killed Philip?' Theo asked.

'Yes,' Monroe bit out, treating her inability to transform as a failure on his part.

'So the last thing she did was taste his blood,' Theo mused. 'Maybe she needs another taste to bring her back.'

I stared. 'I really don't think that's a good idea,' I began. It was too late; Theo had already reached into his pocket and drawn out a thin knife.

Monroe wasn't happy. 'Weapons are not permitted here,' he said. 'Not anywhere in our community.'

'Your body is a weapon,' Theo answered unequivocally. 'I need something to defend myself with.' He raised the blade and sliced it across the palm of his hand. Then he held it out, letting a few drops of bright blood splash on the floor.

Maggie's nostrils flared as she scented the blood and she looked even more scared than before. Her whole body was quivering, as if she couldn't control it.

'Go on,' Theo urged. 'Have a taste.'

A hundred to one this would never work. Why would it? All the same, I watched, fascinated, as Maggie's tongue darted out and she lapped tentatively at the nearest drop.

At first it seemed that nothing was happening but then an expression of oddly lupine confusion crossed Maggie's face and her body contorted and spasmed. She had to be in great pain. The chains holding her in place clanked violently and I drew in a sharp breath. Her tail whipped wildly from side to side and she threw her head back in a keening howl. I made the mistake of blinking and, when I looked again, she was on all fours, her curved naked back presented to us.

'Shit,' I whispered. 'It worked.'

Maggie raised her face and looked at us with tear-stained cheeks. Her human features were strangely reminiscent of her wolf form. I gazed into her pain-filled eyes for a moment then I sprang into action. 'Get those chains off her,' I barked. 'And find her some clothes.'

'We don't treat nudity with the same fear that you humans do,' Monroe said.

Theo spoke at the same time. 'She might look human,' he said, 'but she still killed one of mine.' At his words, Maggie's head jerked up.

'We are not interrogating a young woman who is manacled and naked,' I said. 'Regardless of the circumstances.' I didn't care what was encouraged by werewolf culture or what Theo thought. We were better than that; we had to be.

Soon clothes were found and Maggie was released from her shackles. Julian appeared while she was being allowed some privacy to dress, his expression a grim mask. 'So she finally shifted, did she?'

'It was the vampire,' Monroe grunted, pointing at Theo. 'He worked out what to do. One taste of his blood was all it took.'

I watched Julian's face carefully. There was no indication that this was an expected outcome. 'Is that normal?' I asked. 'Is it something to do with vampiric blood?'

All three men shook their heads. 'It's not anything I've heard of before,' Monroe said.

Theo agreed. 'We've clashed with werewolves before. There have been deaths before, but nothing in our records suggests that such a thing adversely affects the werewolf concerned.'

Julian's body was tense. 'Your kind have killed ours in the past, too. This is not a one-sided conflict.'

'I wasn't saying that it was,' Theo shot back. 'And I wasn't implying that werewolves are bloodthirsty monsters, even if you deserve that reputation more than we do.'

'I think you're forgetting that a vulnerable human woman was the first to die,' Julian replied.

I didn't think that the Valerie I knew would have been too enamoured of being called vulnerable. 'Whatever is going here,' I said, 'it's clearly out of the ordinary. What we have to find out is if it's a result of the magic in the atmosphere or if something else is going on. We have to speak to Maggie and find out exactly what she did and why.'

Monroe put his hands in his pockets. 'And the sooner the better.'

Chapter Seventeen

If anything, Maggie was more cowed and scared than before. Two hulking werewolves, albeit in human form, skulked behind her; Theo, Julian, Monroe and I faced her. It seemed like security overkill to me but I refrained from commenting. I was out of my depth amongst the vampires and werewolves but, if Maggie continued to appear so intimidated, I wouldn't be able to keep quiet. I reminded myself that, whether he'd drained Valerie of all her blood or not, Philip had been torn to pieces by this terrified woman. There was more to her than fear.

'Her alpha has been out on patrol since Tuesday and we've not been able to contact him,' Julian said. 'I've got people looking for him now. Until he shows up, I can speak for him.'

Monroe nodded. In an aside to me, he explained. 'There are seven packs in total. Each one is loyal to their own alpha and individual wolves will ultimately follow their alpha's lead. But beta wolves will follow another alpha's lead as well, unless there is conflict across packs.'

'And some alpha wolves are more powerful than others,' Julian added. 'For example, Monroe might not have a pack of his own any more but the other wolves here will still do as he commands, especially in the absence of their own alpha.'

Monroe did have a commanding air about him, even if he winced at Julian's words. 'That only happens when I'm not being threatened with eviction from the community,' he said, with a steely edge.

If Julian was discomfited by Monroe's words, he

didn't show it. 'I had to do something,' he said simply. 'We need you fit and well.'

Before this descended into a squabble, I changed the subject. 'Maggie's alpha must have noticed that she's missing. Why didn't he get back here and sort out a search party?'

Julian and Monroe exchanged looks. 'Each pack serves a distinct unit,' Julian explained. 'Although we all live together as a community, and tasks are allocated, each pack is only responsible for its own members' safety. They'll have been looking for Maggie but they wouldn't have come back here to get help with the search.' He paused. 'Each to their own, so to speak.'

I stared at them. 'So if one pack is decimated then what? You just shrug your shoulders and get on with things?'

'We've been through this,' Monroe said. 'We have to work on the survival of the whole community, not the individuals. People die.' His tone was flat. 'We should all get used to that.'

I knew he was still thinking about his own pack but it didn't matter. Nobody would survive if we didn't look out for each other. 'That's not how a community works!' I spluttered.

I thought he would argue with me as he always did, but instead his gaze slid away. 'You might be right.'

Both Julian and Theo looked at him in surprise. Monroe tutted in dismissal and folded his arms, ending the conversation.

I rubbed my neck and focused on Maggie. 'Why don't you start by telling us what has happened over the last few days?' I said to her. I glanced at the others. 'Then we can ask other questions to fill in any gaps.'

'Good idea. And,' Theo added smoothly, 'if you don't tell the truth, I'll—'

I interrupted him. 'She'll tell the truth.' From Maggie's body language and submissive pose, I was fairly certain she wasn't capable of lying, even if she desperately wanted to. 'Right, Maggie?'

The werewolf nodded. She licked her lips and kept her eyes trained on a spot somewhere to the left of my feet. 'We all went out as a pack two days,' she began tremulously. Her accent was pure Essex and it was difficult for me to believe that this was someone who'd viciously clawed away chunks of a vampire's pale flesh. She sounded like she'd be better suited to downing Prosecco and canapés at a garden barbecue. 'It was our turn. There'd been trouble with some creatures who'd settled in a street not too far away from here. We were going there before, scouting further afield for any shops or warehouses that still have supplies. I was feeling out of sorts. It was my turn for a bath before we left, but there was blood coming out of the taps so I couldn't clean. It sounds like a small thing but...' She sighed. 'I'd been looking forward to it.'

I glanced at Julian. 'Her turn for a bath?'

'We ration water,' he explained.

I frowned. 'You know that's not really necessary. It rains so often that the reservoir is full. Our combined populations aren't so great that there will be a problem.'

'Until the taps start bleeding,' he murmured.

I scowled. 'We fixed that.' Clearly, Julian – and the other alphas – were somewhat draconian in the way they ran things. If someone wanted a bath, they should be able to have a damned bath.

Maggie appeared faintly embarrassed by the increase in tension and continued speaking. 'Anyway,' she said, 'we cleared out the creatures. It was a nest of rat-like animals. They stank to high heaven and they were rather vicious. There were several other animal carcasses nearby from their recent kills. It was clear that, if we hadn't done something to get rid of them, they'd soon have become a problem for us. There were more than we'd anticipated so it took longer than we expected and it was getting dark by the time we got to Yarburgh Street.'

I stiffened. Yarburgh Street was in the south. That was my territory. While I'd never had a proper discussion with any of the northern dwellers, not even with Monroe, about who could take supplies from where, I was unimpressed to hear that they'd been targeting one of my spots. I suppose that I shouldn't have been surprised; the faster food ran out, the more these things would occur. Monroe had always been adamant that this new world was about survival of the fittest instead of looking after everyone.

Maggie's hands twisted together in her lap before she raised them to scratch at her forearms. 'Mia and I went into an Indian restaurant to check their shelves. There wasn't much there but we grabbed a few old tins and some sauces. She started to carry them out. I was on my way to join her but…' Her voice trailed off.

'Go on,' Monroe prompted, in a surprisingly gentle fashion.

She swallowed. 'I heard a noise. It was somewhere towards the back of the shop. I went to investigate it. It was dark and I couldn't see much. Then,' she shrugged awkwardly, 'I think something hit me on the back of the head. I don't really remember anything else until you were there and there was a dead vampire and I could taste blood in my mouth…'

Theo snorted in disbelief. 'You've lost your memory? Well, isn't that convenient?'

'I remember flashes,' she said hesitantly. She scratched her arms again. She was leaving long red welts on her skin without realising it. Maggie seemed uncomfortable talking about her own state of mind. I had the distinct impression that, although most of her words rang true, she was definitely lying about something – or at the very least omitting some information. I was certain of it. I didn't think she was lying about Philip's death per se, but there was something going on with her.

'Feelings. Not much else. I remember seeing a vampire and thinking that he was evil and that I had to kill him or we'd all suffer. I think he attacked me.' Her eyes filled with tears. 'I'm not sure, though. I don't know.' Her head dropped further. 'I know I wanted to hurt him because if I didn't the others in my pack would get hurt. I had to protect my pack from that vampire. I didn't intend to kill him. I'd never have *wanted* to kill him. I wanted to keep my family safe. He was going to hurt my pack '

'But,' Monroe said softly, 'you'd been separated from your pack. You didn't know where they were.'

Maggie's whole body sagged. 'I can't explain that,' she whispered. 'I can't explain where the feeling came from. All I knew was it was me or him. It was survival at all costs.'

Survival at all costs. That sounded dreadfully familiar. I avoided sending Monroe a pointed look. 'Can you remember anything the vampire might have said? Anything he did? Just the smallest detail might help.'

Maggie's mouth moved but I couldn't hear what she said. The others did; I felt Monroe stiffen beside me and Theo grew stonier faced.

'Pardon?' I asked. 'What was that?'

'He said he was sorry,' she said in another whisper. 'That's all I remember. He said he was so very, very sorry.'

***

We questioned Maggie for what seemed like hours but her story didn't change and she had very little other useful information. When we emerged into the cool night air, all I could do was grind my teeth in frustration.

'We have more questions than answers,' I said. 'It's like one step forward and twenty miles back. We're no closer to an explanation for what Philip did, or even real proof that he did it. And unless Maggie starts to remember properly, she can't explain her actions. Most of what she's saying seems true but I'm sure there's more to her story than she's letting on.' I shook my head. 'Her and Philip. They're both connected and through more than his death – but I can't see how. All I keep thinking is that there's far more to this than any of us realises.'

'Maggie has to answer for what she did,' Theo said, although there was little conviction in his words

Monroe ran a hand through his dark-red curls. 'There's nothing more we can do tonight,' he said. 'We should sleep on it and re-group in the morning.'

Theo raised an eyebrow. 'Sleep? The night is getting started. This is hardly the time for sleep.'

'We'll sleep. You can…' Monroe waved a hand around '…do whatever you want.'

Julian glanced at me. 'There's room at my place. Both you and that teen girl you're with can stay with me. It's too dangerous to return to your home in the south right now.'

Monroe bristled and drew himself up. 'Charlotte will *not* stay with you,' he said icily. 'My quarters are perfectly adequate.'

'You live on the outskirts,' Julian replied mildly. 'She'll be more assured of her safety with me.'

'Safety?' Monroe growled. 'What exactly are you trying to insinuate? That I'm incapable of keeping her safe?'

'There's only one of you. There are dozens in my pack.'

Monroe's hands balled into fists. 'And I don't have my own pack because I let them all be killed. Just like I'd let Charlotte be killed. That's what you're saying, isn't it?'

'I'm not saying anything of the sort,' Julian responded.

Theo looked at me. 'I think what both of them are saying is that with the big bad vampires out on the streets all night long, it's not safe for a vulnerable little woman like you anywhere here. Don't forget,' he sniped sarcastically, 'we're evil monsters.'

'Neither of us said that, vampire,' Julian hissed.

Theo sniffed. 'I have a name, you know, wolfie.'

Unbelievable. I threw up my hands and glared at all three of them. 'Don't you see that this bickering is what got us here in the first place? If we worked together more effectively, there wouldn't be loners like Philip out on the fringes. There wouldn't accusations flying around which are close to causing World War fucking Three! Survival at all costs, right? Even if that cost involves the complete destruction of everything any of us ever knew? I understand that tensions are high, believe me. But this is the time to work together, not to argue and spit.'

I jabbed a finger at Theo. 'The actions of one vampire don't define your entire race.' I turned to Julian. 'In the same way that the actions of one werewolf don't define yours, whether Maggie deliberately killed Philip or it was self-defence. And you,' I hissed at Monroe, before he started looking too smug, 'you can't let the past continually define who you are and how you behave. Learn from it, but don't let it rule you. This is a new world, but it will be a good one if we work to make it that way. All of you, stop worrying about your egos and your self-interest and start behaving like we're all in this together. Because we are!'

I'd probably vented a tad too much. Monroe, Julian and Theo stared at me in open astonishment.

Julian flicked a glance towards Monroe. 'I thought you called her sunshine because she was a happy, optimistic woman who always had a smile and a kind word and she brightened up your days. She doesn't seem very happy.'

'She's not smiling,' Theo added.

Oh for goodness' sake. Patronising, much? 'Nobody is one thing all of the time,' I half-yelled. 'We're all complex. We all have issues. And, as you all keep pointing out, we all should be looking out for ourselves.' I put my hands on my hips. 'I'm going to get my girl and we are going home together on our own. You lot can keep to your enclaves and hidden communities and barely concealed spite. Cath and I will protect ourselves and survive without any of your grudging aid. And don't any of you dare try to follow us or you'll get zapped by full-strength enchantress magic.'

'Charlotte—' Monroe began.

'No. Don't you Charlotte me. It's not one rule for one and something different for everyone else. You can't try to protect me and ignore everyone else.'

'I care about you. I don't care about everyone else.'

I rolled my eyes. 'If you really felt that way, you wouldn't be spending all this time investigating Valerie and Philip and Maggie.' I spun on my heel. I was getting out of this godforsaken place. Then I thought of something else and turned back. 'One other thing,' I spat. 'If this really is survival at all costs and looking out for number one, then stay the hell away from the south. The supplies there are for my community. Not yours.' I gave the three of them one final irritated sweep of my eyes and whirled off. Enough already.

Chapter Eighteen

By the time I reached the makeshift hospital and morgue, I was already regretting my outburst. My intention was to get everyone to work together and look out for each other, not to drive a wedge further between us. I almost went back to say as much to the hapless trio but I couldn't count on not losing my temper again. Tomorrow was another day, I told myself decisively. I'd sleep on today's events and start afresh in the morning.

I breathed in through my nose and out through my mouth and tried to think of happy, shiny things. Maybe once this murder crap was over, I'd take up yoga. Apocalyptic yoga. That had a nice ring to it.

I found Cath in one of the wards, hovering over a bed at the far end. When she caught sight of me, her expression filled with delight. That made a pleasant change. 'Charley!'

I smiled weakly at her. 'Are you ready to go?' I asked. 'We need to head home before it gets too late. It's already very dark.'

'Sure, sure.' She grinned down at a bearded man, who was regarding with what could only be described as a form of bizarre worship. 'You get better soon, Fred. It was lovely to meet you.'

'Come back any time,' he called after her.

'Is he very sick?' I asked as we headed out of the room.

'He's got the clap,' she said cheerfully. 'From what I gather, werewolves are good at exaggerating and making things seem far worse than they really are.' Cath was often more perceptive than she let on.

'Mmm. Did you learn anything about Philip? Did you see his body?'

She beamed. 'Yes! In fact,' she tugged at my arm, 'you should come and see for yourself.'

I really just wanted to go home but this could be important. And given how I'd left matters with Monroe and the others, I might not get another chance to visit. 'Okay,' I said reluctantly.

Cath led me down to a darkened room. She lit a couple of candles, busying herself as if she'd been there for years rather than mere hours. 'The wolf docs are around here somewhere. They've been really helpful. I feel like I've already learned tonnes,' she chirped happily, as if we weren't standing over the rigid corpse of a tortured, murdering vampire. 'Look,' she said. 'They told me about these.' She held one of the candles closer to Philip's face. 'It's difficult to tell because of his other wounds,' she said. 'The werewolf used her claws and her teeth her to tear out his…'

I held up my palms. I could see the details; I didn't need her to describe them to me as well.

Cath grinned, understanding. 'Anyway,' she continued, 'if you look closely enough, you can see this.' She pointed at a spot on dead Philip's cheek. 'It's a scratch mark. It's nearly healed but the docs were certain it was caused by a fingernail. And,' she added, 'even better, they found this.' She reached behind her and grabbed a small transparent jar. 'Part of a fingernail was embedded in there.'

I swallowed and looked closer. The nail was painted – and the colour matched the varnish which Valerie had been wearing. I wasn't sure whether to be relieved or not that we had proof Philip was most likely her killer. Just because we had identified him and his body lay on a gurney didn't mean that the case was closed. I was still concerned about his motives. Not to mention Maggie's, as well.

'It was him, then,' I said distantly.

'Yep.' Cath nodded and dusted off her palms like it was a fait accompli. 'Well done, boss.'

I flinched. I'd not done much. And I really was very tired of being the boss.

The door opened and a white-coated figure appeared, framed in the moonlight. 'Ah, Cath. You're still here. I was hoping to catch you before you left.'

'Hey, doc!' Cath waved. 'This is Charley. She's the enchantress,' she added proudly.

The doctor strode forward and reached out to shake my hand. 'It's a pleasure to meet you finally,' she said. 'Catherine here has been singing your praises.'

I coughed. 'Uh, it's nice to meet you too.' I wondered if it would be bad form to ask the good doctor to abandon her work here and join us in the south. It couldn't hurt to ask, right?

Before I could say anything, the doctor jumped in. 'I'm glad you popped in,' she said. 'I wanted to speak to you about Catherine. She has quite a talent and a great deal of enthusiasm. We could do with someone of her calibre to help out here. Our group does tend to get into quite a lot of scrapes. We can teach her more about the rudimentals of medicine. The more medically trained people we have, the better.'

I couldn't have agreed more. The trouble was that I wanted the medically trained people with me in the south, not on the other side of the city where I couldn't reach them in a hurry. But Cath looked so eager that I was reluctant to say no. Besides, if I prevented her from coming here to learn that made me as bad as Monroe and all the others. I sighed. I was too tired for all of this right now.

'In theory that sounds good,' I said carefully. 'Maybe we can discuss it later? Cath and I are leaving now.'

The doctor glanced me up and down, registering my dishevelled appearance and – no doubt – exhausted eyes. 'Absolutely. You're welcome here any time.'

After my blow-up, I wasn't convinced that was still the case. Regardless, I smiled at her and propelled Cath past her. 'Nice to meet you,' I said firmly. I could still manage some manners, if nothing else. 'Come on, Cath. Time to go.'

We trotted out, weaving through the streets until we reached the main barricade leading out from the northern community. Felicity, the werewolf I'd met earlier in the day, was waiting there. I was prepared to scoot past her with nothing more than a raised hand but she stopped us, her expression serious. 'I have a message for you,' she said.

Here we go. I took a deep breath. 'Go on.'

'Monroe said that he'll leave you in peace if that's what you want, and that he knows you can look after yourself.' She pointed to a car beyond the barrier. 'He wants you to take that and drive home. He was most insistent about it.'

As much as the stubborn side of me wanted to throw the gift in Monroe's face and storm off into the night to prove a point, I knew I had to take it. For one thing, I had Cath's welfare to look after. Besides, we'd get home far quicker with the vehicle than if we were cycling or on foot.

'Tell him thank you,' I said, with more grace than I'd thought I'd be able to muster.

'Can I drive?' Cath asked eagerly.

'No.'

'But…'

'Get into the car, Cath.'

She jutted out her bottom lip but did as I'd instructed. I joined her, remembering everything I'd learnt from my visit here. 'You've done well,' I said quietly. 'That doctor was obviously really impressed with you, and the fingernail you found is invaluable. Well done.' My hands gripped the steering wheel. 'It might be a good thing if you come here again and stay to learn more.' It pained me to say it; I didn't want to lose her, and not just because of her value as a potential doctor. I'd really grown to like her and I enjoyed her company. Cath had free will like the rest of us, though, and she deserved her right to exercise it without other obligations and responsibilities holding her back.

For a long moment, she didn't speak then she turned to me. 'Are you trying to get rid of me?' she asked in a small voice, with more vulnerability than I'd ever seen from her even in the dark days immediately after she'd escaped from Max.

'Never,' I said. 'I'd prefer it if you didn't go. But that's for selfish reasons. You should do whatever your heart is telling you to.'

She blinked at me. 'What does your heart tell you?'

That it was tired and sore and that a certain blue-eyed werewolf with complex issues of grief and masculinity was the only person who would ever make it sing. 'That we should get home and get some rest,' I said.

I started the car engine. I reminded myself to be thankful that I wouldn't have to worry about getting caught in a traffic jam and put the car into gear. *Adios, muchachos.*

***

Most of the journey was uneventful. As mine was the only vehicle on the bumpy, potholed roads, I could flick the headlamps on full beam and accelerate as much as I dared. The main route between the north and the south was fairly clear of trees and dangers. In the absence of a working radio, Cath hummed and sang. She wasn't the most accomplished singer I'd ever heard but her voice lifted my spirits. Before long, I'd pushed my worries away and was bobbing along in time to her beats.

I'd over-reacted earlier, especially with Monroe who I knew was trying hard to soften his approach to survival – and our future together. A few hours' apart would do us good. I'd swallow my pride and return to apologise tomorrow. It was the only thing I could do.

Cath was just reaching a crashing crescendo when a shadow flitted across the road in front of us. I hit the brakes, more out of instinct than logic, bringing the car to a juddering halt and stalling the engine. Cath and I were jerked forward.

'Sorry,' I said. 'Old habits die hard.' These days it was far better to keep moving, especially at night, rather than stop and encourage the beasties to start swarming. I was more than confident of my skills at beating them back, but that didn't mean it was sensible to invite trouble.

Cath was untroubled. 'I told you I should drive,' she said.

'Yeah, yeah.' I smiled. 'You can drive next time.'

'Promise?'

I'd long since learned not to make promises I couldn't keep, so I just winked at her and switched on the engine again. When I tried to accelerate, however, the wheels spun uselessly. The car shook; what it didn't do was move.

I cursed. We must have got caught in a pothole or something. Maybe it was a patch of slimy mud from the increased erosion caused by all manner of magical happenings. I sighed and unclipped my seatbelt. 'Stay here,' I said. 'I'll sort this out.'

I opened the car door and waited a beat to see if this was some sort of trap. I couldn't sense anything waiting in the darkness, and the shadow that had made me slam on the brakes had bounded off into the night. I walked round to the back of the car. The back wheels had snagged in a narrow sinkhole which plummeted down into dark depths that I didn't want to think about.

'Piece of cake,' I muttered. Everything was easy when you had magic. I raised my hands. I'd send out one quick boost to push the wheels forward over the hole and we'd be on our way. Honestly, if all the problems in my life were this straightforward I wouldn't have a single to worry about.

My magic blossomed forth, hitting the tail of the car and lifting it up just enough to do what I needed. It juddered forward and I started to smile in satisfaction. Then something flew out of the darkness and smacked me onto the cold ground.

I gasped, as much from shock as anything else. More magic burst out of me and the thing, whatever it was, squealed. I heard claws skitter away and I breathed out, pushing myself up onto my elbows. The coast was clear. Unfortunately, my attacker had buddies. I'd barely made it into a sitting position when, out of the gloom ahead, dozens of them appeared and leapt towards me.

It was my turn to squeak – actually, it was more of a screech. I covered my head with hands and doubled over to protect myself. I appeared to have come across another colony of whatever those giant rat things were that Maggie had been talking about. They were the size of cats and smelled like a sewer. Apparently they were also incredibly angry. Rats had been my first experience of the apocalypse, way back before I'd understood what was going on. These creatures were akin to those first ones in fur only; these were larger, scarier and considerably more dangerous.

They swarmed over me, claws scrabbling to get into my skin. At least two of them were tugging at my trousers. More were nibbling at my back and I felt a pair of sharp teeth bite into my hands. I concentrated and tried to send out more magic to throw them off. Blast them, Charley, I whispered to myself.

Magic exploded from me. The rats flew off, some tumbling before running off, others shaking themselves then and preparing to attack again. Creepy little shits. I prayed that they weren't carrying any diseases and took advantage of the brief hiatus to scramble to my feet. One more shot of magic should be enough for me to escape to the relative safety of the car. Screw the rats.

My skin tingled. No more Miss Nice Enchantress. I lifted my hands a final time. I'd have managed it as well, if it weren't for the cunning little bastard that leapt onto my back. Its jaws opened and it bit into my neck without a moment's hesitation, as if sensing my human vulnerabilities.

The pain was excruciating and all coherent thought fled. My arms flailed and my magic was all but forgotten in my desperation to get the creature off me. I felt warm blood trickling down my neck but it barely registered. My fingers clutched at matted fur, and tears squeezed out of my eyes.

Suddenly there was a flash of strange purple light. The rat tumbled and landed on its back, its eyes wide and staring. Cath was standing beside the car, gazing at her hands in astonishment.

I heard more skittering to my left. My blood froze and, without any more thought, I barrelled for the open car door and flung myself inside. Cath jumped in the other side and we slammed the doors shut. I revved the engine and we accelerated away. I caught sight of several rats chasing after us in the rear-view mirror before we turned the corner and escaped.

'Bloody hell,' I screeched. 'Those things were massive!'

Cath shuddered. 'Tell me about it. Did you see their eyes?'

I looked at her. 'What I saw was purple. Purple magic.'

She bit her lip.

'That was you, wasn't it?' I asked.

She nodded. 'I think so. I don't know. It's never happened before. I just knew I had to do something and … I don't know. It's like something inside me came bursting through.'

'You've got magic,' I said slowly. 'Just like me.' I squinted at her. Now I looked at her and concentrated, she did indeed have her own blue aura. It was lighter than the shade I'd seen on vampires and werewolves, but it was definitely there.

Her eyes widened. 'No, I haven't.'

'Yes, you have.' I absorbed the news for a moment. The ramifications of this could be life changing. 'Keep it to yourself,' I said suddenly. 'For now.'

Cath looked far more terrified than she had been when she was confronted by a swarm of giant rats. 'Okay.'

I reached across and patted her arm. 'You'll be fine.'

'Okay.' She stared at me. 'You're bleeding.'

I grinned at her. 'I'll be fine too.' Delight

expanded deep in my chest. Now that I thought about it some more, this had actually been an incredibly successful day.

Chapter Nineteen

'I've identified two out of the three men from Valerie's diary,' Anna told me the next morning. 'Both young guys. Or at least a great deal younger than she was. They were both shocked about her death but neither was … devastated by the news. The first one is one of ours. He lives a few streets away but still within our barricades. He met Valerie at the casino. She told him she could teach him magic spells. It didn't take him long to realise she was lying and that she had ulterior motives.'

'Sex?' I guessed.

Anna pursed her lips. 'That, but also companionship. He told me they didn't have much in common but she'd enjoyed playing the role of the experienced older woman with a lot to teach.'

'A veritable Mrs Robinson.'

'Indeed.' She sniffed. 'The other one said he felt a bit sorry for her. He's one of the hotel residents, so he already knew that she'd been murdered. He didn't initially volunteer his, uh, involvement with her when we questioned all the guests but I suspect he was embarrassed. I could be wrong, but I don't think either of them had anything to do with Valerie's death. Maybe it was simply a thirsty vampire who drank too much.'

'Who, by coincidence, was then killed by a werewolf who was seemingly attacked herself and now has memory loss.'

Anna shrugged. 'Occam's Razor.'

Sometimes the most obvious theory is the one that's true – but I wasn't convinced and, from Anna's expression, neither was she. 'You've had no luck with lover number three?' I asked.

'Not so far.' She consulted her notes. 'From what her diary says, she met him at the hotel but he wasn't one of the usual residents. She was also … disparaging about him. Here,' she tapped the notepad. 'Jiggly skin. Bad teeth. She also wrote "know-it-all" and added a little doodle of a knife wrapped in barbed wire. Whether that's relevant or not is anyone's guess.'

'Either way,' I said, 'this third man was not her usual innocent ingénue.'

'No.' She grimaced. 'There's not much to go on to locate him. Lots of people pass through the Travotel. Some, like you, go there for a break for a couple of days and some are just curious about Timmons the faery. Some use it as a meeting place and for socialising. It's safer than venturing somewhere else in the city but more interesting than remaining out here 24/7.'

I pondered over this. 'Neither us nor Monroe's lot keep track of who comes in and out on a daily basis.'

'The barricades are there to keep beasties out,' Anna pointed out, 'not to keep people in. And there are always the loners who don't live in either community. Our missing man could be anybody. And he might not have anything to do with what happened. I'll keep on it for another day or two. There are some punters who frequented the casino with Valerie who might have some useful information to impart. But at this stage it's more about tying up loose ends than coming up with answers.' She looked at me. 'This is often how things go. Even when you find your man, there aren't always reasons. There's not always a motive.' Her expression hardened. 'Sometimes people are just shit.'

'Theo, the vampire I spoke to, was convinced that Philip wouldn't have killed Valerie. That he was too nice and kind and gentle to do such a thing, even if it were possible.'

'If there's one thing I've learnt over the years as a police officer,' Anna said, 'it's that anyone is capable of anything. And we are talking about vampires here. Look at Julie. Most of the time, she's perfectly lovely but she also almost caused the end of the world.'

'She fucked up once. Disastrously so. But I don't think she'd kill anyone.'

'Anyone,' Anna repeated, 'is capable of anything. Julie wanted to be more powerful and the magic gave her everything she desired. Murder is about power, Charley. And so is magic.'

I had to grudgingly agree. It wasn't only Julie: the vampires and werewolves were all stronger because of the magic in the atmosphere. Possibly that magic was affecting their baser instincts too, and encouraging mild-mannered vampires like Philip to take human life and werewolves like Maggie to take a vampire's life. The trouble with that scenario was that it boded very badly for the future. If the magic could make anyone do anything, maybe we were all doomed. I shivered.

Anna pushed back her chair and got to her feet just as there was a sharp knock on the door. No one ever knocked. I knew instantly who it was. I wasn't sure whether to be glad that Monroe had come to me first or dismayed that I'd not had the chance to approach him.

I gave Anna a meaningful look and walked to the door and opened it. Monroe was leaning lazily against the door frame. I didn't miss the flash of relief in his eyes when he saw me. 'Charlotte,' he drawled. 'May I come in?'

I motioned him inside. 'Of course.'

'I was just leaving,' Anna said hastily. 'Good to see you, Monroe.' She gave him an awkward wave and bustled out.

Monroe waited until she had gone and glanced at me. 'She has a crush on me.'

I shook my head. 'No, she doesn't. She was startled by your good looks when she first met you, but she got over that when she got to know you.' I grinned and winked. 'She was in a hurry to escape because I told her what happened between us yesterday. She feels awkward about the situation.'

His eyebrows shot up. 'You told her about us?'

'She's my friend,' I said simply. 'I needed to offload.' Then, more gently, 'You might want to try it some time.'

Monroe smiled faintly. 'I'm not sure Anna wants to hear about my problems.'

I tsked. 'I meant with your friends.'

'I don't have any friends.'

I watched him patiently. 'I'm sure you do. In fact I know you do. I'm your friend.'

'My friend?' he asked softly.

I didn't blink. 'Yes.'

His eyes grew more intense, to the point where it was difficult to look away. 'Even after our … argument yesterday?'

'It wasn't much of an argument,' I said. 'It was mostly me yelling and you listening.'

'Because you were right,' he murmured. 'I am beginning to re-think my policy of isolationism.'

I'd already suspected as much but it was good to hear him say it. A thrill of delight ran through me. Maybe our future was brighter than I'd thought.

'The reason being,' he continued, 'that if everyone is together in the same place, it'll be easier to keep an eye on them all. It'll improve all our safety and ensure all our survival.'

My happiness dissipated slightly. He was still fixated on the idea of survival at all costs. What about the *quality* of that survival? I told myself that I should be happy that he was concerned about everyone's future. I'd had visions of Monroe's community as a series of separate enclaves, with each race protecting itself from the others.

'I was discussing the vampires' situation with Theo,' he said, surprising me. 'We've decided to create covered walkways so they feel more comfortable coming out during the day. They didn't used to be affected by sunlight, not until all the magic shit occurred. It's made them more powerful and more vulnerable at the same time. If we can bring them into the community more often, they'll feel less separate.' He paused. 'And less likely to go out and commit murder.'

I shifted uncomfortably. Monroe was no fool and he gave me a sharp look. 'What is it?'

'I have a theory,' I said. 'One you're not going to like.'

His expression grew grim. 'Go on then.'

'A vampire's natural instinct is to drink blood. A wolf's natural instinct is to hunt. What if the magic in the air is merely amplifying those instincts? What if neither Philip nor Maggie could help what they did?' I started to warm to my topic. 'It's like the old fable of the scorpion and the frog.'

Monroe's eyes narrowed slightly. 'The frog carries the scorpion across a river to save it and the scorpion stings the frog, drowning them both, because that's its natural instinct. That's what you mean?'

'Yeah. Vampires will kill humans because they need their blood.'

'And werewolves will attack because they can't help it. It's not logic, it's just base need.'

———

189

I was relieved that he understood what I was getting at and wasn't upset by it. I bobbed my head enthusiastically. 'Yep.'

'If that's true,' he said softly, 'it seems to me that you've created your own reasons for isolationism to continue rather than to stop.'

Hang on a minute. 'That's not what I meant!' I protested.

'It's true, though. If we can't stop ourselves then you have to stay away to keep yourselves safe.' His mouth tightened. 'Perhaps you're right. All the humans should be kept away from the supernaturals.' He stepped back from me, seemingly already implementing the policy.

'I was not suggesting that!' I glared at him. 'I was only floating an idea!'

'A valid one.' His expression had closed off. Shit, me and my big mouth. Why hadn't I kept my daft theory to myself?

Monroe crossed his arms over his chest, forming yet another barrier between us. 'If your idea is correct, there will be more deaths. Things will get worse.'

'Not necessarily,' I began. 'If my idea is correct, we can work together to find ways to curb those natural instincts and let off steam. Knowledge is power, Monroe. Forewarned is forearmed. You can't use this as a reason to hide away even more – you said yourself that it would be better if we were all together!'

He scratched his chin and his features tightened in pain. 'I'm a wolf, Charley. If my natural instinct is to hunt and to kill and to be a predator, what if you become my prey? What if I can't help myself and I hurt you?' His voice lowered to a whisper. 'What if I killed you? I have enough deaths on my conscience as it is.'

'You wouldn't do that. You wouldn't hurt me.'

'You don't know that,' he said flatly. He looked away. 'I was thinking about therapy. Proper therapy. I thought I could speak to someone professionally then I might be able to sort myself out and be worthy of you. Of this life. I'm tired of fighting myself.' His voice grew more strained. 'Maybe I don't have any choice, though. Maybe the only course of action is to stay away from you for good.'

Fucking hell. In the space of a minute we seemed to have gone from the idea of a happier future for everyone to utter hell. 'Monroe,' I said, 'I think we need to talk about this a little more before either of us jump to any conclusions or do anything we might regret.'

The door slammed open and there was the sound of running feet. 'Charley!' Lizzy whirled into the room. 'You have to come now!'

I shook my head. I couldn't deal with squabbles over rations or water or whatever else was going on right now. 'Someone else will have to deal with it, Lizzy. I'm busy.'

''It has to be you. She demanded it was you. I don't know what's going on but if you don't come now, someone is going to get hurt. Some green-skinned woman is going absolutely nuts. Green skin! She's kicking off at the barricade and yelling for you. You've to get there now. John's got a gun and he's pointing it at her. She's got some kind of sword. There's—'

I was already out of the door and running. Monroe was beside me and overtook me in a heartbeat. He didn't shift into his werewolf form, but I knew from the magic buzzing underneath my own skin that he would in an instant if the situation called for it.

We sprinted towards the noise. There was a lot of shouting and screaming going on. Some people were ducking into their houses for safety; others were running with us to try and help out.

'Charley! Enchantress! If I don't see you in the next sixty seconds, I am not going to be responsible for my actions!'

Monroe slammed through the crowd, ignoring the people he shoved to the side, and I followed him through the ensuing gap. There, standing on the roof of battered-looking van, stood Alora the bogle. Gone was the calm, queenly figure I'd met the other day – now she was a creature of absolute fury. It didn't help that she was brandishing a lethal-looking sword with her right hand, which gleamed as it caught the sunlight. She was also holding a furious Anna by a hank of her hair with her left hand.

'I'll cut her head off if any of you come any closer!' Alora spat. 'And more of my kind will follow after me!'

'Charlotte's here,' Monroe said, his voice raised. 'I'm here. What's the problem? What's happened?'

Alora's wild eyes turned in our direction but she didn't relax at the sight of us. If anything, her fury grew. She twisted her hand, pulling sharply at Anna's hair and forcing the policewoman's neck into an unnatural and painful position. Anna didn't make a sound, but I could see from the grimace on her face how much the action hurt.

'One thing,' Alora spat. 'We only asked you to do one thing. We accepted the mermaid's intrusion. We spoke politely. We came to an understanding. Or so I thought.'

I shook my head in desperate confusion. 'I don't understand,' I said. 'What's happened?'

I wasn't sure she'd heard me because she merely continued with her tirade. 'Did you want them to die? Were you trying to get rid of them? Is that what it was?

Or were you trying to hurt us because we refused to trade? We were never a threat to you. What you've done was completely unnecessary. I thought you were a decent person but you're nothing more than a bloodthirsty bitch.'

I flinched. The vicious hatred in her tone was nothing I hadn't experienced before, but as far as I could tell she was teetering on the edge of sanity. I had to prioritise. Monroe was right – safety first.

When I spoke again, I sounded far calmer than I felt. 'Everyone get back inside and stay there.'

For a second no one moved then Monroe lifted his head and howled. Before he'd finished, they'd all scattered, guns and all. At least now we'd have some breathing space. A fraction of a second of breathing space.

'You might think you're protecting them,' Alora snarled. 'But you can't protect them all. Not after what you've done.' As if to add weight to her words, she tightened her hold on Anna's hair. Shit. Whatever was going on here, it wasn't good.

I held up my palms to indicate that I wasn't fighting her. Not yet, anyway. 'I don't know what I've done. Believe me, Alora, I don't know what's wrong. You have to explain what the problem is.'

'She's right,' Monroe said. 'We don't know what you're talking about.'

'You wouldn't know because she's probably stabbed you in the back as well,' Alora said to him. 'They were human. We know this was her doing, not yours. If this was down to you, you'd have sent wolves.'

Dread spread through me, its icy tentacles snaking through my veins and squeezing at my heart. 'Who are you talking about?' I asked. 'You have to tell us what happened.'

Alora gazed at me. For a strange moment, it felt as if her eyes were searing into my soul. 'So,' she said, more softly, 'you didn't send them after all.' Her mouth tightened. 'It doesn't matter. They could only have known of our existence because you told them. How long did it take for you to break your promise to keep quiet about us? Was it days? Or merely hours?'

'I…' I didn't know what to say. 'Alora, I didn't tell anyone. I mentioned the mermaid, I did explain about Nimue, but I didn't tell anyone about you or the other bogles. I promise.'

'This was an accident?' Her words were calm but her expression was not. 'I find that hard to believe.'

I gestured helplessly. 'I still don't know what you're talking about.'

Alora bared her teeth and waved her sword menacingly in the air. 'Then,' she said, 'come and see for yourselves.'

Chapter Twenty

Monroe and I went with her. Alora released Anna, whose venomous rage at being held hostage even if for a short while, was barely contained. I only just managed to persuade her to stay behind for the good of everyone else. Given the vicious looks and bristling tension I was still receiving from Alora, the fewer of us who walked into the bogles' territory the better.

Alora was calmer now but she still held onto her sword, ready to wield the pointy end at me at any given moment. I kept a wary on her while Monroe drove, wondering if I could defend myself against the unmitigated fury that still bubbled beneath her suddenly serene exterior.

'You have to understand,' she said, continuing to finger the edge of the blade, 'that things have not been easy for us. Even before the apocalypse, we had to be careful. Our skin was not so green then and it was easier to hide, but we were still magical beings in a non-magical landscape.' She jerked her head at Monroe. 'He will have a better idea of what we went through. His experience will have been similar. But his kind have always had their own power. Ours was insignificant.' She smiled without humour. 'Not any longer. Despite all the tribulations of the apocalypse, we are now in a very different position.' Her eyes fixed on mine. 'Now we can defend ourselves properly.'

I licked my lips. 'You certainly look like you know how to use a sword.'

She shrugged. 'It's a traditional weapon of our

kind. We put it to good use against the faeries when they attacked us. They learnt of our skills, ones we'd won by hard work and practice rather than mere magic.'

'You were attacked by faeries?'

'Some of them.' She sniffed. 'Perhaps you've heard of Rubus. He was the faery who wanted to use a little magical sphere to transport his species away from this place. He didn't care what would happen to this world after he used it. He sent some of his minions to us when he was looking for the sphere. They killed several of us – but we killed more of them and Rubus got his comeuppance in the end.'

I shot a glance at Monroe, whose hands had tightened round the steering wheel. I knew that his whole pack had been destroyed because of this Rubus and I felt a surge of sudden, unexpected hatred for the now-dead faery. He was lucky he was dead, otherwise he'd have had me to answer to.

In that instant, I knew I was capable of terrible things. Anna was right: under certain circumstances, anyone was capable of anything.

Alora seemed to understand what we were thinking and her tension eased somewhat as she continued. 'Those faeries' actions are the main reason we did not wish to be part of what you were establishing. Not until we'd recovered ourselves. And not until your own problems were settled.' Her hands clenched. 'But now the issue has been forced.'

My answer was quiet. 'It was not us who forced the issue.' I paused. 'Not deliberately, anyway.'

Alora's lip curled. 'We shall see about that.'

She didn't speak again until we reached the outskirts of her neighbourhood. She turned the blade in her lap over and over again; I couldn't tell if she did it absently-mindedly or whether it was a reminder that she was still a threat. Either way, I was well aware that I was walking into a complex and dangerous situation.

I was glad that Monroe was there, too. His presence was reassuring, even though Alora seemed to feel some kind of kinship with him because of his lupine nature.

She directed Monroe to park at a corner. As far as I could tell, we were at least a few hundred metres away from any inhabited buildings. That made a certain sense; if Alora really believed that I was the devil incarnate, inviting me to stroll along her pavements and pop in for tea probably wasn't her intention.

'We haven't touched his body,' she said in a perfunctory manner.

I stiffened. Until now, there had been no mention of a death. I wasn't sure I could cope with another corpse.

Alora got out of the car and waved the sword at me, indicating that I was to follow. I exchanged a glance with Monroe and steeled myself. It appeared that I didn't have much of a choice.

Girding myself, I climbed out of the car and followed her. Monroe walked abreast with me, his hand brushing against mine to remind me that he was there to help. We rounded the next corner and were confronted with a row of angry, green-skinned bogles. No prizes for guessing where the body was.

My mouth felt painfully dry and I wished I'd brought a bottle of water with me, even though Alora had demanded we leave immediately. It didn't help that each and every bogle was sending me death looks. My skin prickled and I felt the uncomfortable weight of being despised settle across my shoulders. It wasn't much fun; no wonder the vampires tended to be so snarky. This sort of attitude could really get a person down – and I'd only been on the receiving end of it for a flicker of time.

'Are you okay?' Monroe murmured under his breath.

I nodded. 'Are you?' The last thing anyone needed was for him to transform or snarl or generally act like an alpha male. So far he was being calm and controlled. That was good. I could take my lead from that.

'I'm fine. Do you know who we're likely to find up here?'

'Not a scooby.' The dead body was human, though; Alora had been adamant about that. I prayed he would be a complete stranger. If only wishing could make it so.

As we reached the bogles, a cold gust of wind swirled up, catching my hair and making me shiver. Alora gestured at the crowd and they shuffled to the side, revealing the prone figure of a man on the ground. He was face down but, from the unnatural angle of his neck, it was obvious that he was dead.

'We pay attention to our surroundings,' Alora said in a clear voice. 'We have watchers all over this area and we know when someone is approaching.' She looked at us. 'You know that yourselves, from your own visit.'

I spotted Malbus in the group of bogles, the one who'd come across us at Boggart Hole. He was glaring at me with far more hatred than the others. I didn't blame him; when he'd appeared, I'd tried to use humour to defuse the situation. Now we were confronted with a corpse, that pathetic humour seemed like a slap in the face of every bogle. There wasn't much that was funny about sudden death. The way things had been going for me lately, I was starting to think that should be etched on my gravestone.

Alora continued. 'He was making a beeline here. He was coming for us.' She jabbed her finger at one of the other bogles who nodded and darted forward, holding out a gun by her thumb and forefinger. 'And he was carrying this.'

I sucked in a breath. I didn't know a great deal about guns but this one certainly looked lethal.

Monroe held out his hand. 'May I?'

The bogle looked at Alora. She jerked her head and the gun was handed over to Monroe. 'It's already been unloaded,' she said, flicking her eyes to me. 'In case you were wondering.'

As a matter of fact, I hadn't been; I was too dismayed at the sight of the weapon. It wasn't a toy or an antique or a mere curiosity, it was an object designed for only one thing – and that was to kill.

There was a tradition and an art to the swords that the bogles carried, something graceful and beautiful about them despite their lethal nature. Even the guns that I'd confronted when soldiers had entered Manchester to start the evacuations and when Max had tried to take over the city had been of a utilitarian mundanity. The gun that Monroe was holding was a different beast altogether.

If you think it was strange to attach so much to a mere object that was rendered useless by its lack of bullets, that's because you didn't see what I was seeing. You could call it inexperience or innocence: to me it was downright common sense. I recoiled when Monroe offered it to me. No, thank you.

'The bag,' Alora murmured.

Another bogle stepped forward and held out a backpack. He unzipped it and Monroe and I peered inside. It contained at least three more handguns and an array of grenades. Shit. The dead guy had meant serious business.

'Wait,' I said suddenly, as a thought struck me. 'When you came to us, you said "they". You said they were human. Where are the others?'

Alora pointed at a short bogle with thinning hair that looked incongruous on such a young face. He swallowed, his Adam's apple bobbing, and lifted up his chin. I noted the bandages on his arm and his leg and the fresh blood seeping from underneath them. 'They came in from the south,' he squeaked. He cleared his throat and tried again. 'They came in from the south by Winner Street. There were two of them. Him and,' he hesitated, 'another one.'

'Where is the other one now?' Monroe growled.

'She spotted me before I got too close. She said something to this one and then she ran. Then he started shooting.'

Bloody hell. 'What did she look like?'

'It was still dark. I didn't get a look at her face,' he whispered.

Monroe's expression was taut. 'She told him to stay and fight,' he said through gritted teeth. 'And meanwhile she saved herself.'

'Was anyone else hurt?' I asked.

'Andus was shot twice,' Alora said coolly. 'Is that not enough? Far more would have been hurt if Malbus hadn't been nearby and heard the shots. He was able to flank him and take him down, otherwise things would have been far, far worse.'

I sneaked a look at Malbus. He was stony-faced and I suspected that the incident had shaken him more than he was letting on. Killing someone, even in self-defence, would probably do that to you.

'Flip him over,' Alora instructed.

Two of the bogles lurched forward and grasped the corpse, turning him unceremoniously onto his back. I ignored the wound at his neck where he'd bled out and focused on his face. I thought I knew him, although what his name was I couldn't guess. What I did know was that he'd come late to the south, arriving only a few weeks ago after hiding somewhere else in the city. I'd spoken to him briefly at the time and he'd seemed more shell-shocked and scared than anything else. The idea that he could be a threat hadn't crossed my mind.

'You know him,' Alora said, reading my expression.

'Not well,' I admitted. 'But yes. He's one of mine.'

A strange rumbling sound reached my ears. At first I couldn't work out what it was, then I realised it was coming from several of the bogles. They were growling. Uh oh. That didn't bode well but frankly I didn't blame them. Fury mixed with guilt rushed through me. This human had come here to kill. He lived in my community; he was a part of me and mine. And he'd come to this place armed with guns and grenades.

'I don't know his name,' I said in a strained voice. 'Or his history. I have no idea why he did this or who the woman was. I will find her,' I promised. 'I will deal with this. And it won't ever happen again.'

Alora's eyes met mine. 'You can't guarantee that,' she said simply. 'Don't make promises you can't keep.'

I drew myself up. 'I will find her,' I repeated. I tried not to dwell on the fact that I now had not one but two murder investigations to deal with. 'And I swear on my own life that I did not breathe a word about your existence to anyone.'

Alora gazed at me for a long time. Eventually, she gave a curt nod. She believed me, which was something; whether she believed that this would not happen again was a different proposition.

'You weren't the target.' Monroe's words were so

quiet that I barely heard him. I turned towards him and blinked. He repeated himself. 'You weren't the target. Charlotte is not a liar and I did not tell anyone about you either. We have had other … issues on our plate.' He looked at me. 'You said that you did speak about Nimue. You told others about the mermaid.'

I stiffened. No. Oh no.

'Nimue was the target,' I whispered. 'They were heading for Boggart Hole, not here. That dead bastard and his girlfriend were taken by surprise. They weren't expecting anyone to be here. That's why she ran and why Malbus managed to sneak up on him so easily.'

The bogle in question folded his arms. 'I am good at sneaking,' he asserted.

'I don't doubt it. But we're close enough to your neighbourhood for anyone with this amount of firepower to have been prepared for someone like you beforehand. They would have been ready for an ambush – but they weren't expecting you to be here.' I felt an odd measure of relief but it was short-lived.

'Who did you tell, Charlotte?' Monroe asked. 'Who knew about Nimue?'

I didn't want to answer. I didn't want to say the word. But I didn't have a choice. 'Julie.' I closed my eyes, feeling a throb of pain. 'I told Julie.'

Chapter Twenty-One

We took the nameless man's body with us, folding him into the back seat of the car like an unpleasant gift.

I smacked the dashboard over and over and over again as we drove away. 'This was my fault. I should have listened to you from the start. I welcomed Julie in, even though I knew what she'd done before. I welcomed that man in too. They were with me. They were fucking with me. I let this happen.' I raised my hand to punch the window.

Monroe slammed on the brakes and brought the car to a screeching halt. 'Stop it.' He didn't raise his voice but his words were imbued with command. 'You didn't do this. You didn't encourage it. You weren't the one who came here with those weapons. This is not your fault.'

'You said it.' I shook my head. 'You said that to invite all and sundry into the same community was to accept that bad things were going to happen. I was prepared to deal with those consequences – but not like this. Not someone I thought was a friend coming to a peaceful group of people and opening fire on them! Not hunting down a mermaid for no apparent reason! This isn't like Philip or Maggie, this isn't the magic affecting someone's base instincts. This is someone coming out here with guns and grenades and planning to kill.'

A muscle throbbed in Monroe's jaw. 'They'd have done it anyway. Whether they were a part of your community or not, they'd still have done this. You're the one who keeps talking about free will. This was the result of their free will. If Julie did this…'

'If?'

'So far the evidence is circumstantial. Maybe she mentioned Nimue to someone else. Maybe this wasn't her.'

I stared at him. He hated Julie; he always had. A single tear leaked out of my eye because even now Monroe was trying to make me feel better.

I desperately wanted to cling to the thought that Julie was innocent. I desperately wanted someone else to be responsible for this, but I knew the odds. If I were going to gamble on who was responsible, I'd gamble on it being Julie.

My head dropped. Vampire or not, I'd thought I could trust her. 'She almost destroyed the whole world,' I mumbled. 'Why wouldn't she try and destroy everything else we've been working for?'

Monroe grabbed my hand and held it. 'Whether this was her or not, it doesn't make it your fault. You're not responsible for her actions.'

I *felt* responsible. 'You knew this would happen. You saw it coming a mile off.'

'No,' he said, 'I didn't.' He sighed. 'Let's find Julie first and see what she has to say. She deserves that much.'

I looked at him balefully. 'Fine,' I said eventually. 'Drive. Drive as fast as you fucking can.'

***

Monroe did as I asked and we made it across the city to the south in record time. People were standing in the streets, eyes wide, as Monroe stopped the car and we jumped out.

Lizzy and Anna wasted no time in pushing

through to us.

'What happened? What on earth's going on?' Anna asked.

'Are you alright?' Lizzy's nostrils flared and she glanced at the car. 'Jesus. Is that a dead body?'

'It is.' I smiled grimly. 'He deserved it.' I looked at the crowd. 'Where's Julie?'

Anna frowned. 'I haven't seen her today.'

'Me neither,' Lizzy said. 'But I think Cath said something about getting hold of her in the north for a tour. She spends enough time there that she knows the place inside and out.'

Cath. I had a flash of freezing terror that Julie would hurt her. No. Julie had made considerable effort with the bogles to run away and keep her identity hidden. She wouldn't hurt Cath, not when other people knew they were together.

I clambered on top of a car that formed part of our makeshift barricade and raised my voice. 'Listen up!' I yelled. 'Something terrible happened this morning. Another community was attacked…'

Almost immediately my words were drowned out by gasps and calls of dismay. 'Are we in danger?'

'Who was it?'

'It was the vampires!'

'It was the werewolves!'

I didn't have the patience for this. 'It was us,' I yelled. 'People from our community did this! People we know went out with the sole intention of hurting others!'

The crowd fell silent, shock written across many of the faces that I knew well – and many of the faces that I didn't. Some seemed disbelieving, others merely horrified.

'We're supposed to be pulling together!' I yelled, my frustration and anger overtaking me in a tsunami of emotions. 'We're supposed to be looking out for each other! Not killing! Not hurting! Things are hard enough as it is, without us turning on ourselves!'

A woman piped up from the back of the crowd. 'But nobody's died here. It's the other communities that have had deaths – the ones where those magical freaks hang out. Maybe they deserved it!'

A strange stillness overtook me. I swivelled round, picking out her face. She whitened slightly but held her ground. Part of me admired her; at least she was saying what she thought. Judging from the expressions on some of the other faces, there were plenty of people who agreed with her. This was what people did. They told themselves what they needed to hear in order to believe that they were right. The trouble was that there was nothing more dangerous than the delusions of the self-righteous.

'I'm magical,' I said. 'Am I a freak?'

The woman swallowed then she lifted up her chin. 'Maybe,' she said.

She had pluck, I'd give her that. By my side, Monroe growled out a warning. I didn't know if it was for me or for the woman but I didn't care.

I smiled slowly. 'In that case,' I said, 'you're a freak too. In fact, you're all freaks.'

'What's that supposed to mean?' someone called.

I laughed humourlessly. 'This city is filled with magic.' I raised my hands and trailed them through the air. 'It's in the air we breathe. It's in the water we drink.' I took a step forward then thought better of it as I nearly toppled off my perch. But I still grinned. 'I gained magic through sleeping next to a powerful object. I didn't mean to do it. I didn't know I was doing it. But I still did it. Did you all really think you could stay here and not be affected by magic in the same way?'

Several people exchanged glances, their bafflement growing.

'That's right!' I shouted. 'We're all magical freaks now!'

Until Monroe and I went up City Tower, I hadn't fully realised that the blue aura surrounding Monroe's community was only slightly stronger than the blue aura here. The people here had magic running through their veins now, just like I did. Cath's actions the previous night had confirmed it.

My smile grew even wider until I probably looked like some kind of crazed creature. 'It turns out magic is like the common cold. And, like the common cold, there's no cure for it.'

The muttering grew. 'She's nuts. She's finally lost it.' Then one of the younger men flicked out his hand. A bolt of something green shot up into the air and exploded into a cascading rainbow of colour over his head.

'She's right,' he said. 'I thought it was only me but I can do magic. I can do … things.'

A few others nodded. Apparently he wasn't the only one who'd been experimenting.

'You see?' I said. 'By choosing to stay in Manchester, you've chosen to accept the consequences – and the consequences are that we're all enchanters. We're all witches and wizards or whatever the hell you want to call us.' My voice hardened. 'We're in this together, no matter who or what we are.' I glared. 'Unless you try to hurt or maim or kill another person. Do that, and I will find out who you are and there will be consequences. This might be a magical society but it's not a lawless one. Justice *will* be dispensed.' I wasn't sure anyone was paying much attention; they were all too flabbergasted by the revelation that they had their own magic.

Monroe reached over and squeezed my hand. 'Go

on,' I said to him. 'Say it.'

'Say what, sunshine?'

'"I told you so". Say "I told you so".' I looked down at him.

His blue eyes crinkled at the corners. 'I wouldn't dare,' he smiled. 'You're pretty scary when you get going.' His expression altered and his gaze dropped. 'If I wasn't such a dangerous person to be around, we'd be good together.'

I pulled my hand away. 'So now we can't be around each other because of one daft theory? Because you might not be able to contain your wolf? Monroe, if that was an issue, it would have already caused problems. It's not the issue. I was wrong.'

'I told you. I have too many deaths on my conscience. I won't put you in danger too.'

I opened my mouth to continue arguing when there was an inarticulate shout from near the car. It was Anna – and from her tone it was important. I hopped down from my vantage point. All around me, people were buzzing, staring at their fingers, trying to get magic to spout forth. Some were successful; others needed more practice.

I ignored them and pushed my way through. 'What is it?' I asked her. 'What's the problem? Do you know him?'

Anna's body language was stiff and unyielding and her lips were pressed together in a thin, taut line. 'I vaguely recognise his face. But that's not it, Charley. That's not the problem.'

I stared at her. 'Then what?'

She pointed down at the corpse. The car door was open and one of his arms was dangling out of it. It wasn't a pleasant picture – I'll give you that – but I still didn't see what the problem was.

'His tattoo,' Anna said. 'Look at his tattoo.'

I glanced down at the body's bare forearm. It wasn't a large design but it was certainly distinct: a dagger wrapped in barbed wire and dripping blood.

'It's the same,' Anna told me. 'It's exactly the same as the doodle in Valerie's diary. This is the third man she was sleeping with. The one I couldn't find.' Her face was pale as she paused so we could consider the ramifications. 'What are the odds that these deaths are unconnected?'

A grim darkness descended on me. 'Not good. Not good at all.' Just how much blood and sorrow was Julie responsible for? I shook my head. We had to find her before anyone else got hurt. I didn't know what she was doing or how she was doing it, but she was involved. She had to be.

I spun round again and started marching in the opposite direction, ignoring the bustle of excited people. Yeah, they had magic – but we also had a murderer in our midst.

'Where are you going?' Lizzy asked, catching up. Anna was right beside her.

'Julie's house,' I bit out. 'Even if she's not there, there might be some clue or some evidence about what she's done. These deaths are tied together. I can't see how or why, but they're linked somehow.'

Monroe joined us, his features as dark as my thoughts. 'You think she might have persuaded Philip to go after Valerie?'

'Perhaps. Maybe she helped him and that's why every last drop of Valerie's blood was gone.'

'There was only one set of puncture wounds,' Anna reminded me.

I shoved my hands into my pockets and walked faster. 'Perhaps it was all Julie. Perhaps she killed Valerie and pinned the blame on Philip. He was a loner. He would have been a convenient target to take the fall.'

'And the scratches on Philip? What about those?' Monroe asked. 'Or Maggie? What about her?'

'Maybe Julie manipulated Maggie into killing Philip. Julie is an actress – and a very good one. Maybe she managed the crime scene and planted the idea of the scratches into our heads.'

'And then,' Monroe questioned, 'she manipulated that guy back there to go with her to Boggart Hole to kill Nimue? She's on a random murder spree and is getting others to join her as she goes along?'

I stopped suddenly in my tracks. Damn it. There were far too many leaps of logic. 'It doesn't make any sense,' I admitted.

'No,' he agreed. 'And people don't like Julie. They hold her responsible for a lot of what's happened. You're just about her only friend. To imagine that she managed to get these others on her side and follow her into committing these crimes … it doesn't seem credible.'

'It doesn't fit together, either,' Anna interjected. She looked at me sternly. 'The first rule of any investigation is to focus on the hard evidence, not to fill in gaps with ideas and conjecture. Stop speculating. Let's focus on what we know and use that as the basis to work out what we don't know.'

I passed a hand over my face. That made sense. 'Okay,' I said. 'Okay.' I was letting my wild thoughts take over and joining dots where perhaps there weren't any dots to join. I sighed. Jumping to conclusions wasn't going to help anyone. But unfortunately neither could we ignore what facts we already had. 'Right now, it looks like the deaths are connected. Julie is the only suspect we have who's alive, other than Maggie. We have to find her.' I glanced at Anna. 'Agreed?'

She smiled at me. 'Agreed. You'll make an excellent detective yet, Charley.'

I certainly bloody hoped not. I never thought I'd miss the day when all I had to deal with were petty squabbles and complaints over gluten-free cereal bars. I managed a smile. Just about. 'At least we're getting somewhere,' I said. 'We have more information now than we had an hour ago. Whatever is going on here – and whatever we're dealing with – we have more of the puzzle pieces.'

'That's my ray of sunshine,' Monroe murmured. He smiled at me but I could see the sadness in his eyes. Once this was done, I knew with absolute certainty that he would cut all ties with me. He'd already decided there wasn't any choice. I reckoned I only had until these deaths were solved to change his mind.

I set my jaw. I wasn't alone. I could do this. All of this. The alternative wasn't worth thinking about.

Chapter Twenty-Two

There was nothing to go on in Julie's house: it was empty of both the vampire actress and any clues that she was involved. Unless vast quantities of gin could be counted as a contributing factor to murder.

I wasn't sure whether I should be relieved or dismayed at lack of hard evidence. 'Monroe and I will have to go to the north and see if we can find her there,' I said decisively. 'Maybe she's still with Cath.'

Monroe coughed. 'I'll go alone.'

No way. I had the distinct feeling that if he did, I'd never see him again. 'I'm not arguing with you,' I told him.

'Good,' he began.

'I'm coming with you.'

Icy fire sparked in his blue eyes. 'Stay here. From the revelations about the magic and the reactions of your people, you've more than enough to deal with.'

'Anna and Lizzy can stay. They'll keep the peace at this end.'

'Actually,' Anna said, 'I was going to come too…'

'No,' I said. 'Monroe and I will deal with the north. And Julie.'

'The north is mine. I'll go alone.'

I glared at him. 'Julie is mine. I'll go with you.'

'She's a vampire.'

I shrugged. 'So? She's still part of this community. And if she's not actually involved in any of this – and the evidence so far is purely circumstantial –

it's better that I'm there to avoid any hotheads prevailing.'

He regarded me coolly. 'So far, I've been remarkably calm. You're the one who's been the hothead.'

I pretended that I hadn't heard him. He did have a point. 'Either way,' I said, 'you can't stop me from coming with you.'

Monroe growled. 'Yes, I can.'

No, he couldn't. 'What's the worst that could happen?'

A deep snarl rumbled in his chest. 'You've proved that the magic in the city has affected everyone. All those people who never had anything supernatural about them before have been touched by it, fundamentally changed by the atmosphere. It stands to reason that if that same magic is affecting vampires and werewolves, I could turn on you at any second. I might not be able to control myself. Not only that, you'll be walking into a part of Manchester that's filled with other predators. I won't allow it.'

'You're not my boss,' I said.

Lizzy nervously put her hand into the air. 'Um, what's going on? How is the magic affecting vampires and werewolves?'

'We're all more powerful than we used to be,' Monroe explained.

Lizzy considered this for a moment then nodded. 'I'm a bunyip,' she said quietly. 'Every day I feel it more.'

Monroe's head jerked towards her. 'You're right.' He stared at me. 'Lizzy can come with me. You can stay here.'

I rolled my eyes in irritation. I knew exactly what he was thinking. Sometimes the man was a complete idiot. 'Lizzy wouldn't attack anyone.'

She started. 'What? Why would I attack anyone?'

'The magic isn't just making us stronger,' Monroe said. 'It's speaking to our natural predatory instincts and causing reason, logic and emotion to fly out of the window. It explains why a vampire, whether it was Philip or Julie, would drain Valerie of all her blood and why a werewolf like Maggie would kill Philip. The magic is growing within us to a point where we can't control ourselves.'

'It's only a theory,' I bit out. 'And not a very good one.'

Lizzy frowned. 'I don't feel like killing anyone.'

'I wasn't feeling like that but I'm starting to feel rather murderous now,' Monroe said, directing his words at me.

I smiled serenely at him. 'I'm coming with you,' I said, 'whether you like it or not. If you turn into a wolf and rip my throat out along the way, then you're absolved of any responsibility. I have my big girl pants on and I know what I'm getting into.'

He snorted. 'Big girl pants?'

'Lacy. Pink. Delicate. They're very pretty.' I paused. 'Would you like to see them?'

Monroe's eyes darkened and he turned away. 'No.'

Just as well. They were actually cotton, grey and very holey.

'We're going now,' Anna said hastily. 'We'll leave you to it.'

'Lizzy should come with me to the north,' Monroe grunted.

'Lizzy is staying here,' I told him.

Lizzy grabbed Anna's arm and started to walk away quickly. 'Lizzy is leaving!' she called out to us.

'Don't kill Julie unless you really have to! Good luck!'

Monroe sniffed. 'Now look what you've done.'

'I haven't done anything.' I grabbed his shoulders and forced him to look at me. 'You know me, Monroe. You know what I believe in. I want to protect everyone and keep them safe. If I thought Lizzy was a threat, I wouldn't let her waltz over there to hang out with everyone else. She's not going to hurt anyone. Neither are you. You've already changed a lot of your ways. You've been calmer, you've been thinking of others. Lately you've been far more thoughtful than I've been. Those aren't the actions of someone who's about to flip out.'

'We've been through this. You make me calmer.'

I threw up my arms. 'All the more reason for me to stay with you!'

He shook his head. 'It's not worth the risk.'

'It's my risk to take. Besides, I can protect myself. Even against you.'

'You couldn't.' He looked down at me, his eyes narrowed. 'Not if I really wanted to hurt you.'

'Try me,' I said.

His head dipped lower and he bared his teeth. He let out a low snarl and yanked himself away from me. 'We can't do this. I can't let myself hurt you. We don't have to separate from each other for good, but we need to do it until your theory has been disproved.'

I was certain that if Monroe's pack were still alive and this had come up as an issue, he'd have laughed in my face at the very idea that his wolf side would take over his other instincts to the point where someone would get hurt. He'd lost far more than just his family when they were all killed. I dropped back and considered. I had to be smarter about this. If this was all about base instincts, perhaps those were what I should be addressing.

This was about Monroe wrestling for control with himself.

'Do you know what?' I said thoughtfully. 'Upon reflection I think you're right. We should stay away from each other. You're a predator and you're dangerous. Once we've established what's really going on with these killings, we should avoid each other for good.'

Monroe's eyes narrowed. He seemed to think I was toying with him. Which I was. 'You changed your tune quickly enough.'

'It's for the best. Maybe we should build a wall between the south and north to avoid any further complications.' My eyes dropped deliberately to his lips and then lower, travelling slowly down his body. 'And temptation,' I husked.

Monroe blinked. 'I'm glad you finally see the light,' he said stiffly.

'I do,' I told him cheerfully. 'And despite how much I feel for you, there are plenty more fish in the sea. There are still lots of good-looking men hanging around the city. Now we know they all have magic, I can enjoy any number of powerful partners.'

Monroe's expression darkened and I thought for a moment that I'd taken things too far, but he simply turned on his heel. 'Let's solve these murders so you can get on with your love life then,' he spat.

Behind his back, I smiled. He was perfectly happy to have distance between us when he was the one putting it there, but when I did the same thing his natural instinct was to fight against it. There really was something left of the old manipulative poker player inside me. Monroe didn't appreciate how good I could be at bluffing when I tried. But was I also a winner – and this was one match I was most definitely going to win.

***

We found Cath in the hospital, chattering away to the same doctor as the night before. She hadn't seen Julie since the morning, and she was so bright-eyed and enthusiastic to be finally learning from a real medical professional that I didn't want to distract her and ruin her day with the details of what Julie might have done. Relieved that she was safe, I told her to stay put.

Monroe and I went off to search the rest of the district. Julie wasn't hiding from the afternoon sun in any of the vampire-friendly pubs and she wasn't in any of the public buildings. And when we arrived at the vampire enclave, the new guard at their barricade denied having seen her. 'Look,' he said, 'I know what happened the last time we helped you out. I'm not protecting that bitch, though. If I knew where she was, I'd tell you. She doesn't come here.'

There was nothing that suggested he was lying. Julie didn't have a lot of friends, even amongst her own kind. While facing the fact that she might be some master manipulator with a penchant for corpses, I felt the need to defend her.

'Listen,' I said to the vamp, 'I appreciate that she could have caused the end of the world but you weren't there at the time. You came to Manchester because the power in the magic makes you feel powerful. It was a similar thing with Julie. She had a moment of madness where she almost helped to bring about the apocalypse by forcing too much magic into the city because she was tired of being hunted and feeling like prey. What you have to remember is that the world didn't end. And she feels really bad about what she did.'

He looked at me curiously. 'Is that why you think I don't like her? I'm not bothered about what happened there. We're all allowed our moments of madness.'

Are we? I raised an eyebrow.

He tutted. 'Whatever this world is now, whatever this city is, until the apocalypse occurred our kind had to hide. Do you have any idea what it's like to be so alone that you can't tell a single soul what you are?' He gestured at Monroe. 'We're not like werewolves. We don't usually live in packs like this. Most vampires are only living here together because we have the wolves to contend with, and this is the time for a display of might and numbers. It won't last.' He shook his head. 'No. Until all this occurred, even the faintest hint of our true nature could bring vampire hunters to us. They don't just kill us – they want to capture us, keep us alive, study us.' A pained expression crossed his face. 'You've not experienced what it's like to feel you're a monster until you've seen the bodies of your parents after they've spent a few years being tortured by the hunters.'

I felt an overwhelming desire to hug him tightly but I doubted he'd appreciate it. 'Julie experienced the same thing. She's like you. She had to hide from them, just like you did.'

'She was an actress.' The guard spat on the ground as if it were a dirty word.

I scratched my head. 'Uh…'

Monroe got it. 'Broadcasting her face to millions on a daily soap opera. Doing interviews. And not growing old.'

'Exactly.' The vampire folded his arms and nodded. 'Sooner or later some clever bastard on the internet would have worked out that there was more to her longevity than Botox. It was only a matter of time. Because she wanted to be famous, she risked exposing us all. There weren't many vampire hunters because there weren't people who knew about our existence.' He sniffed. 'But imagine an entire world knowing you're out there. Looking for you.'

'The entire world knows you're here now,' I pointed out.

He shrugged. 'Perhaps. But they're out there and we're in here.' He glanced again at Monroe. 'Dealing with wolves is far preferable to the life we had, the pitiful existence that Julie Chivers threatened.' He set his jaw and I knew the conversation was over. There was deep-seated pain and trauma amongst all the vampires. Yeah, every single one of us was messed up in our own way.

Monroe and I walked away. 'The vampire is right, you know,' he said. 'Julie's desire to be on television put all of them under threat.' He grimaced. 'If any werewolf tried to do the same...'

I wrinkled my nose. 'Why weren't hunters after you guys? I mean, you're supernatural too. In theory, werewolves should have also been a target.'

'We live in close-knit packs. We don't have the unnaturally long lives that vampires do, so we don't draw as much attention to ourselves. And when someone gets too curious, we're excellent hunters and trackers.'

I stared at him. 'You'd kill someone who discovered your true nature?' I asked, aghast.

'It never happened,' he said quietly.

'But if it did?'

'Then, yes. For good of my pack and the others out there, yes, I would indeed do that.' He stopped walking. 'You know I'm not lying.'

I shivered. Unfortunately I did.

'I told you, Charlotte,' he said softly. 'I'm dangerous. It's a good thing that you have all those other fish in the sea to choose from.'

Shit. 'Monroe, I...'

He held up his hand. 'Don't.' He raised his head

and scented the air. 'I don't think Julie is here. There's no trace of her. I know her scent and her presence is not usually difficult to locate. I don't think she's here or in the south.'

This did not bode well. 'There's no one else who might know where she's gone. From the way that guy was talking, all the vampires feel the same way about her. They all hate her.'

Monroe stilled. From the look on his face, he'd thought of something hugely important.

'What is it?'

He clicked his fingers. 'You might be onto something.' He grinned at me so suddenly that I was taken aback. 'Good work, sunshine.' He took off in the opposite direction, jogging away. 'Come on, then!' he called to me.

I gazed after him for a moment. 'Please let us find her,' I whispered to myself. Then I ran too.

Chapter Twenty-Three

I was some distance behind Monroe. When I entered the pub he'd disappeared into, he already had Carter, the barman, by the collar and was yanking him over the counter. 'Monroe!' I yelled. 'She's not here! We've already checked this place!'

He paid me no attention. 'I'm looking for two vampires,' he snarled in Carter's face. 'Both of them are tall, thin and balding. One has a scar on his cheek. The other is a Metallica fan.'

From the way Carter's pupils flared he was scared, but he was doing a good job of standing up to Monroe. 'I was never a fan of doggy breath,' he spat. 'Get your face out of mine.'

Monroe tightened his grip and shook him. There was an odd snapping sound and, for the briefest moment, Monroe's face changed into a wolf's muzzle. With a wolf's teeth. Then his features smoothed back to their human form. 'Believe me,' he said, 'I can give you more than dog breath if you keep this up. Tell me where I can find them. You know exactly who I'm talking about.'

Carter straightened his back. 'You can't keep doing this. You can't keep coming in here and threatening me and my punters whenever you like. I won't stand for it.'

'I'm trying to solve a series of murders,' Monroe said. 'I think that supersedes a couple of shitty drunks.'

'Because you're trying to pretend that you care? You don't give a flying fuck about who's died, Monroe. You like to pretend that you're the big man. You got us all here months ago after your big speech about creating a community where people would be safe and protected as long as they toed the line. You suggested that your ways were better than her ways.' He jerked his head towards me. 'Then you ignored the lot of us. Don't start acting like you're surprised and you give a shit that people are getting killed. There are easier ways to get into a woman's knickers. Have you thought about flowers?' he sneered. 'I mean, how hard can it be to fuck a blue-haired—'

It happened so quickly that I couldn't even react. Monroe snapped his head forward, headbutting Carter. The vampire barman staggered, blood streaming from his nose. 'Fuck you,' he snarled.

Monroe's body shook. He was a wolf's whisker away from shifting completely. I doubted that would help matters so I stepped forward hastily. 'Please, Carter. I understand that you're upset. You have reason to be. When all this is over Monroe will listen to your complaints, but right now we're on a clock. The last thing we need is for more people to die, whether they're human or wolves.' I paused. 'Or vampires.'

Carter wiped away the worst of the blood with his sleeve. 'All you had to do was ask nicely,' he spat. He looked at me. 'You got any room in the south for a vampire bar?' he asked.

'Please, Carter,' I said. 'Help us out.'

He looked away, his mouth twisting. 'The two you're looking for are called Ben and Jerry.' He winked at me but there was little humour in his expression. 'Not their real names, darling, that's what they're known as. They're always together. They live smack-bang in the middle of the enclave. Terraced house. Blue door. It's next to an old Chinese restaurant.'

Monroe was heading for the exit.

'You probably won't find them there,' Carter called. He raised his eyes to mine. 'You'll remember that I helped you.'

I nodded. 'I will.'

He stared at me for a long moment, trying to ascertain whether I was telling the truth, then he grunted. 'They have a hideout near the River Irwell,' he said. 'North east. They've been setting it up for weeks. They want somewhere to hole up when all this community business goes to hell. Smart move, if you ask me.'

'Where?' Monroe asked, more softly. That was something at least. 'Where exactly near the river?'

'Beside some old cemetery. Kinda creepy if you ask me, but they've always been like that.'

Monroe gave him a long look, filled with mixed emotion. 'Thank you,' he said finally, inclining his head.

Carter glared. 'You're welcome.'

For no other reason than that it seemed fitting, I nipped over and pecked him on the cheek. 'I really appreciate it,' I whispered. 'Monroe does too.'

The vampire grunted. 'Get the fuck out of here.'

I smiled at him before Monroe and I vamoosed.

'I don't know what's going on here, or what these two vamps have to do with anything,' I said as I struggled to keep with him. 'But I don't think headbutting a vampire is the way to win friends and influence people.'

'Maybe I should have kissed him instead, like you did.' Monroe's voice vibrated with barely checked anger. 'Besides, he shouldn't have insulted me. He should show more respect.'

'Should he?' I asked. 'He's disappointed, Monroe. It's written all over his face.'

We veered round a corner and out towards the edge of the community. 'Disappointed with what? He's got nothing to be disappointed about.'

I wasn't sure whether I should answer or not but concealing the truth didn't seem like it would do anyone any good. 'He's disappointed in you. He was expecting more from you. It's not your fault that you've not lived up to his expectations but…' I grimaced. 'It's obvious that's how he feels. I know it because I see the same look on the faces of the people in the south every time they come to talk to me.'

Monroe slowed his steps and turned to look at me.

'You see?' I said. 'We're all fuck-ups.' I paused. 'But let's not fuck up this investigation. What are you onto? Who are these two guys?'

I could see him wrestling with himself, torn between what was going on with Julie and what had happened with Carter. In the end, the investigation won out. It had to. 'When Julie came to me to talk about you, before I saw you at the reservoir, she only stayed until two other vampires showed up.'

'Ben and Jerry?' I guessed.

Monroe nodded. 'Indeed. As far as I could tell, they were looking for her and she wasn't happy about it.'

'So if they've been keeping on tabs on her, they might know where she is.'

'Searching for them when we have their address makes more sense than trailing aimlessly through the city searching for Julie.'

'Agreed.' Whether it proved fruitful or not, having a destination was the best thing we could hope for right now. 'I think I know where this cemetery is,' I told him.

He pointed ahead. 'Lead the way.'

***

There were quite a few buildings dotted around the

cemetery, any one of which could have been chosen by a pair of vampires as a back-up hidey-hole. Most of them looked desolate and dark, and most had blacked-out windows, but only one of the buildings had voices raised in dispute coming from it. It was an old industrial warehouse that had seen better days. Hadn't we all?

Monroe and I looked at each other. 'Definitely vampires,' he told me, his nostrils twitching.

I smiled in grim acknowledgment. 'So how will we play this? We seem to keep switching roles. One minute you're the calm one and I'm the crazy, the next minute it's the other way around.'

His gaze was steady. 'I suppose it's like that,' he said quietly, 'because we actually work well together.'

'Mmm. It's a shame that will stop after all this.'

Monroe shifted his eyes away. 'From the brief impression I got of this pair, they'll respond better to brute force and intimidation than the nicey-nicey approach.'

I brightened slightly. 'So we both go in with guns blazing?' I was more pleased about that than I should have been; recent events were getting me down more than I'd realised. 'Fabulous. On a count of three.'

'Don't get hurt,' he said, his eyes flashing.

'I might say the same to you.' I smiled. 'Three. Two.'

'One,' Monroe finished. In the next beat we were both running towards the warehouse.

Whatever Ben and Jerry were arguing about, their emotions were running high. Although their words were inaudible, their tone was not. Even with the warehouse doors and windows firmly shut, it was obvious that they were yelling at each other with gusto. When Monroe and I reached the front door and their shouts continued unabated, neither of us wasted time speaking in whispers.

'The sun is still high,' I said. 'Once we open that door, they'll know we're here. Unless we find another way in and opt for a stealthy approach to take them by surprise.'

'Honestly,' Monroe said. 'I can't be arsed.' He raised his foot and kicked in the door. It crashed open and Ben and Jerry's argument stopped. 'Vampires! Ready or not, here I come!'

I smiled, raised my hands and sent a bolt of magic towards the centre of the warehouse. It sizzled when it hit the ceiling, causing a cascade of dust and wooden splinters to rain down onto the cement floor. 'Me too!' I shouted. And with that, both Monroe and I loped in.

There was a row of shelves laden with tinned goods against one of the far walls. Ben and Jerry were certainly preparing themselves for every eventuality. I wondered whether there should be a word for a person who, after an apocalypse, continued to prep for the possibility of a second one. Re-preppers? Post-preppers? Selfish idiots who stockpiled goods that other people needed and who deserved a sharp kick in the nuts?

Something came flying out of the gloom. Monroe shoved me slightly so I stumbled out of its path and the missile didn't smack directly into my skull. I already had it covered, though, and flicked out an explosive magical shot to pulverise the object – whatever it was – into a cloud of dust.

'Nice move,' he murmured.

I grinned at him. 'I know.'

Part of me wished I'd dressed up for the occasion. I liked the idea of stalking through the building with a long leather coat flaring out behind me. Despite the darkness, I'd be wearing stylish sunglasses and I'd have skin-tight clothes to show that I meant business. More to the point, so would Monroe. I guessed I'd have settle for jeans and a shabby jumper. It didn't really matter: winners come in all forms.

There was a loud bang somewhere to my left. Even with my inexperience in stalking, I wasn't stupid enough to fall for such a diversion. Instead of leaping to investigate, I twisted in the opposite direction and smiled grimly as I spotted something. Monroe caught the same flicker of movement and smirked, displaying his white, even teeth. Then he transformed, his clothes ripping off as he changed into his wolf form. Honestly. He would have to do something about that; there were only so many boiler suits and changes of clothes in the city.

He leapt forward, his fur bristling in the stale air. A second later there was a strangled shout, whether from Ben or Jerry it was impossible to say. Either way, one down, one to go.

I swivelled the other way. If they had any nous, they'd have split up; that meant the other one had to be somewhere over there. I was right; unfortunately I hadn't factored in that they might have a hostage.

'Come any closer,' shouted a shaky voice, 'and I'll slit her throat! It won't be easy for her but she'll die all the same. Regardless of the magic around us, we're still not immortal.'

Before I could see who either Ben or Jerry was talking about, I knew.

'Darlings,' Julie's strained voice said, 'I'm really rather parched. I don't suppose there's any chance of a drink?'

I walked forward, keeping my pace even and slow and counting on the fact that Monroe had the other one covered. 'Are you Ben?' I called. 'Or Jerry?'

His face contorted. 'I fucking hate those names.'

'So what would you like me to call you?' I asked. I kept my palms raised, to avoid any erratic movements that might trigger his anger even more. 'Abductor? Criminal?'

'How about hero?' he snarled.

I felt something chill inside me. Was that because Julie had dared to become a television actress? Or was it because he knew something else about her? Like the crimes she might have committed recently?

'I'll just run with Jerry,' I said. I moved forward out of the patch of shadows and my gaze snagged on Julie. She was suspended upside down from the ceiling on a chain which was coiled round her ankles. It didn't look a particularly comfortable position. Neither did it look easy to get out of. There would be no snatching her and making a run for it.

Jerry, if that's who he was, gave an irritated snort. 'I don't know why you're even here. This bitch doesn't deserve a rescue mission.'

'But she does deserve to be hung upside down like a piece of meat?'

He took a step backwards and nudged Julie in the ribs. She started swaying from side to side, her arms dangling uselessly and her fingertips trailing on the floor. 'If it hadn't been for the apocalypse, every vampire in the country would have ended up like this. Her actions would have seen to that.'

'How?' Julie demanded. 'The only person I was putting in danger of discovery was myself, and I was prepared to retire before anyone got suspicious.'

Jerry bent down until his face was in hers. 'Once the world knew what you were, they'd have come for all of us.' He angled his head towards me. 'Have you killed Billy?'

Eh?

He tutted and straightened up. 'Ben,' he hissed. 'His real name is Billy.'

228

Oh. 'We're not actually in the business of killing people,' I said. Although given Monroe's temper these days, I wondered if I was telling the truth. Fortunately, a moment later, Monroe himself padded up, dragging Jerry's unconscious partner by the arm.

'Two against one, Jerry,' I said. 'You should give this up. Besides, it's all moot now. With what's happened to Manchester, no one has to hide their true nature any more. You can be a vampire and tell the world and it doesn't matter. Not in this city. You're upset over something that happened in the past and can't be changed.'

'Exactly,' Julie said. 'Let me down, darling, and this will all be in the past too.'

Jerry kicked her, clearly more for effect than to cause pain. 'Shut up.' He put his hands on his hips and faced me again. 'The past defines us. The past colours everything we do. No, it can't be changed but that doesn't mean we should forget it.' He nodded at me. 'Doesn't your past follow you?'

If I closed my eyes for a moment, I knew I'd find myself back in my parents' house, scrabbling to get up the smoke-filled staircase to rescue my little brother Joshua, who never had a chance. Because of me. 'Yes,' I said quietly. 'Yes, it does.'

'And what about what might have been? If things had been different and the apocalypse hadn't occurred, I could be the one being tortured right now. *She* can't get away with that.'

I drew in a deep breath. 'But you weren't tortured. You weren't exposed.'

Jerry sniffed. 'That's not the point.'

'Of course it is.' I walked forward until we were almost toe to toe. Monroe growled in warning but I ignored him and put my hand on Jerry's shoulder. He flinched but he didn't move away. 'You can't live your life focusing on what might have been. We can't forget the past, and we shouldn't – it's there for us to learn from. Memories help us avoid making the same mistakes again. But just because there are things in those memories that might be sour doesn't mean they should sour our whole life. You won't feel better if you hurt Julie.'

'Yes, I will.' There was a stubborn set to his jaw.

'Okay,' I conceded, 'maybe you'll feel better for a while, but it won't last. Guilt will set in sooner or later. After all, Julie didn't actually hurt you – and she's carrying around her own guilt. I bet she has those snarky thoughts herself. You know, the ones that keep you awake at night, that your mind keeps churning over and over again.'

'It's not enough,' Jerry spat.

'Don't mess yourself up over this,' I advised. 'You're fine. We're all fine. This life we live now is not the life we lived before. There's nothing Julie can do now that will hurt you. Hurting her will hurt you in the long run. Give this up. Move on.'

'I'm not fine,' he told me.

'But you will be,' I answered simply. 'You've been fixating on Julie as someone to blame for all your woes. Sometimes blaming others is helpful, but sometimes it's not. Now it's not. Nothing about this new life is easy to deal with. Don't make it harder, Jerry.'

Indecision warred within him and his eyes shifted back and forth. I was aware of the coiled tension in Monroe. I could only pray that Jerry would make the right choice; I didn't need more spilled blood to deal with.

In the end he turned to Julie, reached into his pocket, pulled out a small blade and held it up to her face. 'Remember,' he said, 'I could have done this. I could have killed you.' He pulled back. 'But I have chosen not to.' He heaved in a shaky breath. 'We all pay for our crimes in the end.'

He put the knife away and glanced at Monroe and me. When neither of us moved, he strode over and took his partner's body, hauling him into a fireman's lift. He walked towards the exit.

Despite what Jerry may or may not have been about to do, I was glad we were letting him go. He'd stopped himself before things got too bad; he'd listened and reflected and altered his course. Sometimes that was the best any of us could ask for.

The sound of cracking bone filled the space. When I glanced back, Monroe was straightening up. He was human again – as well as naked and surprisingly vulnerable. 'Wait,' he called out.

Jerry froze in his tracks.

'I'll give you a lift home,' Monroe said gruffly. 'Your friend is in no state to be carried through the streets, not with all the beasties around. We'll clear this place out later. You don't need a back-up hiding place. We're all going to look after each other in the north. We're a community, when all is said and done.'

I blinked, surprised. Then I smiled.

Jerry slowly turned. 'I'm shocked you care,' he said.

'Well, I do,' Monroe muttered. He gave me a fleeting glance. 'I've not been doing a very good job lately. It's time that changed.' He took a shaky breath. 'We all need to put the past behind us if we're to move on.'

We stayed where we were, none of us speaking but all of us appreciating a shared moment of total understanding.

'He would never actually have hurt me,' Julie

said, breaking the spell. 'They were arguing before you got here. The other one thought they'd scared me enough and that they should let me go.' She scoffed. 'As if they could scare me!'

She'd looked pretty scared from where I was standing. My insides churned. This wasn't over. Not yet.

'Let me down, darlings,' Julie drawled. 'This position is doing nothing for my dignity.'

I shook my head. 'No.'

'Charley, dear…'

I balled my hands up into fists. 'Was it you?' I asked quietly. 'Did you manipulate Philip into killing Valerie?'

Even upside down, I could tell that she was stunned. 'No. Good heavens! What would make you think such a thing?'

'And Maggie?' Monroe interjected. 'Did you hit her over the head and then get her to attack Philip?'

'What?' she spluttered. 'How would I manage that? Why would I want to?' Her arms flailed as she tried to gesticulate. 'I can't believe you're asking me that!'

I steeled myself for what was to come. 'We know you went to Nimue yesterday. Or tried to go. You took Valerie's lover and you both went there with guns to hurt her. With *grenades*.'

'Darling,' Julie said. 'I have no idea what you're talking about. Who on earth is Nimue?'

'The mermaid. The one I told you about.'

Jerry hissed in surprise. 'A mermaid? Seriously?'

'This is a joke, right? You're having a laugh.' Julie waved her hands towards me. 'You're trying to lighten the atmosphere and have some fun by accusing me of … what? Murder?'

'It's no joke,' Monroe said. 'We need to know exactly what you did and why you did it. Was it the magic in the air? Did it override everything else and make you want to kill?'

'Darlings,' Julie began. 'I…'

'Where is this mermaid?' Jerry asked.

'Over on the east side,' I told him. 'Near a place called Boggart Hole.'

'I've never been to Boggart Hole!' Julie exclaimed. 'So this isn't me! You're looking for someone else. Let me down and I'll prove it to you.'

'How?' I asked. 'How will you prove it, Julie?'

'She doesn't have to,' Jerry said quietly. 'We've been following her for days. She's not gone anywhere near the place you're talking about. She's certainly not gone near any mermaids. The only people she's spoken to are you two and some teenager who's helping out at the hospital.' He raised his eyebrows. 'Believe me, I wouldn't lie about this. If she's been causing any more trouble, I'd tell you about it.' He paused. 'I might be walking away from her now but I still despise her and everything she's ever stood for.'

That was his prerogative. I knew without checking his face for tells that he wasn't lying. He was the most unlikely alibi I could think of – and that made him all the more reliable.

I breathed out and met Monroe's eyes. 'We're back at square one,' I said. 'Again.'

Chapter Twenty-Four

Julie was more shaken than she wanted to admit. Her hand trembled around the glass as she raised it up to gulp down her gin. For a moment I was tempted to offer her some of my blood, if only to calm her down, but fortunately the temptation was brief. I liked my red stuff where it was, despite the tales of feeder euphoria that had been described to me.

'Much as I hate to admit it, that was rather a close call, darling,' she said. 'Far too close for my liking.' She shuddered delicately. 'That Jerry was out to get me. I'm sure his partner would have persuaded him to let me go in the end, but it wasn't much fun. I might have been a tiny bit frightened.' She flashed me a smile. 'Don't tell anyone that. I'm sure I can trust you. But how could you entertain the idea that I'd manipulate people into committing murder? It's too much to think about. I'm going to need therapy after this. For obvious reasons therapy wasn't something I could think about in the past, but things are different now. I can pour my heart out without fear of reprisal or disbelief.' She pursed her lips. 'There's definitely something to be said for all this apocalypse business.'

'I'm glad you're alright,' I said. 'And I'm sorry for flying around making accusations. The evidence pointed to you, but I'm truly glad that you're not involved in any of these deaths.' I wondered if Julie would hold it against me. It didn't look like it; we'd all learned not to dwell too much on the past.

I ran a hand through my hair and teased out a few knotted tangles. 'Someone *is* involved in these deaths,' I sighed helplessly. 'Goodness only knows who or why.'

Julie fixed me with a look. 'Are you sure you're not looking for links between the killings when they've actually got nothing to do with each other?'

'No,' I said. 'They're connected. I know they are. I can feel it in my bones.'

'And Monroe?' she enquired. 'Does he feel the same?'

'I think so.'

'Are you and he…' She made a rude gesture with her forefinger and thumb, which was definitely not what I'd have expected from her.

I shoved her playfully shove. 'No!'

'Well,' she sniffed. 'You should be.' She took another sip of her drink. 'I've seen him naked now, you know. That's not the sort of thing you see every day, darling. He's yours for the taking – and if you don't take him, I will.' She grinned at me. 'Unless he's not for you. You could always take a leaf from Valerie's book and sort yourself out with your own well-stocked harem.'

I laughed. 'I don't need that kind of hassle.' Besides, the only man I wanted was Monroe, no matter how dangerous he might turn out to be. I traced a random shape on the table top. 'Julie,' I began.

'Uh oh,' she said. 'Here we go.'

I smiled weakly. 'You've experienced loss of control before,' I said. 'You know, when you…'

'Almost caused the destruction of the world?' She inclined her head. 'Yes, darling. I remember.'

'Do you think you've ever felt close to something similar? I mean,' I added hastily before she mistook my meaning, 'do you think the magic that's around us would speak to your vampire self and you could be unable to control your bloodlust?'

Julie frowned and took the question seriously. 'No,' she said simply. 'I've never felt like that either before or since. Yes, I'm more powerful now. Blood has more of an effect on me than it ever did, and it's so irksome not to be able to enjoy the sun's rays like I used to. But the magic isn't so strong that it affects my inner self. I was … overwhelmed that first time. I was easily swayed by the magic's pull. But things are more stable now. If I were going to do anything crazy like that again, it would have already happened. The apocalypse was an explosion of magic. Since then, things have settled down. You're talking about a gradual build-up.' She shook her head. 'I just don't think it's possible.'

'Thank you,' I murmured. 'I needed that.'

'Any time, darling.' She watched me for a moment. 'He's scared, you know,' she said suddenly. 'He's terrified by how you make him feel. He's even more terrified that something will happen to you. But you're both sensible people when you don't have other problems to deal with. You'll work it out.'

I massaged the back of my neck. 'The trouble is,' I sighed, 'there are always other problems to deal with.'

The corner of Julie's mouth lifted. 'Then get someone else to deal with them.'

I smiled sadly. Easier said than done.

***

The next morning I was at a loss. The investigation had all but stalled. I couldn't think of where to go or what to do next, and the idea of dealing with the usual mundanities of post-apocalyptic life made me feel like I'd swallowed a ten-tonne weight that I'd never get rid of.

I'd have to return to that life sooner or later, even

if the others did help me out more. In this new world, life wasn't about excitement and thrills and seat-of-your-pants, death-defying bids for survival. It was about clean water and enough food to eat and ensuring nobody killed anyone else in a fight about nothing.

Julian seemed to have the post-apocalyptic infrastructure down to a fine art in the north, but he took it all a bit too seriously and things there could do with some serious tweaking. If it weren't for Monroe's fear about the magic, I'd suggest that we all moved in to the same neighbourhood rather than staying in separate ones. We could learn a lot from each other if we allowed ourselves to do so. If I hadn't floated my stupid theory, Monroe might have agreed. Unfortunately I doubted that Julie's assertion that the magic wouldn't affect the vampires in any more ways would be enough. Monroe needed proof that they could hold their natural instincts in check; I had no way of getting that proof.

'Hi-de-hi!' Lizzy trilled, strolling into the room. 'How is my lovely enchantress this morning?'

'Peachy,' I grunted.

'That's what I like to hear.' She smiled at me and I couldn't help but smile back. I needed some sunny Australian optimism to brighten up my life. 'Anna asked me to drop by and fill you in,' she said. 'The name of the dead guy you brought back, the one with the tattoo, is Craig Featherstone. I helped her search his house yesterday. There wasn't much there, unfortunately. Lots of bits of paper but no indication about why he might have done what he did, or who the mysterious woman was that he was with.'

Big surprise. I sighed. 'Thanks anyway.'

She nodded. 'How's Julie?'

'She'll be okay. She's pretty resilient. She said was she was thinking about getting some therapy but that might have been a joke. We hardly have psychiatrists hanging round every corner. We can't even find plumbers.'

'You'd be surprised. One of the scraps of paper we found at Craig's place was a leaflet for a counsellor. I mean,' she shrugged, 'I doubt it was anyone who's medically trained but they clearly had experience. They were advertising hypnotherapy.'

I blinked. 'What? You get hypnotised into … self-affirmation?'

'Don't knock it till you've tried it.'

True. I raised my cup and then I froze. 'Wait,' I said slowly. 'What did the leaflet look like?'

Puzzled, she raised her hands. 'About this big,' she said, indicating the size. 'Handwritten. Why?'

'Was there any sort of picture or drawing?' I asked. 'Some kind of symbol?'

She stared at me. 'There was, actually.'

I leapt to my feet and darted over to the window, breathing out to create condensation before drawing the outline of a head with a spiral where the brain would be located. 'Did it look like this?'

Lizzy licked her lips. 'Exactly like that.' She was growing nervous; golden fur was starting to sprout across her arms. She patted it down absently and continued to look at me. 'How did you know?'

'Philip,' I ground out. 'Philip had a bookmark with the same design.' My stomach flipped. 'Get Anna,' I said. 'Get hold of her and tell her to meet me at the Travotel.'

'You think this has something to do with it?' she asked. 'Hypnotherapy?'

For once I wasn't going to jump to conclusions. Not yet, anyway. 'Just tell her to meet me there,' I said. 'As soon as she can.'

***

The alarm on Timmons' face when I careened at full speed into the Travotel lobby was obvious. 'No,' he said. 'Just no.'

'I have to see Valerie's room again,' I bit out. 'Now.'

'I've been losing guests left, right and centre!' he told me, flapping his arms. 'You can't come in here and disturb them again! People think it isn't safe here. I've been doing everything I can, but they say they can't trust my magical alarms. They say they can't trust me! Having you here again is not going to help!'

'What if your alarm wasn't at fault?' I said.

He blinked. 'Pardon?'

'If Valerie invited her killer in and didn't feel any fear, then the alarm wouldn't necessarily have gone off, would it?'

He stared at me. 'I don't suppose so. But it was a vampire who killed her. She didn't like vampires. She fought back.'

'Only in her last moments,' I said. 'We already know that to drink that much blood from her would have taken hours. If she didn't start fighting until she knew she was dying, the alarm wouldn't have been gone off until it was already too late. When I was downstairs having a jam sandwich.' I tried not to think too hard about having strawberry jam smeared across my face while Philip the vampire had Valerie's blood smeared across his.

'She wouldn't have invited a vampire in to drink from her.'

I grimaced. 'She might have if someone else persuaded her to.'

'Who would do something like that?'

'I'm working on it.' I folded my arms. 'Let me see her room.'

Timmons sighed. 'Fine. You know where it is.'

I flashed him a quick smile of thanks and darted through the door and up the stairs. I was onto something. I just knew it.

Valerie's room remained untouched. There was an indentation on the mattress indicating where her body had lain, and a few spots and smears of blood. Other than that, you'd have been forgiven for thinking she'd merely popped out. I ignored the bed and strode to the desk, flipping through various bits of paper. There were all sorts of scribbles, drawings and gambling-related notes, mostly to do with poker plays which I assumed she'd been trying out. I resisted the urge to focus on them too closely. I wasn't looking for tips – not for cards, anyway.

I'd started on the drawers when Anna appeared in the open doorway. 'What's going on, Charley?'

I looked up from the mess I was making. 'Thank you for coming.'

She walked in. 'You know I always would. Have you thought of something? Or found something?'

'Not yet, but I think I'm onto something. Was there anything in Valerie's diary about going for counselling?'

'Counselling?' Anna pursed her lips. 'Not that I recall.'

'What about hypnotism?' I started rifling through the first drawer again. There had to be something there. There had to be proof somewhere.

She wrinkled her nose. 'No. Charley…'

I let out a high-pitched squeak.

'What is it?'

I pulled out the grubby piece of paper and held it aloft. 'This,' I said. 'This is it.'

Anna squinted. 'I don't get it.'

I jabbed at the paper. 'This picture. The outline of a man with a swirl where his brain should be. Philip was using the same picture as a bookmark. Craig Featherstone had the same leaflet amongst his belongings. I'll bet my last penny that Maggie does too. This is what links them together.' I waved the paper with its neat doodle and spidery handwriting. 'This is what we've been looking for.'

Anna took it. '*Are you feeling vulnerable?*' she read. '*Is the apocalypse too much for you to deal with? Are you struggling with the new city and your place in it? Then hypnotherapy could be for you.*' She raised her head, her sceptism obvious. 'Hypnotherapy?'

'Imagine hypnotising a reluctant vampire to drink more blood. Or,' I said, pointing at Valerie's empty bed, 'hypnotising a human to allow themselves to be drunk from.'

Her brow creased. 'But hypnotism doesn't work like that. You can't hypnotise someone to do something against their will. You can't swing a pendulum in my face and tell me to go and kill, and then I go and do it. It's not possible.'

I stood my ground. 'It wasn't possible before the magic,' I said quietly. 'But if you draw on the magic in the atmosphere to bolster what you are doing, then I bet it would work. Especially when you're using the hypnotism to speak to someone's inner nature and deepest desires. A vampire *wants* to drink blood. Werewolves don't like vampires and some of them think they're unnatural creatures who need to be put down.' Anna winced. I warmed to my topic. 'Valerie might not have liked vampires, but she did have a desperate need to be loved. She could have been persuaded to offer her blood to a vampire who would love her in turn.'

'Craig Featherstone,' she murmured. 'From what I've been able to find out, he was ex-army.'

'So he knew guns.'

Anna nodded. 'And it could be argued that the ultimate goal of a soldier is to attack in order to protect.'

'If he were hypnotised with a dose of magic for extra strength, he could be persuaded to shoot first and ask questions later.'

Anna sucked on her bottom lip. 'So it's plausible,' she said finally.

'We're all feeling vulnerable. We're all a bit fucked up,' I said. 'A therapist could gain our trust, learn our darkest desires and weakest spots and work on them for their own means. You told me that murder was all about power.' I jabbed my finger at the leaflet. 'Well, this is the ultimate power. Persuading others to commit crimes without lifting a finger yourself.'

'But Charley, a therapist's goal is to help people.'

'I'm not saying that it's not twisted, I'm just saying it could be true. This isn't about jumping to conclusions, this is about the evidence we have in front of us. It fits. You know it fits.'

Her expression was sombre. 'You're right,' she said. 'I think you're onto something.' She held up the paper. 'But there's nothing here. There aren't any contact details. There's no name. Whoever passed out these leaflets might have done it deliberately to maintain deniability. They would have suggested times and places verbally for the sessions to take place. Without workable computers or Google, I don't see how we can tell who created these leaflets.'

'The therapist made a mistake though, didn't she? She left Maggie alive. Maybe she hypnotised Maggie into remaining as a wolf so she couldn't talk about what happened. But she made a catastrophic error and didn't count on a vampire's blood being enough to turn Maggie back into her human form.' I balled my fists. I knew Maggie had been hiding something. This had to be it.

'She?' Anna questioned.

I breathed in. 'The bogles saw a woman with Craig Featherstone. It fits. This is someone who might not have the physical strength to kill someone on their own but who can do so vicariously through others.'

Anna's skin looked white. 'She's still out there. She'll keep doing this until we stop her.'

I swallowed. 'We need to get to Maggie now.'

Chapter Twenty-Five

'You're not coming in.' The two werewolves at the barricade to the northern community were stony-faced and adamant.

I threw up my hands, my furious movement a complete contrast to the wolves' stoic facades. 'What?'

'Boss's orders.'

'You mean Monroe,' I spat. The fucking idiot. 'Look,' I said, trying to calm myself, 'he thinks that the magic means he can't control himself. That his wolf might emerge at any second and attack me. That you are the same.' I put my hands on my hips. 'Do you feel like that?' I demanded. 'Do you feel like you're about to turn rogue despite your best intentions?'

'You can yell all you want,' the first werewolf said implacably. 'We're only following orders.'

'Get him here,' I said through gritted teeth. 'Let me talk to Monroe.'

She crossed her arms. 'He's gone out.'

What the hell? 'Gone where?'

'Dunno. It doesn't matter. Unless I hear directly from him, you're not coming in.'

This was unbelievable.

'Then let me in,' Anna said.

'Nope. You're human. We can't do it. No humans are to be given access under any circumstances.'

I drew in a ragged breath. 'Monroe thinks he's protecting everyone by doing this.. Instead, while we're out here twiddling our thumbs, someone else could be dying.'

Anna was a great deal calmer than I was. 'Lizzy's not human. Neither is Julie. We can go back to the south and get one of them. They can speak to Maggie for us.'

'No.' I folded my arms. 'It'll take too long. Our killer therapist is already escalating. We can't afford to waste any more time.'

The werewolves appeared unperturbed. 'You should leave this place,' the second one said.

I hissed under my breath and spun away, but I wasn't leaving. Not until I'd spoken to Maggie. Magic prickled under my skin. If that was what it was going to take, then so be it.

'Charley.' Anna sounded nervous.

'Don't worry,' I told her. 'Everything will be fine.' I turned slowly to face the werewolves again. Just beyond them, hovering in the lowlight of the oncoming dusk, was Theo. There was a smirk on his face, suggesting he knew exactly what I was planning. If he got in my way, he'd suffer the consequences as well.

'Charley,' Anna persisted. 'Two wrongs don't make a right. I really don't think this is a good idea.'

For the first time, the wolves appeared less than confident. Good.

'I'm not really human,' I called out to them. 'Not any more. None of us are.' I gazed down at my fingers and wiggled them. 'Magic can be used for good,' I said, 'or for absolute evil. And sometimes for what lies in between.' I flicked my wrists, spiralling out two gentle plumes of smoky-green magic.

The first wolf ducked, hoping the barricade would save her. The second wolf faced it head on, his teeth bared. He started to shift but he was no Monroe. By the time he'd sprouted fur, the magic had reached him and was swirling round his body and binding him tight. There was a choked cry from the other barricade and I knew the same was happening to his colleague. Huh. It wasn't exactly what I was going for, but it worked all the same.

'You can stay out here if you want,' I said to Anna.

'I can't,' she muttered. 'I have to stay with you, if only to save you from yourself.'

I considered her words. 'I'm not the one being obstructive here,' I pointed out.

'If you say so,' she replied. 'How would you feel if someone did that to any of our people?'

Hmmm. I ignored the guilty stab and offered a blithe shrug. 'You reap what you sow. I'm not the one who separated our communities, and I'm not the one who's causing problems now.'

'That's a matter of perspective,' Theo said from the opposite side of the barrier.

I looked at him. 'Do you want to try and stop me too?' I asked. 'Because I'm hunting down a killer so I have no qualms about wrapping you up like a Christmas present, just like them.'

He smiled. 'I'm fine as I am, thank you.' He glanced at the two fallen werewolves. 'But you know what I will do?' he said softly. 'I'll stand here and keep guard for the wolves while they're incapacitated. After all, we all live in this community and there is a killer on the loose.'

I watched him. He might have been amused by the situation but there wasn't a trace of guile in his expression. 'You're a good man,' I said finally.

'Remember to tell Monroe and Julian that when all this is over,' he murmured.

'Done,' I promised.

I paid scant attention to the furious glares emanating from the magically trussed-up wolves. That's what you got when you messed with the enchantress.

Anna and I scooted past the barricade. I avoided the temptation to stroll down the street as if I were starring in an old Western film and made the sensible decision to stick to the shadows along the edge of the buildings. It wasn't worth garnering unwanted attention if we could help it. We trotted past the makeshift shops and the scattered bars, including the Blood and Bones, and headed across the square. I hoped that Maggie was still being kept there, or there might be problems.

Tripping up the steps and pushing open the door, I pulled back my shoulders and acted for all the world like I was supposed to be there. I had permission; I was *allowed*. There were a few people scattered around but none of them paid Anna or me any attention. In fact, we made it all the way to the room where Maggie was being kept before we were challenged.

'I've got this,' Anna said to me when a pair of green eyes narrowed in our direction and Felicity, the unyielding werewolf, started forward. 'Besides,' she added, 'I can't let you have all the fun.'

I grinned.

'I'm Anna Jones,' she said, striding forward with her hand outstretched. 'I'm investigating the killings from the southern side and I have a few questions for Maggie.'

'You're not supposed to be here,' Felicity snapped. 'Do you think I'm stupid just because I'm a wolf? The order went out hours ago and it's not been rescinded. Whoever you are and why ever you're here, you're in the wrong place.' She pointed at me. '*She* is most definitely not supposed to be here.'

'I'm a police officer,' Anna began.

'Not here you're not.' Felicity crossed her arms. 'Not now. But if you want to talk to Maggie, go ahead. But don't hurt her. She's been through enough as it is.'

My mouth dropped open and Felicity gave a

short, unfriendly laugh. 'Do you know why humans aren't allowed here any more?' she asked. 'It's because there's a chance that the rest of us supernatural beings won't be able to control ourselves. That we'll let the magic get the better of us and we'll attack or even kill you without provocation.'

'It's just a theory,' I managed, still unsure what was really going on inside Felicity's head.

'And a stupid one at that,' she snorted. 'Magic won't overpower me. It won't change who I am. Nothing will force me into shifting and attacking you. If I do that, it's because I choose to do it. I don't like vampires. I think they're vicious, nasty creatures who don't belong here, but that doesn't mean I'll hurt any of them. I'm not a monster and I can control my own urges. Besides,' she added, 'you're the enchantress. If you want to protect yourself, I'm sure you're more than capable.'

I frowned. 'I thought wolves always followed orders and maintained the hierarchy, no matter what.'

'Maybe more than one thing around here is changing,' she said with a crooked smile She turned on her heel and started walking away. 'I've not seen you. I don't know where you are.'

Well, well, well. I watched her go before exchanging a baffled glance with Anna then opening the door into Maggie's cell. I could only pray that we were going to get some answers.

Maggie was still chained up but she appeared considerably healthier than before. There was a glow to her cheeks and her thick dark hair looked shiny, giving the impression that she'd taken a long shower with some expensive conditioner. When she clocked Anna and me, she seemed surprised but not overly dismayed. That was a good start.

'Hey,' I said softly. 'Remember me?'

'I'm not likely to forget.' She glanced behind me, no doubt expecting Monroe or Julian to stride in after us. When it was clear we were alone, I could tell her interest – and her trepidation – was piqued. 'What can I do for you?'

Softly, softly, Charley. 'Have you been treated well?'

She shrugged, making her chains rattle. 'I can't complain.'

'Are the restraints necessary?' Anna enquired.

'Don't ask me,' Maggie said. 'I only work here.' She curved her mouth into a smile as if she were merely telling a light-hearted, albeit not very funny, joke. When we didn't chuckle, her smile disappeared and she sighed. 'I can't be trusted. I can't even trust myself.'

I stepped close to her then sat down cross-legged and within her reach. Not only did it bring me down to her level, it also indicated a level of trust on my part. I didn't think Maggie would attack me and I was willing to prove it.

'I'm DI Jones,' Anna said. I turned my head to look at her and she shrugged. 'I've given myself a promotion. I think I'm entitled.'

I wasn't about to argue. 'Why stop at Detective Inspector? Why not go for Commissioner?'

'Too much paperwork,' she said, without a trace of irony. 'Now, Maggie, we would like to ask you a few questions, if you're willing.'

Maggie's eyes shifted between the two of us. 'Sure. I've gone over it several times, though. I'm not sure there's anything new I can tell you.'

'It's not the incident itself that we're interested in,' Anna said. 'It's what was happening before.' She paused. 'With you and your state of mind.'

For the first time Maggie looked faintly nervous.

'Oh yes?'

Anna pressed ahead. 'How have you been finding the aftermath of the apocalypse?'

Maggie shifted uneasily. 'It's great,' she said unconvincingly. 'I have a lot more strength than I used to. My wolf responds to the magic in the air. She likes it.'

I found it interesting that she separated herself from her werewolf form. I'd not heard Monroe do that.

'Mmm-hmm.' Anna nodded. 'So everything's hunky-dory? Couldn't be better?'

Maggie's tongue darted out to wet her lips. 'Yes.'

Anna didn't say anything. Neither did I. The silence stretched out until I could almost see the prickles of discomfort across Maggie's skin.

'Well,' she said eventually, 'it's not perfect. I mean, nothing ever is, right?'

I leaned back and rested my weight on my hands.

Maggie swallowed. 'I'd never been to Manchester before the apocalypse. I'd never spent much time in a city. Our pack is from the countryside. We lived near a forest and hills and...' She looked away. 'Not buildings and roads. I know the city here is virtually empty but it's still different.' Her hand went to her throat. 'Sometimes it can be quite constricting.'

'Did you talk to anyone about how you were feeling? I understand that wolf packs can be quite close knit.'

'They are. Of course they are. My pack is my family – they mean everything to me.' Her voice was so fervent that I couldn't help wondering who she was trying to convince. She seemed to realise that herself because her body sank slightly. 'But it's not always good to show weakness. We have to be strong. There are a lot of nasty creatures out there. If we don't put on a strong front, they could take advantage.'

I suspected she was talking about the vampires within the barricades of Monroe's north rather than the magical beasties who lived outside its limits.

'So,' I probed, 'you didn't talk to anyone in your pack about feeling a bit … claustrophobic?'

'It wasn't claustrophobia.' She glared, although it seemed to be directed at herself rather than at me. 'The magic makes us strong but it's also an unknown quantity. What if we come to rely on it too much and then it vanishes? What if there's another magical surge and it overtakes us? We have a balance right now but things might not stay that way.'

'There's a lot to worry about,' I said quietly.

'Yeah.' Her head dropped. 'I wasn't feeling right. I couldn't sleep.' She touched her temples. 'I've been getting headaches. I've been…' she struggled for the right words '…just not right.'

I wanted to hug her, and I probably would have if Anna hadn't spoken up. There was a reason why she was the professional and I was the amateur. 'It must be really hard. Is there anyone else you've been able to talk to? Maybe not in your pack. Maybe you found someone outside your pack. Someone who's not a werewolf.'

Maggie's expression changed almost imperceptibly. It wasn't much, merely a faint tightening around the corners of her mouth, but it was enough. I knew we had her and I knew we were on the right track.

Anna knew it too. 'Maggie?' she asked gently. 'Was there someone you found to talk to?'

Maggie balled up her fists and her knuckles whitened. 'I'm not ashamed of it,' she declared defiantly. 'I'm not ashamed of going to therapy. It's better to talk things through, to get help when you need it. It takes a strong person to ask for help. It's not a weakness.'

I did my best to batten down my exultation at her

admission. 'No,' I said. 'Asking for help is not a weakness. Going to therapy is a good idea.'

Maggie blinked. Perhaps she'd expected us to laugh at her.

This was what we'd come to. By focusing on physical rather than emotional survival, we'd allowed this to happen. We'd allowed this bastard of a counsellor to sneak in and destroy our house of cards. We should have known better. All of us.

'Maggie,' Anna said, 'who was the therapist you saw? Who did you talk to?'

'A human guy,' she muttered. 'I didn't want someone who lived here and I found a human guy who had a lot of experience. He was nice. Gentle. We met at an abandoned café in the city centre, not far from the Travotel.'

My bubble burst. We weren't looking for a man. The bogles had been certain that Craig Featherstone's companion was female. This couldn't be another dead end, it just couldn't be. Unfortunately it seemed that it was.

'He knew what he was doing,' Maggie said, registering my expression. 'He was great at hypnotherapy!'

I stopped breathing. Anna knelt down beside me and fixed her eyes on Maggie. 'This is important,' she said. 'Who is he? What's his name?'

'I don't know his last name,' she said. 'I just called him Albert.'

'White hair? Bushy eyebrows?'

Maggie nodded.

'He's quite old,' Anna said, half to herself and half to me. 'He won't have a lot of physical strength. He'd need help if he wanted to actually hurt someone. Or kill them.'

'What?' Maggie squeaked.

I exchanged a look with Anna. 'Sometimes,' I said quietly, 'he wears a kilt which, in the darkness, could be mistaken for a skirt. He could be mistaken for a woman.' Then I thought of something else and I could have slapped myself. 'He was there.' I swore. 'When I told Julie about Nimue the mermaid, Albert was there too.' I slammed my hand onto the floor.

'I think,' Anna said, 'we've found our guy.'

Chapter Twenty-Six

Albert was just one man – and a man in his seventies, at that. For all the power that he'd wielded over others, he wouldn't be a physical match for Anna or me. All the same, we approached the café where he held his sessions stealthily. Although it was in a central location, it was tucked away down one of the side streets where there was less chance of any passers-by growing too curious.

It bothered me that the café's door openly displayed a poster that included the outline of a man with a swirl for a brain. I might not have passed directly in front of it but I'd been in the vicinity of this place on more than one occasion in the last few days.

Anna produced a baton and a set of handcuffs. 'You should let me handle this,' she advised. 'Unless he tries any freaky magic hypnotherapy stuff. Then you can let rip with your own powers.'

Somehow I doubted that Albert worked like that. I reckoned his clients were in a relaxed state and entirely willing to be hypnotised. He'd need a calm and therapeutic atmosphere in which to start; it wouldn't be something he'd spring upon the unsuspecting. Then again, who knew what people were capable of these days?

I nodded agreement. With any luck, we'd bring to Albert to his knees with a minimum of fuss. I knew that Monroe would be jealous I'd done this without him, but that was his fault for trying to shut me out.

Anna reached for the door handle. I drew in a deep breath. A moment later, she shoved open the door and started yelling, 'Police! Nobody move!'

It wasn't so long since Manchester had been turned on its head that we'd forgotten all our old habits. If Albert – and indeed anyone else – had been inside, they would have either frozen or made a run for it. When we burst in, however, nothing happened and nobody moved because nobody was there.

Anna sprang towards the back, checking both the kitchen and the small toilet. She came out shaking her head. I let out an inarticulate yell of frustration and kicked at a coffee table, sending the books on top of it onto the floor. Then I sat down on an overly-squishy sofa and was almost swallowed up by the cushions.

'He's probably at home,' Anna said. 'It'll be easier to nab him in the south than it would be here. He'll have nowhere to run to, and our own community will back us up.'

'Yeah.' I scratched my nose. Anna was right. 'I just wanted to get him here and now, you know? To maybe even catch him in the act.' I struggled to sit up again and gazed round the room. Inspirational posters covered the walls. There was the heady yet calming scent of lavender. This was a space designed to put someone at ease. It was the sort of space you'd want to go to if you opted for therapy. That made me all the more angry. 'He's supposed to be helping people,' I ground out.

'I know.' Anna was considerably calmer than I was. 'We'll get him, Charley. Don't worry. In less than two hours' time, he'll be in custody.'

I nodded and pushed myself to my feet, my toes kicking one of the fallen books as I did so. A scrap of paper underneath it caught my eye and I knelt down to pick it up.

My blood chilled when I read what was on there. It was a list of names. And vulnerabilities.

Valerie. Lonely. Desperate for male attention.
Philip. Scared. Desires blood.
Margaret. Feels trapped. Dislikes vampires.
Craig. Impotent. Wants to feel powerful.
Mermaid. Unknown.

There was another name at the bottom of the list. My eyes swam when I saw it and my insides clenched.

Monroe. Grieving. Guilty. Afraid of losing control.

Wordlessly, I passed the paper to Anna. She scanned it and her face whitened. 'Monroe went out,' she said.

I nodded, unable to speak.

'They didn't know where he was going.'

I nodded again.

'Would he have come here?' she asked. 'Would he have sought out Albert?'

My chest was rising and falling with increasing speed. I'd only ever felt true fear like this once before. I thought about all that Monroe and I had discussed over the last few days, and nodded at Anna for a final time.

She exhaled. 'Okay,' she said. 'Okay. Neither of them are here now. We need to assume that they're together and that Albert is planning something. We have to work out where they might have gone.'

My mind flailed, panic fluttering across my bones. That wouldn't help: it didn't help me save Joshua, and it wouldn't help me save Monroe. I squeezed my eyes shut and allowed myself three seconds of outright, blood-trembling terror. Then I opened my eyes and straightened my shoulders.

'He started at the Travotel,' I said, my voice clear. 'But he was surprised when the alarm went off and had to make a run for it with Philip in tow. He wouldn't try there again.'

'Philip died at the casino.' Anna pursed her lips. 'That was neutral ground. It would be safer. Albert could have used Philip's own home without worrying about any of the northern guards or other vampires, but he was probably nervous after the Travotel experience. He wanted somewhere he could control.'

'Except,' I said slowly, 'he took Craig to Boggart Hole. Or at least he tried to.'

'He didn't bank on the bogles being there too,' Anna mused. 'Until Alora showed up screaming her head off, only you and Monroe knew the bogles were there. You're right, though. Unless he'd visited Boggart Hole before, he couldn't have controlled an open-air environment in the same way as the casino. That was proved when he messed up there, just like he did at the Travotel. He'll be looking for somewhere else enclosed. Somewhere else he can control.' She met my eyes. 'The pair of them could be anywhere. I don't know how we can find them in time to stop whatever is about to go down.'

I pinched the bridge of my nose. 'What you're saying should make sense but the casino was linked to Valerie. Maybe he chose that location as nothing more than a nod to her.'

'Either way,' Anna said, 'he's not going to be stupid enough to go there again.'

'Perhaps not. But the Albert I know is gruff and cantankerous and likes to have things his own way. He doesn't appreciate failure. He failed with Maggie to an extent because she's still alive. He must have wanted her to die too. But she's also out of his reach now – and she wasn't his only screw-up. He also failed with location. He didn't reach Nimue before the bogles got in his way. This time he has Monroe with him, who's been there before and knows where to go. If Monroe is truly under Albert's spell, he'll be able to direct him towards Boggart Hole while avoiding the bogles' neighbourhood. Albert will get a second shot at Nimue and bring Monroe down at the same time.'

'So,' Anna asked, 'is his target the mermaid or Monroe?'

'Maybe both.' I gave her a grim look. 'It doesn't really make a difference.' Except I didn't care about Nimue. Monroe had my heart.

'I suppose not.' She touched my arm. 'Are you alright?'

'Yes.' And I was – for now. Either my hunch was correct and we still had a chance to get to Albert and Monroe in time, or it wasn't and we didn't. I didn't want to think about that scenario unless I had to. 'We have to get there as quickly as we can,' I said.

So far all we were doing was running around the damned city at full speed and falling short whenever we got somewhere. This would be our final destination. I'd stake my life on it. 'We have to stop Albert.' And possibly Monroe too, if he'd already been set on his own collision course.

'We will, Charley.' We both pretended not to hear the doubt in her voice. 'We will.'

***

Monroe's little car was parked in the same spot as it had been when Malbus thrust his sword in my face. I should have been relieved at the proof that Monroe was here, but I was just annoyed. It meant that Monroe had driven

Albert and the old bastard was pulling all the strings. He even had the strongest werewolf in the country acting as his chauffeur. He probably thought that getting Monroe to drive to his own death was some kind of poetic justice. Well, he'd learn. I'd show him what justice really meant.

Anna parked behind, effectively blocking Monroe's car so that Albert would have to run if he tried to make a quick getaway. I could run down a seventy year old, that much I knew.

Trying to be quiet, I opened the passenger door and stepped out. Anna did the same on her side. I spotted the fresh footsteps in the mud straight away, two sets, both leading towards the lake.

I held my finger up to my lips and pointed. Anna nodded grimly. She started forward, ready to follow wherever the tracks led, but I grabbed her back.

'You have to go and talk to the bogles,' I whispered. 'We've caused them enough trouble already. Explain to them what's going on and that they have to stay away from here. I'll deal with Albert.'

She tried to be stern. 'I'm the police officer, Charley.'

'I know. But magic is involved in all this. If it weren't, Albert wouldn't have been able to manipulate his victims to the extent that he already has. You might have that magic inside you now like everyone else, but I have more.' I wasn't boasting, merely stating a fact. 'I have the magical experience, too. Besides, the last face the bogles want to see again is mine. Once you've spoken to them, you can come back here. Either it'll all be over and I'll have stopped Albert, or you'll need to do it yourself because I'll have fucked up.'

'Charley…'

'This is my responsibility, Anna. I have to do this.'

She hissed with obvious reluctance but I knew she'd do what I asked. 'You said the bogles live only a few streets away from here. I'll run. I'll be back here in less than twenty minutes. I guarantee it.'

I smiled at her. 'I'd expect nothing less.'

She tutted then she spun on her heel and sprinted off. That meant I had only minutes to resolve this situation. I couldn't put Anna in danger; if all this went tits up, everyone would need her around for whatever else came in the future.

I lifted my head and strode forward. Coming, Albert. Ready or not.

I heard him before I saw him. His voice was surprisingly low and mellifluous. 'Where is she, Monroe? Where is the mermaid?'

'She's in there. She has to be in there.' Monroe's answer sounded distant.

'Call her.'

I stepped out from the trees just as Monroe moved robotically to the lake's edge. 'Hello, Albert,' I said.

For a moment or two, he didn't move then he slowly turned towards me and smiled. 'Charley. It's good of you to join us.'

'The game's up,' I said. 'Your time is over.'

Albert arched an eyebrow. 'Is it indeed?'

'You're coming with me and you're going to pay for what you've done.'

Rather than being intimidated, he appeared amused. 'Am I? What exactly have I done then? Hmmm?'

It was the 'hmmm' that got me. It was both patronising and degrading at the same time, as though by dint of his age and gender he was automatically superior to me.

'You freak!' I spat. 'You think I don't know what

you've been doing? How many people you've killed?'

Albert's expression was mild. 'My dear girl, I've not killed anyone. My hands are clean.' He held them up for inspection. 'And that's no mean feat, given how long it took you to sort out the water problems we were having.'

'Nimue,' Monroe called, oblivious to my presence. 'Nimue, come out.'

'You see?' Albert enquired. 'I'm standing here. It's that wolf who's doing all the work.'

'Yeah, but you're yanking his strings.' Furious magic sparked at my fingertips. 'Get him back.'

The older man tapped his mouth thoughtfully. 'Let me think about that. No.' He smiled. 'I don't think I will bring him here.' He leaned towards me. 'Do you know that you cannot hypnotise anyone to do anything their moral core wouldn't permit them to do under normal circumstances? It's why I couldn't hypnotise dear Val to kill a vampire. She didn't hate them as much as she thought she did. She was a bit fearful of their kind.' He chuckled. 'Although in the end she had every reason to be.'

'She went to you for help! All you did was get her killed!'

'But I *did* help her. She was deeply unhappy. I made that better for her.' He shrugged. 'I didn't do anything to any of these people that they didn't want. The male vampire wanted blood. The female werewolf wanted the vampire's blood.' He gestured in the air. 'And so on and so forth. All I did was give them permission to achieve their heart's desire.'

'Through hypnosis supplemented with magic!' I half yelled.

Albert's eyes narrowed. 'I was helping them. You're just like the others.'

I tried to control my breathing. 'The others?'

'The so-called Council for Psychotherapy deregistered me.' He rolled his eyes in disgust. 'They didn't agree with my practices.'

'I wonder why.'

Albert didn't hear me. 'But,' he continued, 'in this new world, they don't exist. It's why I stayed in Manchester, you know. I offer freedom in the same manner that the magic does.' He reached out to pat me on the shoulder but I flinched away. 'I'm better at it than you are.'

'Nimue,' Monroe called again, this time with a trace of frustration. 'I need you to come out of the water.'

'You see?' Albert grinned toothlessly. 'He was yours but now he's mine. And he feels so much better for it. He came to me, you know, not the other way around. They all did.'

I couldn't help myself. I thrust my hands forward, sending harsh green magic slamming into Albert's chest. He was knocked backwards into the mud, expelling a loud oomph of air as he fell. He struggled to his feet, disdainfully wiped off a smear of mud from his face and glared. 'You see?' he said softly. 'Now I'm giving you what you want, the opportunity to strike down an old man who challenges your authority.' His lip curled. 'Such as it is. You're not doing a very good job of running our community. Effective or not, all leaders become tyrants in the end.'

I drew in a ragged breath. 'No,' I said. 'They don't.'

Monroe was wading into the water. 'Nimue! Nimue!'

'He'll keep going,' Albert remarked. 'Even if you end my life here and now, that wolf will keep going after the mermaid. It's his heart's desire. He's an animal.

Better than that, he's a predator and his purpose in life is to kill. He will kill the mermaid and then he'll be at peace because he'll truly understand his own nature and his own needs.'

I lifted up my chin. 'Monroe isn't like that.'

'Yes, he is. And deep down, you know it just as much as he does.' A knowing look flitted across Albert's face. 'He spoke about you. I do believe he's in love with you, but he can't deny the beast inside himself.' He smirked. 'I'll prove it to you.' He turned towards the lake. 'Monroe,' he called. 'Listen to my voice. Leave the elusive little mermaid for now and come over here.'

Monroe didn't hesitate; he swung round and walked out of the water, trudging towards Albert and me.

'Monroe! Stop listening to him and look at me!' I shouted.

He glanced in my direction. 'Hello, Charley,' he said. 'You look lovely.'

I reached over and grabbed his shoulders, staring him in the face. His pupils were dilated and he had a dreamy expression, but he was still my Monroe. He would still listen to me. 'Stop this,' I said sternly. 'You're better than this. Give yourself a shake and become yourself again, not whoever this bastard wants you to be.'

'Listen to my voice, Monroe,' Albert repeated. 'Charley is suffering. She's in pain. You need to help her in the same way that I'm helping you. Kill her, and all her pain will disappear. She'll be in a better place, a calmer place…'

'Monroe, don't you pay any fucking attention to him!' I shouted. I shook him as hard as I could but he just continued to smile at me.

'Kill her, Monroe,' Albert repeated. 'Make things better and ease her suffering. The wolf inside you wants to do it. It wants to tear into her soft flesh and rip her white skin. It wants…'

I slapped Monroe hard across the face. He blinked but his expression didn't change. With desperation clawing at my insides, I gathered up all the magic inside me and flung it hard in Albert's direction. At the last moment, Monroe nudged me and knocked off my aim, giving Albert the opportunity to sidestep. All that force went slamming into a tree behind him instead, splitting its trunk in two.

Albert's voice hardened. 'Do it, Monroe. Now.'

Right in front of me, Monroe shifted, his human form giving way to a massive wolf. He landed on the ground on all fours and bared his teeth, growling.

I started to back away. 'Monroe, don't do this.' Almost of its own volition, magic flared again around my hands, ready to be dispensed at any moment.

'Oh,' Albert laughed, 'this is too perfect. If you kill him, Charley, what does that make you? Go on,' he urged. 'Destroy the wolf before it destroys you. He's already eating away at your insides. His death will save you from a destructive relationship that will do no one any good. Maybe once he's gone, you'll be able to concentrate on the rest of us in this city. You'll focus on what's important, not your pathetic love life.'

Albert's words were becoming an incessant drone so I shut them out. I reached for Monroe, my fingers curling into his fur. He snarled once, a brief sharp burst, then he sprang towards me and his massive paws knocked me off my feet. I landed on my back, physically winded and emotionally destroyed.

Monroe's body straddled mine, holding me in place. Then his jaws opened.

I squeezed my eyes shut. Make it fast, I prayed. Just make it fast. I held my breath and tensed as something wet and soft landed on cheek. I recoiled and felt my scream rising.

Wait.

A lick. That was definitely a lick. I peeked upwards, one eye open. Monroe winked. He lifted his head and howled for one blood-curdling moment. A second later, he turned and lunged at Albert.

I scrambled up as quickly as I could. I wasn't sure I wanted to see this but I had to bear witness; the victims – and Monroe himself – deserved that much.

Monroe advanced on Albert, paw by soft paw. Albert had his hands up and, for the first time, looked strained and fearful. 'Listen to my voice. You need to back away.'

Monroe shook himself, his red-tinged fur rippling.

'Monroe…' Albert said, his voice shaking. 'You're in pain. You're afraid of yourself and what you might do. But you don't want to do this. Not to me.'

Monroe growled, a vicious sound filled with unquenchable anger. I swallowed as his fur blurred. A second later he stood there, naked as the day as he was born and with his hands on his hips. 'Oh,' he said, 'I do want to do it. I want to do it so very badly.' He tilted his head downwards. 'But I won't. Because you can't control me. I'm not a monster – at least, I'm not the monster you think I am. And you're not worth it.'

Albert stared at him, his eyes wide. 'It worked,' he whispered. He began to smile, a sickening expression that did nothing to reassure me. 'My therapy worked. You're cured! You can move on with your life.' He spread his arms. 'Look at what I did! I saved you!'

It happened so quickly that I didn't have time to react. A delicate hand, with one piece of straggly moss trailing down its wrist, reached up from the water, curled round Albert's ankle and yanked. One second he was standing there, beaming with pride; the next second he was gone. There were so few ripples on the surface of the lake that I wasn't sure he'd had any time to fight back.

I gaped and shuddered. Monroe marched over and wrapped his arms round me. I leaned into him and we stared at the water. It didn't take long. Nimue's head broke the surface. 'Thank you for my gift,' she purred. The faintest smear of blood still clung to her lips

I found my voice. 'You shouldn't have done that. You shouldn't have killed him.'

She smiled. 'It's in my nature. I can't help it. Besides,' she added coyly, 'you both wanted me to.' She raised her hand in a wave. 'Don't forget to come and visit,' she called before she disappeared beneath the water once more.

Monroe and I stood there in silence. When I finally spoke, I didn't turn my head to look at him. I wasn't sure I wanted to. 'Were you ever under his control?'

'For a time,' he murmured, his lips close to my ear. 'He was very … persuasive. His words made sense and he understood which buttons to press. He was a wily bastard. Just not wily enough.'

'You see?' I said quietly. 'You're not the predator you thought you were.'

Monroe's arms tightened round me. 'Oh, I am, I'm just more in control than I thought I was. I know who my targets are. In a way, Albert's therapy worked. I know my limits and my boundaries, regardless of the magic.' He pressed his lips to my cheek, the heat of his mouth searing into my skin. 'I win.'

There was the sound of running feet. From beyond the lake and the woods, Anna appeared with at least a dozen bogles at her back. 'We're all here!' she roared. 'We're all going to…' Her voice faltered as she took us in. 'Isn't he here?'

I glanced out towards the now still water. 'He was,' I said. 'But he's not any more.'

Epilogue

Timmons had a knowing smile on his face as he pressed the key into my hands. 'Your room is on the top floor,' he said. 'It's out of the way of the others. You won't be disturbed.'

'Thank you.'

He handed me a plate covered by a silver dome. I frowned and lifted it. Underneath was a jam sandwich, cut into neat diagonal shapes. 'In case you get peckish,' he told me. He gave me a little nudge. 'Off you go.'

The door to the hotel room was already ajar. I pushed it open with my free hand and walked in, carefully laying the sandwich on the side table where a television would once have stood.

I turned and regarded Monroe who was lying spread-eagled on the bed, surrounded by rose petals.

'We have chocolates,' he said, without taking his eyes off mine. 'And wine. Clearly, the faery has been holding onto his own secret stash. I'll have words with him about that later.'

'No, you won't,' I said. 'Besides, we're all in this together.'

He smiled at me, a secret smile that I'd never seen him bestow on anyone else. 'That we are.' He licked his lips. 'These trysts will be a lot easier to manage once you all move into the north.'

'Everyone is pretty much packed up.'

'Good. Has there been much argument?'

I shook my head. 'Not as much as I expected. I think everyone gets it. Before it was about survival, about making it past the apocalypse and adapting. But now we've moved past merely surviving – we have to start living too.'

He stretched his arms behind his head. 'I'm glad you came,' he said softly.

I breathed in deeply. 'So am I.'

'If you don't want to be here…'

I didn't give him a chance to finish. 'I do. This is all that I want.' I squinted at him. 'Do you want to be here?'

His answer was quiet. 'Like you wouldn't believe.' He looked away as if he were suddenly nervous. 'I'm sorting myself out properly, too. Albert's not the only counsellor in town. It turns out that Theo the vampire is a also a fully-qualified therapist. In fact, hypnotherapy is one of his specialisms. I've signed up for a month.'

I smiled. 'I think that's a really good idea.'

Monroe seemed to relax. 'I'm going to get over this. I'm going to be the person you deserve.'

I walked over and forced him to look up at me. 'You always were.'

His eyes flared, their blue light darkening to a stormier grey. 'Not always.' The corners of his lips curved slightly. 'I like your plans for different clubs and societies. Julian was particularly enamoured by the thought of amateur dramatics.'

I blinked. 'Really?'

Monroe laughed. 'No. Although he would make a fabulous pantomime dame. He is keen on taking poker lessons, though.'

I rubbed my palms together. 'Excellent. I could do with some easy targets. I'd have thought that Julie would be interested in some theatre but she's decided to offer Pilates instead.'

Monroe raised an eyebrow. 'It's a strange new world.'

'It is indeed.' I sat on the edge of the bed. 'Do you think we'll manage?'

He sat up and tugged at my collar, drawing me towards him. 'Yes,' he breathed. 'I do.'

Then his lips descended onto mine.

*Thank you so much for reading Brittle Midnight!
I really hope you enjoyed it. It would mean a huge
amount if you could leave a review – any and all feedback
is so very, very welcome and hugely important for
independent authors like myself.*

Find out more about me and my books at
http://helenharper.co.uk

**The third and final book in The City of Magic trilogy,
Furtive Dawn, will be released on May 3rd, 2019**

mybook.to/FurtiveDawn

About the author

After teaching English literature in the UK, Japan and Malaysia, Helen Harper left behind the world of education following the worldwide success of her Blood Destiny series of books. She is a professional member of the Alliance of Independent Authors and writes full time, thanking her lucky stars every day that's she lucky enough to do so!

Helen has always been a book lover, devouring science fiction and fantasy tales when she was a child growing up in Scotland.

She currently lives in Devon in the UK with far too many cats – not to mention the dragons, fairies, demons, wizards and vampires that seem to keep appearing from nowhere.

You can find out more by visiting Helen's website:
http://helenharper.co.uk

Other titles

The complete *Blood Destiny* series

Bloodfire

Bloodmagic

Bloodrage

Blood Politics

Bloodlust

Blood Destiny Box Set (The complete series: Books 1 – 5)

Also
- **Corrigan Fire**

- **Corrigan Magic**

- **Corrigan Rage**

- **Corrigan Politics**

- **Corrigan Lust**

The complete *Bo Blackman* series

Dire Straits

New Order

High Stakes

Red Angel

Vigilante Vampire

Dark Tomorrow

The complete *Highland Magic* series

Gifted Thief
Honour Bound
Veiled Threat
Last Wish

The complete *Dreamweaver* series

Night Shade

Night Terrors

Night Lights

Olympiana stand - alone

Eros

The complete *Lazy Girl's Guide To Magic* series

Slouch Witch
Star Witch

Spirit Witch
Sparkle Witch

Wraith stand-alone

The complete *Fractured Faery* series
    Box of Frogs
    Quiver of Cobras
    Skulk of Foxes

The *City Of Magic* series
    Shrill Dusk
    Brittle Midnight
    Furtive Dawn

Printed in Poland
by Amazon Fulfillment
Poland Sp. z o.o., Wrocław